Keeper Of The Harvest

THE GENTLE HILLS

Far From the Dream
Whispers in the Valley
Keeper of the Harvest

(All available in large print.)

THE GENTLE HILLS / BOOK THREE

LANCE WUBBELS

KEEPER OF THE HARVEST

BETHANY HOUSE PUBLISHERS
MINNEAPOLIS, MINNESOTA 55438

Cover by Dan Thornberg,
Bethany House Publishers staff artist.

Published by Bethany House Publishers
A Ministry of Bethany Fellowship, Inc.
11300 Hampshire Avenue South
Minneapolis, Minnesota 55438

Printed in the United States of America.

Library of Congress Cataloging-in-Publication Data

Wubbels, Lance, 1952–
    Keeper of the harvest / Lance Wubbels.
        p. cm. — (The gentle hills ; bk. 3)

     1. World War, 1939–1945
2. Married people
3. Farm life—Minnesota—Fiction. I. Title.
II. Series: Wubbels Lance, 1952–   Gentle hills ; bk. 3.
PS3573.U39K44   1995
813'.54—dc20   95–486
ISBN 1–55661–420–9 (Trade Paper)   CIP
ISBN 1–55661–685–6 (Large Print)   AC

To

Nils

and

Ingerlisa

———— ∾ ————

You are
the great loves of my life.
Thanks for
being so wonderful.

LANCE WUBBELS, the Managing Editor of Bethany House Publishers, taught biblical studies courses at Bethany College of Missions for many years. He is the author of *One Small Miracle*, the heartwarming novel of the profound impact a teacher's gift of love makes on the life of one of her struggling students. He is also the compiler and editor of the Charles Spurgeon and F. B. Meyer Christian Living Classic books with Emerald Books. He and his family make their home in Bloomington, Minnesota.

CONTENTS

1

ALL THINGS NEW

A light summer breeze tugged lightly at the corners of the clean white sheet as Marjie Macmillan pressed the last of the wooden pins into position on the clothesline. Stepping back to enjoy the sight of the morning's wash fluttering in the bright sunshine, she breathed a sigh of satisfaction to have such a large task done so early in the day. *What a magnificent morning!* Marjie thought as the gentle wind tossed loose strands of her wavy brown hair from side to side.

The quiet sound of footsteps behind her startled Marjie, and she spun around just in time to catch her husband before he leaped to grab her.

"Shoot!" Jerry exclaimed as he gathered her into his strong arms. "I almost had you!"

"Don't you ever do that again!" Marjie warned, laughing and hugging him tightly. "You scared me to death."

"Poor thing! I better carry you to the house," he teased, gently lifting her into his arms like a precious bundle, then laughing along with her. "I love you, Marjie Belle Macmillan," he said. "Your wish is my command."

"Really?" Marjie whispered.

"Anything."

"How about two wishes?"

"Two it is."

Marjie smiled. "First, a kiss to make this a perfect morning."

Nodding, Jerry leaned over and kissed her firmly on the lips. "Mmmm . . . mmmm," he said softly, shaking his head. "How was that?"

"Delicious," she replied, reaching up to wipe some hay dust from his cheeks. "But I think I need another. Don't be in such a hurry, farm boy."

Jerry pulled her up closer to his face and made sure his second kiss did not disappoint her. Then he slowly let her back down to the ground.

"What else?" he asked, still holding her close.

She looked up into his clear blue eyes, loving the boyish glint in them. "You're sure you want to give me another shot?"

"Try me."

"Okay," she said, pulling back and glancing over at the clothesline. "Did you ever notice that by noon the clothes get lost in the shadow of the big maple tree?"

Jerry nodded. "I've hung my share of laundry there, if you recall. What about it?"

"I'd like you to move the line closer to the cellar door so it's out from under the tree and I don't have to carry the baskets so far," she said. "Plus, I need you to add another section of clothesline. You and your father obviously weren't using the line to hang diapers." She hesitated. "Do you think Benjamin would mind if we moved it?"

"I don't know. . . ." Jerry muttered, already studying what it would take to move the clothesline. "What difference does it make if he did?"

"Well, he might—"

"It's *our* farm now, remember?" Jerry said. "If we want to move a clothesline, that's our business. Dad and your mother have their own clothesline to do whatever they want to with."

"I still can't believe Benjamin's gone and he and Ma are married," Marjie said. "That's going to take some time to get used to."

Jerry nodded but didn't answer.

"So," she said, "can you move it?"

"No."

"What?" Marjie cried. "Why not?"

"Because it's not worth moving," Jerry said with a smile. "Those wooden posts are too old to bother with. I'll make you something better out of the angle iron that's in the shed."

Marjie gave a delighted cheer and hugged Jerry again. "You're wonderful," she murmured in his ear. "And you're right about making this place ours. I've got a few other ideas that—"

"No more wishes today!" Jerry broke in and pulled away from Marjie. "A fella shouldn't overdo a good thing."

"You said—"

"I said two wishes, and you spent them," Jerry persisted. "Save the others for a rainy day. I've got too much fieldwork right now."

"Just as long as you don't forget that I've got more things I'd like to change around here," Marjie said. "Which reminds me that I forgot to ask you what you were working on yesterday afternoon. I took Martha out for a ride in the wagon and I could see the tractor way down by the sinkhole, but I didn't see you. Where were you?"

A sheepish grin crossed Jerry's face, and he reached up to stroke his chin. "Where is Martha? I'd—"

"You know full well that she's taking her morning nap," Marjie scolded, grabbing Jerry by his tattered blue work shirt. "And stop avoiding the question. Where were you yesterday?"

Jerry looked toward the barn and smiled. "I was doing what you said. Making this place our own."

"What's that supposed to mean?"

"I'll spoil it if I try to explain it," Jerry replied, putting his arm around Marjie. "But I got you something yesterday that I think you'll like."

"From the junk you've thrown into the sinkhole?"

"No, no, no," Jerry said. "I just parked the tractor down there so I wouldn't have to walk so far."

"What in the world are you saying?"

"How about if I show you what I got, then explain later?"

"Good idea. Where is it?"

"The barn."

"The barn! You must be—"

"Come on," Jerry ordered, holding her tight and marching toward the barn. "Take a look before your mouth gets you in trouble. It's something for you, but it's just what this farm has needed for years."

Marjie walked silently beside her husband but was unable to guess his mystery. Entering the barn through the milk room and passing through the milk parlor, she saw nothing out of the ordinary—whitewashed wood, pitchforks, gunnysacks in piles, cobwebs, empty stanchions. A steel-blue barn swallow nesting on a wooden beam above them swooped down toward Marjie; she jerked backward as it darted past her head.

The only hint she was given came from Blue. The small cow dog stood eagerly by the door that opened to the pen where the Holstein bull had been kept. The closer they got to the door, the harder his tail wagged.

"What is it, Blue?" Marjie called out.

The Australian cattle dog let out an excited bark and jumped up against the door.

"Get down, Blue!" Jerry ordered, giving the dog's head a scratch, then pointing for him to sit. "Any guesses before I open the door, Marjie?"

"Don't tell me you've gone and gotten me another bull," she lamented. "We may need—"

"Not even close," Jerry announced. "This is truly a gift for you from yours truly."

Marjie saw a shadow move past the outside of the barn window, but the window was so dirty that she couldn't make out what it was. "Show me!" she cried.

Pushing open the top half of the barn door, Jerry stepped back and burst out laughing.

"What's wrong with—" Marjie said, then gasped as the golden head of a palomino saddle horse poked through the opening and looked her right in the face. Marjie's mouth opened, but no words escaped.

Instinctively, Marjie lifted a hand to the horse's velvety pink nose and let him sniff her, the wiry guard hairs tickling her skin. Then her hand rose to touch the horse's silvery mane and then the white streak down the center of its face. "I don't believe it," she finally whispered, looking over at Jerry, who was now laughing in tears. "What's going on?"

"He's yours!" Jerry sputtered through his laughter. "His name is Charlie, and he is your horse."

"Mine?"

"Yes!"

"How can he be?" Marjie protested. "We could never afford to buy a horse."

"Almost true," Jerry said, reaching and scratching behind one of the horse's ears. "Not quite."

"Jerry, I take care of the books," Marjie stated. "We simply don't have anything extra for buying a horse."

"Not in cash," Jerry replied, still not looking at Marjie.

"You didn't borrow—"

"No!" Jerry exclaimed. "I'd never borrow money for a horse. I got him from Tom Metcalfe as a payment for a past debt."

"What? The strange man whose family lives back in the woods down the road?"

"That's him," Jerry replied. "Two years ago I spent a couple weeks helping them get their corn out of the field Tom had broke his foot. He couldn't afford to pay me nothing back then, and he still can't pay."

"So he offered the horse?"

"Nope," Jerry said and smiled. "I heard he'd bought the horse for his daughter, but she got spooked once and wouldn't go near him. Figured Tom might be sick of feeding an animal no one rides, and I guessed right. You've always said you love horses, Marjie. So I thought you might like him."

That Jerry was telling the truth finally began to dawn on Marjie. She started to laugh and cupped her hands over her mouth. Then she put her hands around the horse's face and looked into its large, liquid eyes. "I've always dreamed of owning my own horse," she said softly. "He's really mine?"

"Signed for," Jerry said proudly, pulling an envelope out of the big pocket in his overalls.

Marjie took the envelope from him and quickly looked over the document and the signatures. Then she threw up her hands and let out a restrained scream, scaring the horse back from the barn door and sending Blue on a tear of laps around the rows of milking stanchions.

"How can I thank you?" Marjie cried, hugging Jerry and shaking with joy.

"You can simmer down for starters," Jerry urged. "And you can thank me by enjoying him. Want to ride him?"

"Now?"

"Why not? He belongs to you. Only one problem, though. I couldn't get Metcalfe to add his saddle to the repayment. Can you ride without a saddle?"

"I've never ridden with a saddle," Marjie replied, resting her elbows on the bottom half of the door to get a better look at the fine tall gelding with the four white stockings. "Nobody around our place could afford a saddle, but there were plenty of horses to ride."

"You want to try?"

"Sure. Did you ride him home?"

"Yesterday," Jerry replied with a nod. "He handles smooth as silk even though he hasn't been ridden much lately. You go up and check on Martha while I get him bridled. Better change to slacks, too. I'll bring him around to the front of the house."

Marjie had forgotten all about Martha. Slipping quietly through the front door and up the stairs, Marjie was relieved to find her baby still sleeping in the crib. Leaving the door to Martha's room open a crack, Marjie hurried into her bedroom and changed quickly from her light cotton dress to a white blouse and blue jeans. Then she headed back out of the house, holding the screen door so it wouldn't slam behind her.

Jerry was leading the palomino down the driveway from the barn and stopped as Marjie approached. "You're sure you're ready?" he asked.

"Don't look so worried," Marjie said, reaching up to pat the horse's neck and feel his strong shoulder muscles. "I promise to take it easy. Did you say his name is Charlie?"

"Yep," Jerry replied. "He's five years old, and he loves to run. You're gonna have to hold him back. Keep him in the driveway for now, okay?"

"Help me up?" Marjie asked, moving to Charlie's left side.

Taking the reins from Jerry and placing them into her left hand, Marjie put her left foot in Jerry's cupped hands and sprang up over the horse's back. Jerry stepped back as Marjie shifted her position until she was comfortable.

"How's it feel?" he asked.

"Good," Marjie announced with a confident smile. "Here goes nothing."

She squeezed her legs against the horse's sides. Charlie gently moved forward and began to walk down the driveway toward the road. "This is great!" she exclaimed and waved down at Jerry.

"He'll move to the right when you press your left leg against his side, and vice versa," Jerry called out.

"I know, I know," Marjie called back. "I can do this."

When the horse and rider got to the road at the end of the driveway, Marjie pressed her right leg against Charlie's side. He made a complete turn and walked down the Macmillan driveway like he'd done it a thousand times. As they approached the place where Jerry was standing, Marjie said, "Here we go again."

Lightly touching the horse's sides with her shoes and making a clicking sound with her mouth, Marjie felt Charlie rise up a bit as the horse began to trot. The motion threw her off balance for a moment, and she reached up with her right hand and took the horse's mane until she steadied herself.

"No faster!" Jerry warned as she trotted past him, following the circle of the farmyard driveway.

"What's it worth to you?" Marjie called back, then headed on up the driveway and turned back at the county road. Rather than riding past Jerry this time, she shifted her weight, pulled back on the reins, and brought Charlie to a stop. "I'll keep him to a trot if you say it's okay for me to take him out into the fields."

"No chance!"

"You'd rather see him gallop now?"

"No, but can't you wait a few days?"

"For what?" Marjie asked with a laugh. "I'm ready."

"But I'm not!" Jerry exclaimed, throwing up his hands. "Please keep him in the yard until you've practiced a little more. Give him a chance to get to know us."

Marjie scrunched her mouth together and closed one eye as she thought it over, then a baby's cry from the house broke the deliberation.

"Saved by the bell," Marjie said with a sigh, patting Charlie's right shoulder. "Two days more in the yard, big fella, and then we're taking you out where you can stretch your legs!"

2

SIXTY BIG ONES

"Guess what treasures I unearthed in the attic this morning," Marjie said as Jerry walked into the dining room from washing his hands.

"Oh, you're not gonna drag out those baby photos of me in the stupid baptismal dress, are you?" Jerry groaned as he took his place at the table. "And not for tonight's birthday party!"

"What's it worth to you?" teased Marjie, lifting Martha into her high chair. "Those are precious. And I found some other cuties of you."

"Don't tell me, please," said Jerry. But then he asked, "What specific treasures are you referring to?"

Marjie flashed him her patented smirk. "I found your mother's and your grandmother's diaries."

Jerry looked up from his steaming bowl of beef and vegetable soup and rolled his eyes. "Wow! Nothing like reading Grandma's diaries. Talk about exciting."

"You might be surprised, mister smarty-pants," bantered Marjie. She paused to make sure she got the next spoonful of soup into Martha's mouth. "I liked the time you and Billy played hooky from school when you were ten years old. I take it your mother was not pleased."

"Correct," Jerry said with a laugh. "I got two spankings that day. Mother got me when I first walked into the yard with the

17

note from my teacher. Then Dad got me when he came in from the field. That was a burner I won't ever forget."

Marjie echoed his laugh. "My pa used to wonder if the day would ever come when I discovered how much more pleasant it was to obey than to have our meetings in the woodshed. I was a slow learner."

"Talk about slow," Jerry said, "did my mother's diary tell how they caught us?"

"No," replied Marjie. "She just said that the two of you got caught and that she warmed your fanny with the wooden yardstick."

Jerry laughed again and shook his head. "We'd found a spot down along the creek where the water had cut an overhang. We figured we could crawl under it and hide there all day and the teacher would just think we were sick. The problem was that Billy's sister snitched on us, even though he'd given her some candy to keep quiet."

"Can't ever trust a girl," Marjie joked. "She got the goodies and probably settled some other score with Billy."

"Probably," said Jerry. Reaching over to Martha and squeezing her plump cheeks, he said, "Don't you ever think about sneaking out of school. Daddy's going to die if you make him give you a spanking."

"You just wait," Marjie said, lightly tapping Martha's soft brown curls. "This little girl's already got the look of mischief in her eyes. Say, I almost forgot. You got a letter in the mail."

"You're kidding," Jerry replied as Marjie jumped up and went into the kitchen. "Who from?"

"John . . . Spalding," Marjie came back in reading off the envelope. She handed it to Jerry. "Wasn't he on the *Wasp* with you and Chester when she was sunk?"

"Sure was," Jerry said, pulling out his jackknife and cutting open the envelope. "It's been so long, I didn't think I'd hear from any of those guys again."

"Might make a difference if you tried writing a letter yourself once," Marjie responded. She sat back down alongside

Martha and started to spoon in a mouthful of applesauce. "What's he got to say?"

Jerry had one finger slowly moving across the paper and was wrestling to decipher the illegible handwriting. "Not much," he finally answered. "He and a lot of the guys from the *Wasp* got the same orders I came home with. They're on the new carrier, the *Essex,* and out in the Pacific, but he doesn't give any details about what they're doing. Sounds like he mostly wanted to say he misses Chester and me."

"That was nice of—oh, Martha, no!" The baby had managed to intercept the next spoonful of applesauce with a chubby fist and dumped the whole load down her front. Marjie wiped Martha's fingers with a towel and refilled the spoon. "You don't talk much about it," she said.

"About what?"

"The other men," she said. "You coming home and not going back. What it feels like."

Jerry leaned back in his chair and stretched his neck. Then he stared absently out the large picture window in the dining room.

"It still bothers you, doesn't it?" asked Marjie, wiping Martha's mouth and hands with a towel and untying her bib.

Still not answering, Jerry sighed and kept staring out the window.

Marjie pulled the wooden tray back on the high chair and lifted Martha out, then she handed the baby to Jerry. "Here, I'll get her bottle, and you can finish her meal."

When she came back into the dining room, Jerry was gently bouncing Martha on his knee. "This the way the mommy rides, the mommy rides, the mommy rides. . . ."

"No more horsey rides," Marjie said, handing Jerry the bottle. "I would've thought that after what happened yesterday you'd let her food settle before playing games."

Jerry laid Martha back into his strong left arm and put the bottle to work. "Like I said, you weren't the only slow learner."

"So, why did the letter bother you?" Marjie asked.

Jerry's lips tightened. "I don't know. I guess I feel bad about being home when they're still out there fighting. Sometimes I feel like I ran away. I know, I know it's not true. But it still don't seem right."

"You didn't have any choice," Marjie offered, searching the sadness in Jerry's blue eyes. "Your dad just couldn't handle the farm anymore."

"Hmmm," mumbled Jerry. He twisted his mouth some more, then met her eyes. "That's what I thought . . . but Dad's all right now. So maybe it would've worked out without me here."

Marjie's eyes squinted. She reached out and put her hand on his knee. "We would not have made it, sweetheart. The only reason Benjamin got better was because you were here and he could rest. Without you, we might not be celebrating his sixtieth birthday tonight."

Jerry nodded and looked back out the window. "I've said that to myself a hundred times, but I still feel guilty. It just don't want to go away."

"So why didn't you say something?" asked Marjie. "Have you talked with Chester or Billy about it? Maybe they're feeling the same way."

"Nope, I ain't brought it up," Jerry replied.

"Why?" scolded Marjie, shaking her head. "Why don't you boys talk about things like this? What if it's bothering them, too?"

"Why should it be?" Jerry asked. "Both of them had medical problems. They had to come home."

"Their reasons are no more compelling than yours," Marjie argued. "I want you to talk to them about it tonight."

"I don't—"

"I'm not going to let you bury this, Jerry," Marjie broke in, then she smiled. "Either you can talk to them, or I will. Which way would you like it?"

Jerry looked over with saggy eyes and said, "I love it that you care for me, but let me see what happens tonight. I don't want to wreck Dad's party with my problems."

———— ∽ ————

Billy Wilson and Ruth Buckley were the first guests to arrive at the Macmillan farmhouse that evening. Jerry walked out of the house to meet them as Billy parked the green Plymouth next to the garage.

Stepping out of the car, Ruth called out, "Where's the birthday boy? Don't tell me we beat him here."

"Yep," Jerry answered. "It's been a long time since he was late for anything. But he's a newlywed, you know."

"That's right," said Ruth. "Can't expect much from him for a while. Is Marjie in the house?"

"She's just finishing up with Martha's bath," Jerry said. "If you hurry—"

"I'm on my way," Ruth broke in and hustled past Jerry. "Maybe she won't have her out of the water yet."

Billy had made his way slowly around the side of the car and was walking with a slight limp toward Jerry.

"Scars must be bothering you tonight," said Jerry.

"No," Billy said, reaching down and rubbing his right knee. "It's this bum knee. Must be a change in the weather coming. It started throbbing after I got off work."

"Is it bad?"

"No. Not enough to fret over. Just slows me down a little."

"How's your job going?"

"Swell," Billy replied. "I'm still learning my way around the bank, but I think I'm going to like it."

"So if we need some cash—"

"Don't call me, I'll call you," Billy interjected and laughed. "Say, Ruthie tells me you got Tom Metcalfe's horse for Marjie. Where is he?"

"Come on," Jerry said, nodding toward the barn. "He's in the pen on the west side of the barn."

Billy fell in step beside Jerry, and the two friends headed for the barn. "What'd you pay for him?"

"Nothing," Jerry said as they entered the barn through the milk room. "You remember when Tom got hurt a couple years ago and I helped get the corn out of the fields?"

Billy nodded.

"He never paid me," Jerry continued. "So I went down and offered him to trade the time for the horse. Tom didn't care much for it, but he finally gave in."

"You're kidding!" exclaimed Billy as they got to the barn's west door. "Metcalfe's never been one to pay up on his bills."

"Don't I know," said Jerry, pushing the door open. The palomino was standing just outside the door, one white foot cocked in a resting position. He turned his handsome gold and white face to look at them.

"That's why I offered a trade. What do you think?"

"Would you look at that!" Billy stepped into the pen and offered Charlie a hand to sniff, then rubbed the horse's mane. "He's a beaut. Marjie must have flipped."

"She practically did cartwheels across the lawn," said Jerry with a laugh. "You should see her ride him. I had no idea she loved horses this much. Says her big brother Paul taught her to ride."

"That the brother who's still in the service?"

"Yep," Jerry answered. "Actually, both of her brothers are in the army, now that Ted's joined up. But as far as we know he's still stateside. Paul's over in Sicily, where the fighting's pretty bad."

"That's what I heard," Billy said. "Is Ted the one that was in so much trouble?"

"That's Teddy," replied Jerry, shaking his head. "He was drinking and fighting all over the county. Maybe the army will straighten him up."

They stood quietly for a minute or two, each caught up in his own thoughts. Then Billy gave the horse a gentle slap.

"Well, Jerry, you got a steal. Bet you'll enjoy him as much as Marjie."

Jerry nodded, putting on a grin that quickly slipped. "I think I will. I hope so."

Billy stepped back and ran his fingers through his short dark hair. "Is something else wrong, buddy? You and Marjie aren't having trouble, are you?"

"No," Jerry groaned. "We're fine, but . . . well, I got a letter today from a guy I served on the *Wasp* with. John Spalding. He's on the *Essex* now, and . . ."

He stopped. Billy shifted his weight to lean against the side of the barn, resting his knee. He said nothing, simply waited until Jerry continued.

"It's just that . . . well, whenever I think of those guys, I feel so guilty about not going back. I mean, they're over there risking their lives—John and Paul and the rest of 'em, and here I am on the farm doing what I've always wanted to do. I tell myself I had to come home to keep the farm going, but it still just don't feel right."

"Hmmm," said Billy, pushing himself away from the wall and starting toward the barn door. "You're talking to a guy who knows a lot about guilt. Let's go in the barn and sit down before my knee gives out on me."

Back in the barn, each man found a wooden milking stool to sit on. Billy stretched out his right leg and leaned back against the wooden milking stanchion.

"Do you feel guilty a lot?" Billy asked.

"I suppose it comes up every day," answered Jerry. "Most of the time I can shrug it off, but there are times when it eats away at me for days. Today was real bad."

"I ain't talked to nobody about this," Billy said, rubbing his cheeks with his hand. "When I was in the hospital, for the longest time I felt guilty just to be alive. Most of the fellas I'd gotten to know on the *Arizona* were killed, and it just didn't seem right that I made it off alive.

"When the infection was at its worst, there were times when I thought about how great it would be if I could die like the others. But I lived. Burned legs, bad knee, scar tissue, therapy—none of them were ever enough to take away the guilt. One of the reasons I stayed so long helping at the hospital in San Diego was that I kept hoping I'd finally feel like I'd paid my dues."

"It didn't work?" asked Jerry, sitting forward on his stool.

Billy smiled and shook his head. "You remember that old battle-axe of a nurse I had? Myrtle Wazichozky. I'd probably still be there if it hadn't been for Myrtle. She finally pulled me aside one day and told me it was time to start acting like a man."

"What?" Jerry sputtered.

"Myrtle never minced her words, and she was seldom wrong," said Billy. "She told me I had to be man enough to let go of the past and start living in the present again. She reminded me that I hadn't been responsible for what happened at Pearl Harbor. I couldn't help it that I lived. All I could do was take responsibility for the life I had now. She said I owed it to those guys, and to myself."

"Whew!" exclaimed Jerry, rocking back on his stool. "She gave you both barrels!"

Billy nodded and wrinkled his forehead. "It was just what I needed to hear. I can't tell you how much it helped. There are still moments when it all crashes back in on me, but then I see Myrtle sticking her finger in my ribs and telling me to be a man. She can scare anything off!"

Jerry and Billy laughed, and Jerry was reminded of many other times when they had sat laughing together and talking about their problems. "Thanks," he said, getting up off his stool and offering a hand to his old friend. "I feel better already. We need to talk more often, Billy."

"I'd like that," Billy said, taking Jerry's hand and slowly standing. "Sounds like the other folks are here. We better get up to the house."

Two more cars had joined Billy's in the yard, and a small crowd had already gathered in the living room by the time Billy and Jerry got there. Jerry's father, Benjamin, had already taken his old comfortable chair and was saying something to Chester Stanfeld, Jerry's navy buddy. Sarah, Marjie's mother, newly married to Benjamin, sat on the davenport, holding tight to Martha's hands and helping her stand up. Margaret Stanfeld, Chester's Scottish war bride, was busy stacking plates and coffee cups on the dining room table.

" 'Bout time you boys got in here!" called out Benjamin from his seat of honor.

"That's right!" exclaimed Marjie, emerging from the kitchen with Ruth behind her. "You're holding up the big show."

She carried an angel food cake covered with a deep coating of whipped cream and decorated with six brightly lit red candles. She carefully placed it on the dining table while everybody gathered around, then raised her hand for quiet.

"Henrietta Macmillan's diary reads that on the sultry evening of June thirtieth, 1883, she gave birth to a fine baby boy whom she and Garrit named Benjamin Gerald. Lest you think sixty years ago constitutes ancient history, first consider that Edison had already given us the light bulb and Bell had invented the modern telephone.

"To a really modern fella that we really love a lot," Marjie declared, pausing to kiss Benjamin on the cheek, "Happy sixty big ones, and may your next sixty be even better!"

3

LIGHTNING

"This heat's a killer," Jerry said as he stood at the dining room picture window holding Martha and looking out toward the western sky. "The cows were about as miserable in the barn tonight as I can remember, and the flies were biting anything that moved. I don't know how they do it, but they were even biting through my socks!"

"The static's really cracking on the radio, but I listened long enough to get the weather report," Marjie commented, setting a dish of potatoes on the table. "Sounds like a storm's moving our way."

"No surprise," Jerry added, looking back at Marjie. "You could feel the pressure building all day. Something's gotta give."

Marjie stepped to the window and put her arm around Jerry. "Martha was miserable this afternoon. She just about drove me crazy with her fussing and crying. Couldn't get her to take a nap. I thought that she might have another tooth coming in, but she just got crankier as the air got worse. Don't get too close to me tonight—I've joined the grouch club."

"That makes three of us," Jerry said and laughed, then looked back out toward the west. "If it's going to storm, you couldn't tell from the sky. Just one big doughnut cloud. Looks like a gigantic smoke signal. That's a strange sight."

"Sure is. I don't like it, though, and I hate all the flies on the screens." Marjie pointed to one of the windows. "I think I want to move Martha's crib in with us tonight. Got a feeling we're going to get it in the middle of the night."

"Good idea," Jerry agreed. "Supper ready?"

"Right behind you," Marjie replied, taking the baby from Jerry's arms. "She's almost out. How do you do it? You should have come in this afternoon and put the magic touch on her." She laid the baby against her shoulder and patted her soothingly. "I think I'll take her upstairs and put her down before she comes to again. Go ahead and start. I don't feel much like eating, anyway."

Marjie had no sooner laid Martha in her crib than she heard the telephone ring. She could hear Jerry's muffled voice down the stairway but couldn't make out what was being said. And it wouldn't have mattered if she could, for Martha went into one more extended round of fussy crying before she finally dropped off into a sound sleep.

By the time Marjie made it back down to the dining room, Jerry was seated at the table waiting for her.

"I said to not wait," Marjie said, sitting down at the table and exhaling a frazzled sigh. "What's wrong?"

"Nothing's wrong. Just didn't want to eat by myself."

"Who was that on the phone?"

"Banker Billy."

"And. . . ?"

"You're not going to believe this," Jerry mumbled, taking a sip of his cold Lipton's tea. "His boss at the bank, Mr. Stockdale, wants Billy and me and Chester to put on our navy uniforms and ride in the back of his fancy '39 Mercury convertible for the Fourth of July parade. I'd like to wring his neck."

"What a great idea!" Marjie exclaimed. "And you agreed to do it?"

"Didn't have much choice," lamented Jerry. "Chester already said yes. I couldn't think of any excuse."

"Good," Marjie said and giggled. "I'll bet Ed Bentley will be taking pictures. Maybe I—"

"Why don't you ask Chester if you can borrow his camera

instead of hounding Bentley?" Jerry interjected.

"That's a great idea. I forgot they had one. Better dust off your uniform again and make sure it's pressed."

"We have a week. Let's talk about something else."

———————— ∽ ————————

By bedtime, the dark horizon to the west of the farm was almost a continual flash of lightning. Even though the storm appeared to be moving to the north, Jerry and Marjie decided to sleep in the first-floor bedroom off the living room, the one that had been Benjamin's. They moved Martha's crib down so she'd be close as well.

Shortly after midnight, Marjie awoke with a start as a deep rumble shook the house. It sounded like a freight train going by. She and Jerry jumped out of bed at the same moment and tried to figure out what was going on. Marjie's first reaction was to check on Martha, while Jerry dashed to close the window. The bedroom curtains were thrashing wildly in the breeze, but as Jerry got to the window, the curtains suddenly were sucked back up tightly against the screen.

"This is a bad one!" Jerry called out as he tugged on the curtains and pushed the window down. "The wind just did a complete switch-around. You take Martha down to the cellar, and I'll get the windows closed."

Jerry rushed out of the bedroom, running from room to room to shut the windows. Marjie scooped Martha out of the crib, gathered up a diaper and several small blankets, and headed for the stairway to the basement. The house was so bright from all the lightning outside that Marjie thought for a moment the lights were on, and she couldn't believe that the sudden drop in air temperature had already cooled the house.

Flicking on the cellar lights and racing down the stairway, Marjie placed Martha in a large laundry basket on an old oak table, propped the blankets around her, and covered her with another blanket. To Marjie's amazement, the baby had slept through all of the noise and flurry.

Through the cellar windows, Marjie could see the swaying

trees against the backdrop of lightning. But the cellar muffled the outside sounds enough to add an eerie sense of unreality to what was happening. Then she felt the ground rumble again and heard the windows shake as another huge wave of thunder rolled through. Marjie reached out and put her hand on her baby until the thunder passed, then she tried to gather her thoughts on what to do next.

Although she hated to leave Martha for even a second, Marjie couldn't stand not knowing why Jerry had not come to the cellar. Picking up the laundry basket and setting it carefully under the table, Marjie dashed up the stairs and shut the door behind her. All the windows were closed, but she didn't see Jerry anywhere.

"Jerry!" Marjie called out as loudly as she could yell.

She heard the sound of heavy shoes racing down the stairway, and she came around the corner into the dining room just as Jerry jumped the last couple of steps. He had pulled on his work clothes and was carrying her shoes, a blouse, and a pair of slacks.

"Is Martha all right?" Jerry cried, handing Marjie the clothes.

"Yes!" Marjie responded, grabbing Jerry and holding on. "What can we do?"

"Nothing!" Jerry replied, hugging her tightly. "All we can do is get in the basement and wait it out. You better get those clothes on, though. We may have to—"

Suddenly they both felt the air electrify and the hair on the back of their necks stand up. Jerry pushed Marjie to the floor and covered her with his body, but not before an explosion hit outside that rocked the house and filled the room with a burst of light. The noise from the lightning strike was deafening. Marjie felt like it passed straight through her.

As the crack finally subsided and the thunder rolled down through the valley, the room went silent and dark for a moment. Jerry and Marjie lay motionless on the floor, waiting to make sure it was really over.

"Are we alive?" Marjie whispered.

"I hope so," Jerry spoke softly, then pushed his body weight off her and sat up on the floor. "I think the house took a direct hit. I better look around. You check on the baby."

Marjie sat up as Jerry jumped to his feet, but she was still too stunned to get up. A tremble shook her from head to toe, and she decided she had best put on the clothes Jerry had given her before something worse happened.

Jerry cautiously stepped out the front door and onto the lawn to see if the house was damaged, but it was the acrid smell of fire that first caught his attention. The house appeared to be untouched, but something close by had definitely been struck. Running to the corner of the house, he saw orange flames shooting from the roof of the old wooden garage.

"The garage is on fire!" Jerry shouted out above the noise of the wind. "Call the operator and get some help!"

Marjie dashed to the phone with one shoe still flapping from her heel. Panicked, she tried to ring the operator, but the phone was dead. "Oh, God, help us!" she cried as she bent to pull the shoe on her foot, then flew out the front door.

"Jerry! Where are you?"

"In here!" came the response from inside the garage. She saw flames dancing across the wooden shingles of the roof.

"The phones are dead!" Marjie cried. "What are we going to do?"

"Come to the front of the car and help me push!" ordered Jerry. "We've gotta get the car out of here before the roof caves in—no time to get the keys!"

Jerry had already taken the car out of gear, but by himself he couldn't rock it up out of the dirt ruts where it usually sat. Marjie ran inside the burning garage, got on the opposite corner of the car, and pushed with all her strength. With both of their efforts, the old black Ford slowly inched backward out of the ruts, then caught the downward pitch of the driveway and rolled out the door.

"That's it!" Jerry yelled. He jumped into the driver's side to stop the car from rolling all the way across the yard and into the side of the machine shed.

Marjie turned and saw that nearly the whole garage roof was

already blazing away and the sparks were flying high into the sky. Jerry dashed back toward her. "We've got to get the gasoline out of there or it could blow and start the house on fire."

Following Jerry into the smoke-filled garage, Marjie helped Jerry push the fifty-five gallon drum of gasoline upright from its stand. Then Jerry tilted it on its edge and started to roll it out toward the garage doors.

"Grab the other can and get out of here!" he shouted.

Tears were pouring down her face from the smoke, but Marjie was able to spot the five-gallon can. She grabbed it, then ran past Jerry and out the garage doors. By now black smoke was rolling out the doors, and Marjie found herself choking and coughing as she reached the car and fell to the ground. Turning to the garage, she was relieved to see that Jerry had emerged through the doors and was rolling the large drum of gasoline to safety.

When he'd gotten the drum far enough away from the flames, Jerry set the drum down on the ground and slowly turned back toward the burning wreckage.

"Don't you dare!" Marjie shouted then coughed. "The roof is already sagging. Let her burn. We can't do any more!"

Jerry turned back to Marjie, and in the bright orange flames Marjie could see the defeat written all over Jerry's face. He trudged slowly back to her side, starting to cough and wiping the tears from his smoky eyes. Flopping down beside her, he shook his head in disbelief but didn't try to speak.

"We saved the car," Marjie sputtered. "It could have been the house."

Jerry nodded reluctantly and said, "Good thing the wind's blowing away from the house. Those sparks would set the house on fire like a torch. But we can't afford to build a new garage."

"We'll get along," Marjie said. "That garage was so rickety it wasn't going to last much longer anyway. We're lucky we didn't have much of anything else in it."

"Just some tools," Jerry said, rubbing his eyes again. "I think there was enough gas in there to reach the house if it would have blown. Reminds me of when the ship was torpedoed."

Marjie took Jerry's arm and stroked it lightly, then she remembered that her baby was still alone in the cellar. "I need to see about Martha. But I think the worst has passed over, don't you?"

Jerry nodded, then he stood up and helped Marjie to her feet. "Better get her. I've got to stay and watch what the fire does."

Marjie kept watching the garage as she walked to the house. The entire structure was now in flames, and the sparks were shooting high into the stormy sky. Thunder still rolled around them, but more gently than before, and occasional flashes of lightning showed huge thunderclouds standing watch over them. Marjie felt relieved that all they had lost was the poorest building on the property.

Rounding the house and pulling open the front screen door, Marjie was so absorbed in her thoughts that she barely heard a desperate voice calling out behind her.

"Marjie!" Jerry yelled. "Come quick!"

4

BOUND TOGETHER

Marjie let go of the screen door and turned to see what was wrong. A glance at the angry night sky told her that the winds were shifting again. The airborne stream of hot orange sparks and smoke from the garage was being pushed closer and closer to the barn.

"Oh no!" Marjie gasped. Her memory flashed back to her childhood and a night scene of her father's barn in a blazing inferno, of her father's sobs as the cattle and horses inside bellowed and screamed to escape, of the charred carcasses of the majority that didn't make it. "Please, God, not the barn!" she prayed.

Jerry came running around the corner of the house. "Marjie!" he cried, "we're going to have fight for the barn! If the sparks catch the wooden shingles, we'll lose it!"

"What can I do?"

"Get a bunch of those old heavy horse blankets from the machine shed and soak them in the water tank. I'm going to get the long ladders out so I can get up on the roof."

With that Jerry turned and sped off toward the shed. Marjie followed him as fast as she could run, but by the time she got there he was already dragging out the first section of ladder. She picked her way around the machinery and found the pile of dusty horse blankets in the back of the shed.

Gathering as many blankets as she thought she could carry, Marjie maneuvered her way back out of the shed and headed for the water tank. It was on the south end of the barn. From the shed, she would have to travel well over the barn's full length. With every step the distance seemed to stretch and the weight of the bulky blankets grew. Halfway to the tank, Marjie stepped into a dip in the driveway and down she tumbled.

She could feel the gravel tearing at her knees as she landed, but with her arms loaded, there was nothing she could do to stop it. Marjie hit so hard that for a second she saw white lights, then she rolled on her side in the dust. She couldn't seem to catch her breath, and her knees hurt so badly that she wasn't sure she'd be able to move again—wasn't sure that she wanted to move.

But suddenly she heard Jerry's voice and felt his strong arms lifting her up. "Are you hurt?" he cried, steadying her as she stood.

"I think so," Marjie mumbled. She looked down at her torn slacks and bleeding knees, then moved them slowly up and down. "I'll be okay. Help me with the blankets."

Jerry scooped up the blankets and piled them in Marjie's arms. "Hurry!" he exclaimed. "The sparks are getting closer!"

Then Marjie felt a surge of energy and took off as fast as her feet would carry her. "I can do it!" she yelled into the wind.

When she got to the water tank, she tossed all of the wool blankets into the tank and pushed them under the water. Leaving them there to soak, she ran to where Jerry was hooking on the fourth section of ladder. "I'm going inside to let out the animals and to get Charlie out of the pen. He's too close to the barn."

"I'll get the blankets up on the roof!" Jerry called. "Be careful with Charlie. He might be spooked by the lightning and smoke!"

Marjie ran to the milk room door and pulled the handle down. The door flew open as Blue and the two other dogs pushed and scraped their way through the narrow passageway out of the barn. Seeming to sense the danger, the dogs nearly knocked Marjie to the ground as they made their chaotic exit.

Stepping into the barn and turning on the light switch, Marjie breathed a sigh of relief that the electricity was still on. She wasn't sure how she would find all the animals and get them outside without a light. Quickly glancing around the inside of the barn, she could see only a couple of calves that Jerry was keeping in a pen because they were sick.

She made fast work of opening the gate to the pen and chasing them out the barn door that would take them to the pasture. "Head for the hills!" she yelled at them as they kicked up their heels and disappeared into the darkness.

Then Marjie crossed to Charlie's door and slowly pushed it open. In the dim light from the barn she could see the palomino backed up against the fence, pawing at the ground, with his nostrils flared. As she stepped out the door toward him, the horse reared and struck his hoofs wildly at her.

"Whoa, boy!" Marjie called out, stepping back into the doorway. "It's okay. Settle down."

Charlie seemed to calm a little, but his frightened eyes and continued scraping of the ground told her it wasn't safe to try to get him out. He still didn't know her well enough to trust her in such frightening circumstances. Looking over to the side of the barn, Marjie could see that the sparks were starting to land on the barn's roof. "Please, help!" she whispered. Then she stepped back into the barn, moved several feet from the door, and leaned up against the wall. She hoped and prayed that if she got out of the way, Charlie might go through on his own.

It wasn't long before she heard a nervous snort close to the door, then she watched as Charlie's golden head slowly poked through the doorway and surveyed the inside of the barn. When his gaze fell upon her, he stopped.

"It's okay, boy," Marjie said calmly, frozen in place. "Go ahead."

The horse's eyes blinked a couple times before he moved, but he finally gathered his confidence and stepped into the barn. Seeing the open door that led to the pasture, he trotted toward it and broke into a canter as he disappeared through the dark exit.

Marjie puffed a big sigh of relief, then ran out through the milk room to help Jerry. She stopped to look for him and discovered he was already on the upper half of the roof, knocking out sparks with the wet horse blankets.

"Jerry!" she screamed.

Jerry stopped his work momentarily and looked down. "Get a big rope from the shed and come up the ladder!" he shouted. "The lower part of the roof is too steep for me!"

Marjie wasn't sure what he meant, but she dashed to the shed and grabbed the coil of long, thick rope that was lying by the door. Dragging it behind her, she went to the ladder and began the long climb up. Marjie had never been afraid of heights, but the ladder seemed to stretch up into the heavens as she climbed.

When she reached the top of the ladder, Jerry pulled her over the edge and grabbed the rope from her hand. Tying one end of it around his waist and the other end around Marjie's waist, he tried to catch his breath. "Where the barn slopes down sharply, I can't get to the lower sparks without falling off the roof," he gasped. "You're going to have to position yourself over the peak of the roof and hold me as I go down the steep side."

"What if I can't hold you?" Marjie cried, looking over the peak where the sparks weren't reaching yet.

"It has to work!" Jerry answered, grabbing a soaking wet blanket. "I've got to get down there, or the shingles will catch fire!"

Jerry inched toward the edge where the roof slanted sharply. Marjie went over the peak and braced her weight back as far as she could. As Jerry took his first step down, Marjie held the rope tightly and wanted to yell with relief that the leverage worked.

Moving as quickly as he could from spark to spark, Jerry worked his way from the south side of the barn to the north side. Every so many feet that he moved, Marjie had to move over as well. But as they worked their way to the end of the roof, the garage continued its discharge of flames and the sparks rained down on the sections of roof that Jerry had already covered. From where Marjie was positioned at the barn's peak, it was clear that they were losing the battle. And she didn't know how much longer she could hold Jerry's weight.

"Okay! I'm coming up!" Jerry finally yelled as he pulled hard on the rope.

Marjie braced her weight against the shingles. But just as Jerry reached the edge of the slant, his feet slipped out from under him and he dropped to the steep roof. His total weight nearly jerked Marjie over. Her only choice was to fall forward on the roof and pray that her weight and the leverage of the barn's peak could hold him. Slamming against the wooden shingles, she clung to the roof and held her breath.

Not being able to see Jerry, Marjie waited and prayed. At first there was no movement on the other end of the rope, but it wasn't long before she felt him tugging again.

"Don't move!" Jerry yelled.

Marjie wanted to yell back and ask him where he thought she might be going, but she didn't dare move a muscle. Then she felt the tension on the rope release.

She heard Jerry shout, "I'm up!" but she was too paralyzed and exhausted to move. Then she remembered the sparks and found the strength to get to her feet.

Jerry had untied the rope and was racing from spot to spot on the upper part of the roof with another wet blanket. Marjie grabbed a blanket and went to work as well, but she knew that the real problem remained the lower part of the roof, where most of the sparks were falling.

"I'm going to have to get down there again!" Jerry called out as he raced back toward Marjie. As he took the end of the rope and was tying it around his waist, Marjie noticed that Jerry's arms were bleeding and shaking.

"I don't think I can hold you a second time!" Marjie cried. "The barn's not worth dying for!"

Jerry opened his mouth to protest, but the sudden sag in his shoulders told Marjie he knew it was true. Slowly he reached down and untied the rope while Marjie worked on untying her end. Both of them looked down at the numerous spots on the sloping roof where sparks were glowing, knowing there was no way they could keep up the fight.

"We tried" was all Jerry said, then he wrapped his trembling arms around Marjie and hugged her as tight as he could.

Whether it was the exhaustion, or the fear, or the relief, or a combination of everything, Marjie began to cry in Jerry's arms. Her tears turned to sobs, and her whole body started to shake, but still he held her tight. Then, as she cried with her face to the wind, Marjie felt something brush against her face. At first she thought it was a spark, but then she felt more.

"Rain!" Marjie gasped, clinging to Jerry. "It's starting to rain!"

Jerry looked up and felt it as well. Mixed in between the wind and the sparks were raindrops. First, small drops. But they felt icy cold and refreshing.

"Come on!" Jerry screamed, letting go of Marjie and raising his hands in the air. "Let it rain!"

"Cats and dogs!" shouted Marjie.

Then it came. Big drops splattering against their faces and washing off the blood and smoke and sweat. Sheets of rain that easily put out the sparks and then went to work on what was left of the burning garage. Within minutes the heaven-sent water had the upper hand on the blaze and the raging flames were tamed to little flickers.

Marjie and Jerry stood arm in arm and watched it all from their lofty perch on the barn roof. The rain poured for less than ten minutes, but when it subsided the winds had died away as well. The garage lay smoldering, and the barn roof was saved.

"I think we just were part of a miracle," Marjie whispered, finally breaking their silent watch. "You must have been praying, too."

Jerry nodded reverently, still awed by it all. "Like the parting of the sea."

For a few moments the clouds parted, and the shimmering stars and a silver moon did their best to cheer the weary couple.

"Carry me down," Marjie said finally, "before I collapse and die up here. I once said I'd follow you anywhere, but you'll never get me to chase you up another ladder."

Jerry burst out laughing and mopped the water from his face. "You just didn't know how exciting I am," he said. "This beats any date we ever went on, eh?"

"It certainly does!" Marjie said. "But I've had enough excitement tonight to last me a year. Now carry me down. I don't think I dare get out on that ladder again."

"How about if I get out on the ladder first, and then I'll help you get down?" Jerry suggested, tugging at her arm. "We can go down together."

"Together," she echoed as she followed him to the edge. "Now, I like the sound of that."

———————— ✍ ————————

Getting back down the ladder was far more difficult than Marjie expected. In the chaotic rush to save the barn, she hadn't noticed how much the ladder shook and wiggled or how high it really was. Once she and Jerry were out on the ladder to make their descent, Marjie found that the only way she dared to move was to shut her eyes and depend on Jerry's instructions.

Once down, they trudged slowly past the smoldering remains of the garage without stopping to inspect what was left, remembering that they had left Martha in the cellar alone all this time. Entering the house and then opening the door to the basement, they were surprised to find that all was silent and still. Father and mother crept down the stairs together and found the baby sleeping soundly in her laundry basket.

"Look at the little dolly," Jerry whispered. "The sky is falling down, and she never even wiggled."

Marjie smiled and tucked the blankets back over Martha. "Maybe it's the basket," Marjie said. "Why don't you carry it up to our room, and we'll leave her in it for the night. If she sleeps through, I'm tossing the crib and getting another basket for the wash."

Jerry chuckled and gently picked up the basket. "I'll take her up," he said softly, "and you open some windows. The air in the house is terrible."

"You think it's going to rain some more?" asked Marjie, limping along behind him.

"Probably," Jerry replied. "I'm too exhausted to care if it rains in."

Marjie opened some of the windows and then went to the bathroom to see how much damage had been done to her body. When she flicked on the light, all she could do was laugh at the ridiculous-looking person staring back at her from the mirror. Her hair was a matted mess, her eyes were bloodshot, her face was blackened with smoke, and her whole body was scratched and bruised, especially her knees and shins. Her clothes were so filthy and ripped that she wouldn't have recognized them as her own.

"Is this really the woman you married?" Marjie asked as Jerry stepped into the bathroom doorway.

"The question is," Jerry said, "who was that powerful woman on the barn roof tonight? Was she my wife or Superwoman? 'Look, up in the sky! It's a—' "

"That's enough," Marjie scolded. "Don't you dare start that going around. The least you can do for me now is be nice. I did save your life, you know . . . and mine."

Jerry shook his head as he wiped some of the soot from his face. "That was too close. I slammed down against the roof and I thought we were goners. Look at my arm."

Jerry stepped alongside Marjie and raised his bloody arm into the bright light.

"Good night!" exclaimed Marjie. In addition to the cuts and scrapes, there were slivers everywhere. "Let's get you cleaned up first, then you go to bed. Couple of hours, and you have to be out choring. I'm going to take a long, hot bath and soak this battered body. Every inch of me hurts."

"I know what you mean," said Jerry. "But there's something we need to do even before we get cleaned up."

"What's that?" she asked.

Once more he gathered her into his arms and held her close, then he pulled back so he could look into her eyes.

"When you've had yourself a miracle," he told her gently, "the first thing you gotta do is say thank you."

5

THE DAY AFTER

Marjie awoke to morning sunshine streaming into the bedroom, a cool, dry breeze chasing the curtains from side to side, and a soft cooing conversation coming from the floor beside her bed. Jerry had put Martha's basket there when he left to do the choring. Marjie leaned over the edge of the bed, reached down, and took her daughter's chubby hand.

"Good morning, sunshine girl," Marjie said. "Time to rise and shine?"

Martha smiled ecstatically, her curly dark hair catching a beam of sunlight. Then she let go of Marjie's hand and began to pull herself up on the side of the basket.

Marjie went to sit up and found she could barely move. "Oooh...!" she groaned, trying to stretch. "Oh ... my. This is bad."

Pulling Martha up into the bed, Marjie said, "Today better not be like yesterday. I can't take it if you're fussy again. Be a good girl, okay?"

Marjie looked at the clock and groaned again. "Seven o'clock already. We better get your father some breakfast ... and your bottle ... and you a bath ... and work on my hair...."

By the time Jerry came into the house, Marjie had his breakfast ready and Martha bathed and fed.

"You alive?" he called out from the back entryway.

"Nope," Marjie replied, limping into the kitchen. "Dead as a doornail. How about yourself?"

"I've been better," Jerry said, stepping into the kitchen and kissing her. "I had to walk all the way to the end of the pasture to get Charlie. He's still skittish."

"You should've seen him last night," Marjie said. "I don't know what I'd have done if he hadn't gone on his own. He wasn't about to let me touch him."

"Glad you didn't try," Jerry said. He intercepted Martha and placed her on his knee as she scooted past him on the floor. "I knew a kid who got kicked in the face by a scared horse. Even his nose was as flat as a pancake."

"Sort of like how I feel," said Marjie. Stretching out one of her bruised and battered legs, she added, "This looks better than it feels."

"I believe it," Jerry said. "Time to eat?"

"Just a second, and granny will have it on the table," Marjie rasped. "Put Martha in the high chair."

"Speaking of grannies, did you call your mother yet?"

"No. Why?"

"Why?" Jerry repeated. "Our garage gets struck by lightning, burns to the ground, and we almost lose the barn, and—"

"All right, already," Marjie said, holding up her hand. "So, I'm in slow gear. But I'll call her now—if the phones are working, which I doubt."

Marjie put Jerry's plate on the table and went to the old-fashioned telephone. She was mildly surprised that the phone company had already restored the lines. But she was not surprised, as the operator made the connection, to realize that someone was listening in on the party line. Sometimes she was sure she could hear the click of at least two other neighbors lifting the receiver to catch up on the latest news. This morning she was too tired to ask them to get off.

Her mother answered the phone, and Jerry was finished with his breakfast and working on his second cup of coffee before Marjie finished. When Sarah hung up, Marjie kept the receiver to her ear and heard two clicks.

"Oh no," Marjie groused as she put the receiver back on the hook.

"Give it an hour," Jerry teased, interpreting the expression on her face as she turned around, "and everyone in the county's going to know what happened here last night. This will be a hot story for the gossips."

"Well, at least we'll have some company," Marjie said. "Ma said she and Benjamin will be on their way over in a few minutes."

Jerry's prediction proved accurate, but his timing was off. It was less than half an hour before the Macmillans' phone started ringing constantly. Most of the callers were people Marjie knew, and they all wanted to know if the reports were true. Before much longer, cars began to roll in the driveway, full of people who wanted to look around at the garage and the barn roof. Marjie and Sarah answered the phone and poured gallons of coffee while Jerry and Benjamin stood in the farmyard and repeated the story over and over.

By midafternoon the phone calls had died down, and Marjie hoped that the last of the curiosity seekers had left. She especially hoped to get a nap in before her mother and Benjamin had to leave to start the evening chores, but the crunching sound of tires on the gravel driveway ended that prospect. Marjie went to the window to see who was coming.

"For crying out loud!" she said, turning to her mother, who was holding Martha at the dining room table. "It's Ed Bentley. You remember him?"

"The reporter from the *Preston Republican*," Sarah answered. "You don't suppose—"

"No!" Marjie exclaimed. "He couldn't."

"He could, and he probably is," Sarah finished.

"Count me out," Marjie said, heading for the stairway. "I said I was going to take a nap, and that's what you can tell him. I'm not talking to him."

"Getting a little jumpy, aren't you?" Sarah called after her. "You come back in here, Marjie. It's your story, not mine, and I'm not doing your talking for you."

Marjie turned slowly around, looking down to make sure her long dress covered most of the bruises on her legs. "What if he wants to take a picture?"

"You were keen on getting some photos last time he was here," Sarah teased.

"I didn't look like I'd been riding in the rodeo then," Marjie reminded her mother. "My face is so puffy that I'll look like I've gained fifty pounds. Maybe he'll just go away."

Ed Bentley was already out of his car and talking with Jerry and Benjamin. Jerry was pointing to the garage, then to the barn, and finally the ladder, which was still propped up against the outside wall. Blue sat nearby, his tongue hanging out, looking up at the ladder along with the rest of them.

"Don't look like Mr. Bentley's going anywhere," Sarah said. "If I was you, I'd get out there and make sure he gets the story straight. You wouldn't want Jerry to start telling him about Superwoman. . . ."

"He knows better," Marjie objected, staring at the men. "But . . . maybe you're right. Jerry might put the wrong slant on it."

Marjie went out the front screen door and waved her greeting to Bentley when he turned. He waved back, then straightened his bow tie and pushed his glasses back into place.

"Didn't expect to see you back here so soon, Ed," Marjie said, reaching out and shaking his hand.

"Guess the farm just keeps calling me back," Bentley joked. "Sounds like you've got another headliner story here. Jerry tells me you're pretty good with a rope."

"Oh . . . who called you, anyway?" Marjie lamented. "You're not going—"

"Sure am," Bentley cut in. "Headlines."

"What if we won't give you the story?" asked Marjie.

"I'll just talk to some of the people that stopped by today," replied Bentley. "Either I get it straight from you and Jerry, or I'll take it secondhand. Stories are always best from the eyewitnesses, though. What do you say?"

"I'd rather have him get the real story from us," Jerry said to Marjie. "Ed's already heard some crazy spins on what happened."

"Sounds good to me," Bentley said, walking back to his car and taking out his camera. "You know what would be a great shot for the front page?"

"Forget it!" snapped Marjie. "You don't have enough money to get me to climb that ladder again."

"It would be—"

"Nope!" Jerry said definitely. "Marjie suffered enough when she came down last night."

"Why don't you climb the ladder and shoot a picture from up there looking down?" Marjie suggested. "You might enjoy the thrill."

The reporter looked up at the peak of the barn and shook his head. "You got the wrong guy," he mumbled. "I'm scared of heights."

They all looked at each other and started laughing together.

"How about a shot from beneath the ladder looking straight up to the barn's peak?" Benjamin asked.

"That just might work," Bentley replied. "I'll give it a look, then I'll meet you in the house and get my notes about what *really* happened here."

"Ed," Marjie said. "There's one condition."

"What?"

"You tell it the way we say it?"

He studied her face, then nodded and walked on muttering, "What else would I do?"

When Bentley came into the house, he brought along his pad of paper and his camera. Sitting at the dining room table, Marjie and Jerry told the story from their different perspectives and Bentley wrote page after page of notes. Parts of it had to be re-told so he could fill in the details.

When they got to the part of what it felt like when the rain came, Marjie looked at Jerry and grinned. "Ed, I want you to write this line down and make sure it gets in your story," she stated. "Write: *We knew that God had answered our prayers with a miracle.*"

Ed looked up and wrinkled his forehead. "You know that when I was here the last time I said—"

"This time you said you'd print it like we said it," Marjie corrected him. "You wouldn't print how Jerry came to believe in God last time, and we didn't fuss. This time you print it, or we'll make a stink about it."

"I don't know," Bentley said, shaking his head. "We try to only report the facts."

"That is the story," Jerry said. "What we did wouldn't have mattered without the rain. For us, it's the biggest fact in the story."

Bentley looked around at the nodding faces at the table and finally smiled. "Okay. I think it will work as long as it's your words."

"Did I hear you say you were going to make this your headline story, Mr. Bentley?" Sarah asked, stirring a spoonful of sugar into a fresh cup of coffee.

"That's right. Big bold letters like we did on Jerry's navy story."

"You like to sell as many copies of your paper as possible, right?" continued Sarah.

"Sure."

"Did you ever think that if you spiced your headlines up a bit you might sell more papers?"

"We've talked about it at the office. Why?"

"Well," Sarah said with a twisted smile, "my guess is that you were thinking of a headline like 'GREENLEAFTON COUPLE SAVES BARN.' Am I close?"

"Very."

"You can do better than that, Mr. Bentley," Sarah suggested. "Besides, that headline isn't even true. Marjie and Jerry never once suggested *they* saved the barn."

Bentley put down his pencil and nodded slowly. "Okay. So what's your idea?"

Sarah's eyes twinkled. She reached over, picked up his pencil, and took his pad. Then she wrote in large letters: "IT WAS A MIRACLE!"

6

'39 Mercury Convertible

"I still can't believe he printed it," Marjie said, pressing down hard with the iron to get the last wrinkles out of Jerry's white navy uniform. "Ma should apply for a job writing headlines for the paper."

Jerry looked up from the floor, where he was playing with Martha. "What I can't believe is that the paper came out yesterday with Sarah's headline and now I have to ride in the parade today. This is lousy timing."

"I'm not so sure about that," she said. "Maybe the timing is just right."

"For what?"

"I'm not sure," replied Marjie, holding up the pants for inspection. "But there must be a reason for all this. It wasn't our doing."

"Funny you should say that," Jerry answered. " 'Cause that's just what I've been thinking. God's done so much for us, seems like we need to be doing something for Him." He crinkled his forehead. "Do you suppose we oughta buy some tents and start holding meetings like some of those preachers we read about?"

"Right!" Marjie laughed, picked up her blouse, and laid it across the ironing board. "You could preach, and I'll sing. For a farm boy that gets all tongue-tied in front of a little crowd and a farm girl who couldn't carry a tune in a bucket, that'd really be a winner. I always said farming's too much work for the little bit of money you make."

"Who's making money?" Jerry asked with a smile. "But don't you understand what I'm saying?"

"Yes," Marjie replied. "And I already said I didn't know the reason why all this has been happening. And I certainly don't know why God has involved us. But He has. Do you think there's something we need to be doing more than what we have done?"

While they were talking, Martha had crawled over to Jerry and pulled herself to a standing position by holding his arm. Then she let go, tried to balance, and tipped to the side. Jerry grabbed her before she could fall.

"Did you see that?" Jerry said proudly. "Won't be long before she's walking all over this place."

"She's not even ten months," Marjie responded, shaking her head. "I can't keep her out of stuff now, let alone when she starts to walk. You're going to have to put nails on all the cupboard—"

"Ouch, ouch, ouch!" Jerry cried, trying to get Martha's hand out of his hair. "Let go . . . let go!"

Marjie laughed as he finally managed to get loose, but Martha came away with a prize of several strands of blond hair between her little fingers.

"She keeps that up and I won't be needing to give you a haircut for a while," Marjie teased. "So what are you thinking we need to do?"

Jerry watched Martha closely to make sure she didn't get a second handful of hair and shrugged his shoulders. "I don't know. Wish I knew."

"Why do we have to do something?"

"I don't know. Just seems like we owe it to—"

"Oops. Wrong word," Marjie objected. "This much I've learned. When God gives, He gives freely. He never expects us to pay Him back. How would we ever repay Him for saving the barn, or sparing your life in the water, or sending Jesus Christ to die for us?"

"So we sit back and do nothing?"

"Nothing to repay Him," Marjie reasoned. "He's asked us to love and obey Him. That we can do. If He gives us some more chances to do something for Him, we'll do it. Right."

"Sure," Jerry said. "I just ain't been too comfortable with all the chances He's already given. Despite the money, I like farming."

Marjie laughed. "I don't see that changing, sweetheart. But farming doesn't mean we never do anything but farm. Yesterday you made the news headlines, today you're going to ride in the parade, and tomorrow you'll be in the field. Just do what He gives you to do."

"I can handle that, sir!" Jerry declared, standing up in his boxer shorts and saluting Marjie. "Please hand me my pants before Martha tears the hair off my legs."

———— ∞ ————

"Glad we're wearing our whites today," Chester Stanfeld said, shielding his eyes against the blazing July sun. "Why's it always a roaster on parade day?"

"Probably has something do with it being July, don't you think?" teased Marjie. She reached over to Martha, who was perched in Jerry's arms, and pulled the baby's bonnet down a bit farther on her forehead to block out as much sunlight as possible. "Where's Billy? Didn't he say to be here by one-thirty?"

"Look behind you," Jerry said, pointing down the street. "What a car!"

Rounding the corner and cruising toward the school parking lot was a black '39 Mercury convertible with the top down and Billy and Ruth in the front seat. Rays of sunlight glimmered off the highly polished chrome, and the dozen small American flags attached to the car fluttered in the breeze as it approached. Other people who were in the parking lot getting their floats and tractors ready for the parade stopped to look over the expensive car.

"Whew!" Chester called out as Billy pulled the gleaming machine to a stop beside them. "Didn't know you were moving up in the world so quickly."

"Don't I wish," said Billy, shutting off the engine with a big grin. "Stockdale let me take her for a spin. She really rolls down the road."

"How fast did you take her?" Jerry asked.

"Fast enough to wreck my hair," Ruth answered, staring into the rearview mirror. "Margaret, can you help me? Mr. Navy turned whatever curls I had into a rats' nest."

Billy shrugged his shoulders, pushed open the car door, and got out. "We hit over eighty, and that's going east up the big hill out of town!"

"Wow!" exclaimed Chester, leaning into the car and looking over the dash. "Any chance we'll get to take her out after the parade?"

"None," said Billy. "Mr. Stockdale's going to meet us here and drive us himself. He's bringing this big banner to drape across the back of the car—'Farmers and Merchants Bank Supports Our Boys Overseas.' Says it's cheap advertising."

"Well, that makes me feel real important," Jerry joked, passing Martha back to Marjie and straightening his uniform.

"Like you need to feel more important," Ruth said. "Newspapers, headlines, speaking engagements, parades—"

"He was even talking about buying a big tent and holding meetings this morning!" Marjie teased. "My man loves the spotlight."

Margaret finished unsnarling Ruth's hair, and added in her soft Scottish lilt, "Someday we can tell our grandchildren that we actually knew Jerry Macmillan."

Jerry's blush was only a pale shade of what it once would have been. He put up his hands in mock surrender. "I get the point. If you open the trunk, I'd prefer to ride in there anyway."

"So what's our part in the parade?" asked Chester.

Billy reached over to pat the top of the convertible's backseat. "The three of us are going to sit up here and wave to all the good people who come out to see whether we keel over from sunstroke."

"Not up there," Jerry groaned. "Can't we just sit in the backseat and do our waving?"

"Seaman Macmillan, orders are orders," Billy replied, enjoying Jerry's torment.

"Meaning, Mr. Stockdale said so," Marjie suggested.

"Correct," said Billy with a wink. "And Jacob Medlow, the chairman of the county war board, is going to ride in the front with him. Maybe we'll get our pictures on the front page!"

"Oh, brother!" Jerry blurted. "What else?"

"You forgot to mention the candy," Ruth stated, emerging from her side of the convertible. She reached over to take Martha from Marjie and balanced the baby on one hip as she continued, "You guys get to toss out handfuls of candy to the kids. Sounds like fun, eh?"

"Now you're talking Jerry's language," said Marjie, looking down the street. "Hey, isn't that your dad, Chester?"

"This is strange," Chester said, grimacing slightly. "What now?"

"How's it been going lately?" Marjie whispered to Margaret.

"Since the wedding, much better," Margaret told her softly.

Bill Stanfeld, dressed in new bib overalls, approached the gathering of friends in his usual brusque manner. Everyone went silent, not knowing what to expect.

"Howdy, howdy!" he called out with a smile. "My, you boys look sharp. Makes me proud just to look at you."

"Thanks," the three friends answered collectively.

"What's up, Dad?" asked Chester.

"I was hoping to catch you all here before the parade," Mr. Stanfeld said. "I read the big story in yesterday's paper about the fire, and I wondered if you've talked it over yet."

Marjie could feel her stomach tightening, and she took a deep breath in anticipation of what Chester's father might say next.

"We've all been out to the farm and talked about it," Chester answered for the group. "What do you mean, exactly?"

Bill Stanfeld laughed, and Marjie exhaled. It looked to her like he was in a very good mood.

"Guess I wasn't too clear," he said, shoving his large hands into the deep overall pockets and jingling his keys. "I thought maybe you'd talked over rebuilding that garage. Figured you guys would pitch in together."

"Guess I hadn't thought about that," Chester said.

"Actually," Jerry said, "we didn't have insurance on the building . . . and we won't have money to build a new garage for a while. I'll be glad to get some help, though, once we do."

"Great!" Mr. Stanfeld bellowed. "Mother was right."

Perplexed looks spread over the faces of all the friends. Fortunately, Chester was not rattled by his father's unexplained elation. "Mother was right about what, Dad?"

"She read the article and said this was our chance to make a repayment on what we owe Jerry for saving your life," Mr. Stanfeld explained. "You remember all them big pines and hard maples we cut into lumber some years ago?"

Chester nodded.

"I got enough dried two-by-fours and four-by-fours to put up the entire frames for a half-dozen garages," his father continued, turning to Jerry. "You tell me what you need, and I'll haul it to your farm myself. Deal?"

Jerry shook his head and mumbled, "You folks don't owe me anything, Mr. Stanfeld. I . . . just—"

"It's a deal!" Marjie piped in before he could say more.

Everyone burst out laughing, but clearly it was Bill Stanfeld who enjoyed this scene the most. He ceremoniously shook Marjie's hand, then squeezed Jerry's hand until Jerry winced.

"Say," Chester said, "why don't we see if we can get the rest of the materials together and put it up ourselves?"

"Why not?" Billy seconded. "I did my share of building before my legs got hurt. I'll supervise."

"Supervise, nothing!" Jerry joked. "Legs or no legs, we'll get some honest work out of you."

"You sign me up, too," Bill Stanfeld declared. "Soon as you get the foundation laid, call me and I'll bring the lumber."

"I can't thank you—"

"No thanks are needed," Chester's father broke in. "My boy's alive. Do you know what that means to me?"

Jerry looked at Martha and smiled. "I think I do."

"Well," Stanfeld announced, "I need to get back uptown and find the rest of the family. They're saving me a spot along the parade route. Before I go, though, I have a question for you, Marjie."

Marjie looked into his face, remembering both the bitter outbursts she had seen from him and the tears of happiness he had shed at his son's wedding. She nodded.

For a moment, he chewed his lip and looked a bit agitated, and Marjie hoped what had been such a pleasant time would not be spoiled with a bad ending.

"That stuff about the barn and the rain—did it really happen exactly like the paper said?" Chester's father asked. His jaw muscles flexed, and his eyes were tightly squinted.

"Exactly," she answered evenly. "There were more details that could have been added, of course."

He opened his eyes wide, then returned to his squint. "And you really believe that the rain you felt splash on your face was a miracle of God?"

Marjie fixed her dark brown eyes on his but could hardly restrain a sudden urge to weep for him. "Yes, sir," she whispered, nodding her head. "Without a doubt."

Bill Stanfeld answered her with his own slow nod, then he turned and headed up the street.

7

CHESTER'S MOM

"I can't believe they could get all those materials together in just a week," Marjie said. "Those guys are really on a tear."

She stood elbow deep in hot, sudsy water, looking out the kitchen window toward the new garage site. Jerry, Billy, and Chester were just finishing up the rafters, and Bill Stanfeld and Benjamin were cutting the lumber. "Looks to me like they're going to get everything done today but the big door hung and the roof shingled. At lunch Jerry whispered something to me about helping him finish it up next week. What do you know about chalk lines?"

"Nothing to it," answered Sarah. Handing Marjie another stack of dirty dishes, she said, "Jerry will mark on the roof where he wants the lines of shingles to go. Then you just hold the chalk string in place on the opposite side of the roof from him, he'll snap the line, and you'll move down to the next mark. Hardest part's getting on the roof."

Marjie looked out at the roof and wrinkled her forehead. "Least it's closer to the ground than the barn roof was. Clare, did anyone tell you that Ed Bentley wanted me to climb back up to the top of the barn so he could get a great photo for his front page?"

"No," Clare Stanfeld said and laughed. She was standing in the dining room with Martha in her arms, looking out at the men working on the garage. "Sounds just like him, though. We went to school together when we were kids. He was always concocting some wild scheme, but he never dared do them himself."

"You hit that nail on the head," Marjie replied. "I told him to be my guest and climb the roof himself if he wanted that photograph. He politely declined."

"No surprise," Clare continued. "Some of the boys once forced Ed to the top of a tree outside the school building, and then he didn't dare climb down. He was so late that the teacher made him sit in the corner the entire afternoon."

"It's too bad Margaret couldn't come today," Sarah said. "I miss her."

"Saturdays are always her busiest day in the bakery," said Clare. "The Olsons go home at noon and leave her to run it by herself. They've really taken a shine to her."

Marjie finished scrubbing the last greasy frying pan and dipped it into the not-so-clean rinse water. Then she looked back around the counter. "Any more dishes, Ma?"

"That's it, thank goodness," answered Sarah, drying the fry pan and hanging her towel on a rack. "I'd forgotten how many dishes you can dirty when there are eight bodies to feed. Seems like I've spent half my life setting dishes out and then cleaning them up."

"And the other half raising children," Marjie continued. "How's my baby doing, Clare?"

"Just about asleep," replied Chester's mother, looking down and smiling. "If you get me a bottle, I think she'll go out."

"Take her in the living room and get comfortable," Marjie said. "I have a bottle warming already. We've got the kitchen clean enough."

"No sense overdoing it," Sarah added, taking off her apron and wiping her hands dry. "Just gonna dirty it up again in a couple hours."

Sarah followed Clare into the living room, picked up her needlework from the davenport, and sat down to the white napkins she had been embroidering before lunch. Clare held Martha in the large chair that had been Ben's favorite and jabbered to the baby while they waited for Marjie and the warm bottle of milk.

"Been a long time since I held a baby," Clare said as Marjie came into the living room and handed her the bottle. "Sure feels good again. Especially to hold a girl."

"Let's see, Clare," Sarah began conversationally. "You have three boys, right, and Chester's the oldest?"

"That's right," answered Clare. She had Martha snug against her arm and the bottle ready to go. "Three big strapping boys who are all just about grown up. I lost a child between Chester and his brother Wendell."

Marjie had sat down with her mother on the davenport and glanced over at Sarah quickly. Clare had been with them most of the morning but had been very reserved. Marjie had wondered if the day might pass and they would still know little about the Stanfelds.

"I'm sorry for you," Sarah said, putting down the napkin she was working on and looking at Clare. "How did it happen?"

"Stillborn."

Clare offered no more except her silence. Her expression was deadpan, and she did not look up.

Marjie stared at Martha, nestled so comfortably in Clare's arm, and tried to gather her thoughts. *What would it have been like to have lost...* But the thought was too painful for her to fathom or to continue.

"I don't mean to pry," Sarah said soothingly, "but was it a little girl?"

Clare only nodded.

Sarah looked down at her needlework, then she reached up and pressed her fingers against her eyes like she was massaging a sinus headache. "My older sister lost her first baby," she finally said. "A beautiful little girl. I was there to help Dinah with the delivery, and her baby looked perfect, but she never took a breath of air. I thought for a long time that Dinah would never get over it."

A slight tremor shook Clare's shoulders, but she did not look up.

"All these years, and I never knew that," said Marjie softly. "Why didn't you ever tell me?"

Shrugging her shoulders, Sarah exhaled a large breath of air. "Hmmm . . . that's a hard one. Guess it always seemed too painful for Dinah to talk about, so I kept it a secret. But once a year or so, usually soon after the snows are melted and the ground has firmed up, Dinah still asks me to go out to their church cemetery with her and visit—"

Sarah choked up and shut her eyes. Clare glanced up quickly, then looked back down as Sarah put her hand over her mouth and sat motionless.

"I never would have imagined it," Marjie whispered. "I would go if Aunt Dinah needs someone."

"No," Sarah replied, shaking her head slowly. "It seems like something Dinah and I need to do alone. As hard as it is, it seems to help. Do you know . . . sometimes I dream about little Jenny. That's what they named her. She'd be a year older than you, Marjie."

Marjie tried to imagine what it might have been like to have had a girl cousin to play with, but Clare broke into her thoughts.

"Her husband never understood," Clare commented, looking up again at Sarah.

Sarah shook her head no. "I think he tried, but . . . I don't know. He never seemed to feel the grief that Dinah felt. Least he never was able to show it . . . or help her. I sometimes wonder if he suffered, too."

"You never get over it," said Clare quietly. "Never."

The two older women stared into each other's eyes and nodded knowingly.

"You grieved alone," Sarah observed.

Clare looked from Sarah to Marjie. "Still do. Mary would be seventeen now."

Martha was asleep, and Clare set the bottle on the coffee table next to the big chair. She seemed to linger, staring at the bottle.

"Do you want me to take her?" Marjie asked. "I could put her in her crib."

"No," answered Clare, and with a smile her expression softened. "She feels good right here. As long as I don't seem to be disturbing her, I'd like to hold her."

"Do you think about Mary a lot?" asked Sarah.

"Not usually," Clare said, shaking her head and taking a deep breath. "Seems to come in spurts. First couple of years were bad. Now I can go weeks and nothing bothers me, but then something comes up and I can't get her out of my thoughts. Like Chester and Margaret's wedding. I get to wondering about what Mary would look like, how much she'd be enjoying herself, how nice it would have been to . . ."

Clare's words wandered off, and she looked down at Martha again.

"If you'd rather we didn't talk about it," Sarah said, "just say so. You hardly know us."

"I'm all right," Clare replied softly. "I haven't talked to anyone about this in years, but to hear what your sister's gone through makes me feel, well, normal again. My mother-in-law told me that I'd forget about Mary when I delivered Chester's brother, but she was wrong. Seemed to only make it worse for a while."

"Sounds like everyone wanted you to pretend like your daughter didn't die," said Marjie.

"Or like she wasn't a real baby," Sarah added. "That's how my sister felt."

Clare nodded. "Sometimes I feel like I'm the only one in the world who holds Mary as precious. Maybe that's why I cling to her memory."

"How did your husband take it?" asked Sarah.

"Not good," said Clare, rubbing her cheek slowly. "Bill's an explosive man, as you may have noticed. When life's good, like today, he's happy as a lark. But when something bad happens, he's got a terrible temper. Maybe it was his way of grieving, but when he found out the baby was stillborn, he went into weeks of violent rage. It was frightening."

"Violent—as in striking you?" Marjie asked.

"No, never," Clare assured her. "But he beat the dogs and the cattle and pigs without mercy, and the littlest thing could set him off. I'd be in the kitchen making supper and hear him carrying on out in the barn. I just tried to stay out of his path. I didn't think it would ever end. He still gets angry, but it's never been anything like that spell."

"Didn't he ever talk about what he was going through?" asked Sarah.

"Not really," Clare said, shaking her head. "Except he did talk to me about how much he hated God for taking Mary. It happened not long after we got excommunicated from our church for not being able to pay our tithe—or what they said was our tithe. Bill was convinced Mary's death was God's way of punishing him for holding back money we didn't have to give."

"Oh, my goodness," Marjie burst, feeling the tears well up inside. "What a terrible lie to live under. No wonder he couldn't talk about it."

"I thought your husband didn't believe in God," Sarah said.

Clare nodded sadly. "That came later. After getting kicked out of the church, he started reading literature from the Jehovah's Witnesses for a while. Then he gave that up for *The Book of Mormon*. But that didn't last either. Seems like he sent for some literature from an atheist, then one day he came in from the field and told me he was an atheist. That must be about twelve years ago."

"What did you think when he told you that?" asked Marjie.

"At first I thought he was kidding. I had never met an atheist, let alone having the first one be my husband."

"So you didn't agree with him?" Marjie continued.

Shrugging her shoulders, Clare twisted her mouth and said, "I didn't know what I believed, but I guess I didn't care. Bill was happier than he'd been in a long time. He seemed to be able to live with himself again, and that's made it easier on me and the boys."

"Until Chester started talking about religion," Marjie suggested.

"That set him off, that's for sure," Clare agreed. "When he gets around someone who believes in God, he can't seem to resist attacking them—even people he loves dearly. And then he hates himself so much afterwards that he tries to push them away."

"Like he did Chester and Margaret," said Sarah. "It was too painful to have them near."

Clare nodded. "I think so."

"He loves Margaret, doesn't he?" asked Marjie.

"Adores her," said Clare. "She won Bill's heart, but she lived so true to what she believed that he couldn't take it. And she wouldn't give in to his pressure."

"Makes for a pretty small world," Sarah said. "A hard place to live."

"It is."

"What do *you* think of Chester and Margaret?" Marjie asked. "Their faith, I mean."

"I admire them," Clare replied. "They live what they say, and what they live is love. But it's not for us."

Marjie stared into Clare's eyes and asked, "Why do you say that?"

"Because it would destroy the little that's left of our family," Clare said. "Can't you see that?"

8

CARY GRANT

"Just go!" urged Jerry, pushing Marjie toward the door. "You could leave our newborn alone with my dad, but you think I can't take care of her at ten months for a couple hours tonight? Get moving."

"I'm going, I'm going," protested Marjie. "I'm just afraid you're going to fall asleep, and Martha's going to get out the screen door. You worked like a Trojan from the crack of dawn till now. Besides, what will all your friends think about you baby-sitting? I hate to embarrass you."

"She stays with me," replied Jerry. "And I don't care what they think. Just because we're farm men, why should we get gypped out of spending time with our kids? That's stupid."

"I love the way you say that. I've taught you well," Marjie said proudly as she pushed open the screen door. "The washing machine is down the cellar stairs and to the left, dear."

"I just might surprise you and knock out a couple of loads," Jerry suggested, picking up Martha from the floor and hoisting her to his shoulders. He followed Marjie out the door and down the sidewalk. "By the way, did I tell you the rumor I heard in Greenleafton yesterday?"

"No."

"Word around the feed mill is that you're looking for more roofing jobs. Is that true?"

Marjie broke into a hearty laugh and stopped in front of the garage to admire the work the two of them had done getting the shingles on. "It's a fine-looking roof, that's for sure. I can see how rumors get started. If you could just rustle up enough rationing coupons to go buy the paint, I'd show you what I can do with a brush as well."

"If you had your own business going, we could afford a garage door," Jerry teased. "Can't you see the snow drifting in there in the winter?"

"Snow sounds kinda good right about now," replied Marjie, lifting her long hair off her neck and fanning herself with her free hand. "We are going to need to get a door, though. Anybody else owe you money that you haven't told me about?"

Jerry shook his head no. "I wish. I suppose we could sell Charlie. That animal's been taking up far too much of your time, anyway."

"Very funny," Marjie said. "You're Mr. Jokes tonight, aren't you. Maybe you should come to the movie theater with us and do a stand-up comedy act before the main feature. That might be an easier way to come up with the cash for the garage door."

"What movie did you say was playing?"

"*Once Upon a Honeymoon*," answered Marjie, stepping into the garage. "Sounds romantic, eh? Cary Grant and Ginger Rogers."

"Ginger— "

"Cary Grant," Marjie broke in and laughed. "I have to go, or we'll be late."

"Do you remember our honeymoon?" teased Jerry. "Maybe you should stay home tonight."

Marjie opened the car door and got in. "If you're awake when I get home, we'll see what happens."

Starting the car and backing out of the garage, Marjie stopped alongside Jerry and Martha and stuck her head out. "You are going to listen for any war reports on the invasion of Sicily, aren't you? I'm really worried about Paul."

"I'll have the radio on all night," Jerry said. "Eisenhower landed on the tenth, so it's been a week. We should be hearing something soon about your brother."

——————— ⁓ ———————

"That was so wonderful," Ruth sighed as the three women exited the Strand Theater in Preston and stepped into the warm summer night. "That Cary Grant is the most handsome man in the world . . . next to Billy Wilson."

"Of course, Ruthie," Marjie said with a laugh. "I'll make sure Billy gets the first part of that."

Margaret took Ruth's arm and said, "I forbid you to go home tonight until you've told me every detail of what you and Billy are up to. Marjie promised me the two of you would come up to our house for coffee. It's only two blocks."

"It's going to get mighty late if you want all the details," Ruth joked as they strolled down the dark street toward Chester and Margaret's place. "Is Chester still up?"

"No," answered Margaret. "He gets up so early in the morning that he tries to be asleep by nine. Neither of us are night owls. Night owls—that's the right American expression, isn't it?"

"Perfect." Marjie nodded as they stepped down from the curb and crossed the street. "What time's Chester start work?" she asked.

"He has to be there by seven," Margaret said. "I start at eight."

"So why's he get up so early?" Marjie continued. "You aren't milking cows in the backyard, are you?"

"What—" asked a befuddled Margaret, then she laughed. "No, you silly goose. Chester bought some Bible study books that my father recommended, and he uses the time to prepare for his adult Sunday school class. And then he has his prayer time."

"No wonder the class is so good," said Marjie. "Jerry likes it so much that on Tuesday nights he sits at the dining room table and reads through the lesson so he'll be ready on Sunday. Next thing you know, my charming farm boy's going to be taking notes."

"Speaking of charming," Ruth said, "I've got a question that kept bothering me during the movie. Do older married ladies like yourselves think it's okay to look at Cary Grant and still feel a little dreamy?"

The three friends burst out laughing, and Marjie hollered, "How dare you call—"

"Quiet down out there!" barked an elderly man who was standing unseen in the screen door of the pitch-black house they were walking past. "People are trying to sleep."

"Sorry!" Margaret cried after she recovered from nearly screaming in fright. "We're just on our way."

"Whew!" Marjie whispered, taking Margaret's arm and starting to giggle. "He scared me to death. Nothing like friendly neighbors."

"He's a strange one," said Margaret softly. "The lights are never on at night, but he seems to always be lurking about. Sometimes he's standing out in the garden behind one of the trees. I forgot he might be there."

"Thanks a lot," Ruth said, glancing back nervously. "Can't you older women walk any faster? I've got the creeps."

They collectively picked up their pace until they were well past the spooky house. When they were nearly to the end of the block, they turned onto the sidewalk leading to the large house where Margaret and Chester rented the upper floor.

"It's dark in there," Marjie said as they approached the front door. "Don't we have to walk through the Baxters' entryway?"

"Yes," replied Margaret, stepping ahead and taking the handle of the screen door. "Follow me up the stairs, then I'll turn on the light. But please be quiet."

"Still got the creeps, Ruthie?" Marjie whispered as she reached her hand around Ruth's back and lightly ran her finger along Ruth's shoulder.

Ruth's scream was only partially muffled by her own hand, and Margaret jumped as well. Marjie covered her own mouth as she burst into laughter and nearly doubled over.

"You deserve to die!" Ruth gasped, still covering her mouth with her hand and taking deep breaths of air. "I'm going to make you pay so bad. I should kick you in the shin and—"

"No more!" warned Margaret, who was peeking in the door to make sure the lights hadn't come on. "We can't wake the Baxters, or I'll be in trouble. Follow me."

Margaret quietly pulled the screen door open and silently led the friends through the entryway and up the stairs. Opening the door at the top of the landing, she turned on the light and let Marjie and Ruth into their living room, then she shut the door behind them.

"We made it," Margaret declared with a sigh. "Now you may fight if you like. I'll put the coffee on. Try not to break any of our recent acquisitions. Chester says they're early American."

Marjie and Ruth scanned the sparsely furnished living room. The worn crushed-velvet davenport and chair had not changed since their last visit, but there were two maple end tables that Marjie couldn't remember seeing before. One of the legs on the end table next to the chair was slightly chipped.

Walking to the kitchen door, Marjie said to Margaret, "Nice tables. Where'd you get them?"

"The thrift store. Where else?" Margaret answered and laughed. She set her coffeepot on the gas stove and turned on the burner. "Chester says the good thing about what we buy there is that we don't need to break it in. Most of it's already broken."

Marjie and Ruth laughed, then they turned to take a seat on the davenport. Margaret came in and sat down in the chair while she waited for the coffee to boil.

"So, can you hear the Baxters through the floor?" Ruth asked.

Margaret nodded her head. "Unless the wind is blowing or it's raining."

"And they can hear you?" Marjie asked.

"We assume they can." Margaret couldn't hold back her smile, then she broke into an embarrassed giggle. "We have to be careful. Their bedroom is directly below ours."

"I don't know what you're talking about, Margaret," Ruth joked. "But spare me the explanation. I'm an old maid and I don't care for that kind of talk. Besides, I'm still waiting for you older married ladies to answer my question about Cary Grant."

"Now I remember why I scared you," Marjie said. "I was hoping you might think twice about calling me an old married lady. Don't you dare say you owe me a payback. You deserved what you got."

"Say no more. You will pay," said Ruth, holding up her hand. "The two don't compare. Now, answer the question or you'll have to stay after school and clean the blackboard."

"I can tell you what I think about Mr. Dreamboat," Marjie said. "I'd say I'd have to be blind to not notice somebody as handsome as Cary Grant, and that it's normal to feel a little dreamy about him. I don't think it's a problem. Just natural."

"Is that what you think, Margaret?" asked Ruth.

Margaret nodded. "I can't imagine any woman not thinking he's just grand."

"And what if Jerry knew that about you?" continued Ruth.

"I hope he does know that," replied Marjie. "I would never expect him to see Ginger Rogers in a movie and feel nothing. If he didn't, I'd get real nervous real fast!"

All three women broke out laughing, but Margaret did her best to shush them by pointing in the direction of their bedroom door.

"I thought you said Chester was a heavy sleeper," Marjie said.

"He is, but I don't want to push my luck," replied Margaret, getting out of her chair. "I think the coffee's ready. Sugar or . . . milk? We have no cream."

Ruth and Marjie shook their heads no.

"Black is fine," said Marjie.

As Margaret stepped into the kitchen, Ruth looked over to Marjie. "This may be silly, Marjie, but I did feel a little guilty tonight about being attracted to another man. It made me wonder how much I really love Billy. You don't feel guilty?"

Marjie ran her fingers gently across her lips and considered her answer carefully. "I won't say I never feel guilty. But feeling guilty and being guilty are often a long ways apart. Should I feel guilty that sometimes I wish we were rich like so-and-so and I could afford a whole new wardrobe?"

"No. As long as you don't push it into coveting."

"You know it, and I know it, but I still sometimes feel guilty about it," Marjie said. "Seeing another man we feel attracted to does not need to be a big deal. It's what we do with the attraction. You know that, Ruthie."

Ruth's dark frown faded, and she broke into a frail smile. "I should, but it feels like my whole world's been flipped upside down and I'm having to learn all over again. It's embarrassing, but I've been getting so confused about little things that never bothered me before."

Margaret came back into the living room with steaming coffee cups and an assortment of pastries from the bakery. "Don't forget your good mother's advice," she said to Ruth as she set the tray on the coffee table in front of them.

"What—oh, yeah," Ruth replied. " 'Remember that the greatest distance in the world is between my head and my heart.' I do recall quoting that to you once."

"And it helped me," Margaret said, "to learn what it means to love one man and how it all works. It's like learning to walk all over again."

"Wait until you add children to the equation," Marjie stated and laughed. "There are moments when I wonder if I truly love or care for anyone in the entire world. And I make such bad mistakes. You wonder if you know anything for certain."

"Love's a lot more complicated than I expected," Ruth said. "I just wish I would have been ready for this."

"You'd never be ready," said Marjie. "Never in a million years. Until you jump into the water, you never learn to swim. And once you're in over your head, it can get scary."

Ruth nodded in hearty agreement and took a sip of her coffee.

"So, how deep are you?" Margaret pried. Her round blue eyes fixed on Ruth's flashing dark eyes. "Are you"—she struggled with the expression—" 'over your head'?"

There was an extended pause while Ruth put down her cup

of coffee and settled back onto the davenport with a loud sigh. "How deep is the ocean?" she asked softly.

Marjie and Margaret laughed knowingly, but they stopped quickly because Ruth was not laughing.

"If I show you something," Ruth whispered, pulling a small white envelope from her purse, "will you help me learn how to swim?"

Marjie sat forward on the edge of the davenport cushion and tried to guess what was in the envelope. Both she and Margaret answered, "Yes."

"I wanted you both to see this together," she said. Then she reached into the envelope and pulled something out. "You've got to come closer, Margaret."

Ruth slid to the middle of the davenport, and Margaret got up and sat down next to Ruth.

"What do you think of this?" Ruth asked, slowly opening her hand to reveal a small diamond ring. Quickly she slipped it onto her left ring finger. "We're engaged!"

"Congratulations!" Margaret and Marjie screamed together, taking turns hugging Ruth and taking her hand to study the ring.

"How could you make us wait?" Marjie cried. "You're so—"

"Margaret!" Chester broke in, poking his head out the bedroom door. His eyes were barely open, his hair was matted to one side, and a silly smile had crossed his face. "I thought the roof was blowing off. What's wrong?"

9

RIPPLES IN THE WATER

"We've put this off long enough," Jerry said, parking the car outside the parsonage. "It was months ago that we talked this over."

"You were planting corn," Marjie recalled. "And Teddy had just walked out on Ma. It's going to take me a while to forget that day."

"Now the corn is shoulder deep," continued Jerry, "and Teddy is in the army. How can that be?"

Marjie put Martha's bottle back in the bag and handed it to Jerry. "It's just all those little interruptions. Like your dad falling in love with my mom and getting married; our best friends falling in love; getting struck by lightning and fighting fires. Not exactly a boring summer, I'd say."

"This should add an interesting twist to it," Jerry said, taking the bag and opening his car door. "I wish you'd have called my dad to come along."

"Nope," replied Marjie, pushing open her door and getting out with Martha. "If this is what we're supposed to do, we should do it on our own. You nervous?"

"Little bit," replied Jerry as they walked up the sidewalk toward the large white house. "I never thought Pastor Fitchen liked me much when I was a kid. I was the devil in his catechism class."

"And you expected him to like you," joked Marjie. "You and Billy in the same class must have been sure-fire trouble."

"Unending," Jerry said. He stopped at the door and looked at Marjie. "Ready?"

"This isn't an interrogation," Marjie sputtered. "We're coming to talk to a pastor about being baptized. Isn't that what pastors do?"

"Yes, but—"

The parsonage door suddenly swung open, and Mrs. Fitchen stood in the doorway. Her friendly brown eyes smiled beneath straight white bangs, and her thin arms were raised in a gesture of welcome.

"I thought I heard voices," Dorothy Fitchen said. "Come on in. Marvin is waiting in his study."

"I hope we're not late," said Jerry, following Marjie into the house.

"No, no, no," replied Dorothy. She pointed toward an open door down the hallway. "He's busy working on Sunday's sermon. Now, hand over the little dolly. You can stay in there with the pastor as long as you like. They don't call me Granny just because of my white hair and wrinkles."

Marjie laughed and handed Martha to Mrs. Fitchen. "I appreciated your offer when I called. Make sure you keep your eye on her. She's taken her first couple steps, and she's fast as lightning on her knees."

Pastor Fitchen came to the door of his study and said, "Don't you worry. Dorothy's a professional." Then he shook both Jerry and Marjie's hands and said, "Please come in and have a chair. Nothing's changed in here, has it, Jerry?"

Jerry looked around the large study. "Not much. The chairs are new, though. I like the cushions."

"Beats those hard wooden ones, eh?" suggested the elderly pastor with a laugh. "You boys seemed to have difficulty sitting still on them, if I remember correctly."

Jerry laughed as well and relaxed in his chair. "Marjie and I were just talking about that. We didn't make your job an easy one."

"That you didn't," Pastor Fitchen said, smiling. "But I've been thinking lately that I probably got what I deserved. Did you find those classes boring?"

"Ummm ... I ... don't—"

"I'm too old not to be told the truth," Fitchen broke in, giving Jerry a big nod. "I made the catechism as dull as sawdust, didn't I? You boys were bored silly."

"We were ... pretty bored," Jerry answered. "But we—"

"You were disobedient," the pastor continued, "so I made it all that much tougher. Nothing like putting the joy into religion, is there?"

The three of them laughed, and Marjie wondered at the changes that had come over Pastor Fitchen since the first time she met him. She didn't recall his being the type to laugh or apologize, especially when it pertained to something as serious as the catechism of the church.

"Now, what can I do for you folks?" Fitchen asked. He sat back in his chair and folded his hands. "You didn't come to listen to an old preacher confess his sins, but you got my curiosity up when you wouldn't tell me on the phone what you wanted to talk about."

"With our party line," Marjie answered, "I don't say anything private on the phone. You should preach a sermon about listening in on other people's conversations and then gossiping about whatever is picked up. That would set some teeth on edge."

"My word!" the pastor said to Jerry, raising his white, bushy eyebrows. "Does your wife always hit the nail this hard?"

"Yep," replied Jerry with a twisted smile. "Always."

"I'll give that sermon some thought," Fitchen said. "But perhaps I should wait until I'm a little closer to retiring. So then, what did you want to talk about?"

Jerry looked at Marjie, and she whispered to him, "You do it."

"Well, I know this is gonna sound strange," Jerry began slowly, "but Marjie and I would like to make a public confession of our faith like Billy did."

The pastor was listening carefully. "Some people in the church didn't like it when Billy admitted that his earlier confession of faith wasn't real, but most people seemed to think it was good. It doesn't sound strange to me, Jerry."

"Good," said Jerry, looking a bit sheepish, "but we've got a little more in mind. After Marjie and I have confessed our faith, we'd like you to baptize us along with Martha."

Pastor Fitchen leaned forward in his chair and took a deep breath. "I see," he said softly. Then he reached up and rubbed the back of his neck and slowly shifted his head from side to side. "You are serious?"

"Yes, sir," answered Jerry, sitting up straighter. "What makes you think we aren't?"

"Ummm . . . I'm sorry," the pastor muttered. "I just wasn't expecting this. And I've heard about Marjie's tricks. I thought for a minute I was being set up."

"No, sir," said Jerry, then he laughed at the discomfort on Pastor Fitchen's face. "But you're wise to be on your toes around her."

Marjie smiled. "You're not on my list yet," she told the pastor. "And we really do want to be baptized together. Is it really so strange?"

"Well . . ." Pastor Fitchen drawled out, "let's say that it's irregular for our church. I don't recall anyone ever being baptized in this church as an adult."

"Congratulations, then," Marjie said. "You get to be the first pastor to take a crack at it."

"And perhaps the last," Fitchen added. "Members are going to have a problem with me rebaptizing you, Jerry. Were you baptized, Marjie?"

"I guess," she replied. "My mother says I was, but we weren't ever much on going to church."

"Oh, boy," the pastor mumbled, rubbing his neck again. "This is going to be a big problem to some people. Seeing as you've been baptized as infants, explain to me why you want to be baptized now. Why can't a confession of faith be enough?"

"It's not really a matter of whether it's enough or not,"

replied Jerry, shaking his head. "But I've done a lot of reading in the book of Acts, and when I came to the story about the jailer at Philippi, I read it and reread it. It says that after he believed, then he and his household were baptized."

"And you'd like to do the same," Pastor Fitchen said, looking out his window for a moment. "But this was their first encounter with Christianity. They didn't grow up within the church like you did."

"I know. I've thought about that a lot," Jerry agreed. "Don't get me wrong. I'm not suggesting the church should not baptize babies. In fact, we want Martha to be baptized with us. But for Marjie and me . . . we just feel it's important that we start all over again. Like the jailer, I guess."

Marjie could see the wheels turning in Pastor Fitchen's head. "We realize it's irregular," she added. "But if it's consistent with what was done in the book of Acts, why should it be a problem? And if Jerry and I feel strongly that this is how we want to declare our faith, should we be denied?"

"Not by my way of thinking," the pastor admitted. Then he sat back in his chair and folded his hands again. "I think what you're asking would be a wonderful testimony that's never been seen in this church. But I don't make all the final decisions, and this one . . ."

Pastor Fitchen's voice trailed off, and he puffed out a big blast of air. Then he sat quietly, pondering his options.

"We've put you in a hard place," Jerry said. "Perhaps we should have asked it to be brought before the elders of the church rather than asking you to decide."

"No, no," replied the pastor. "They would have made a mess of it. Anything that looks like something new or different doesn't get the time of day. You were right in coming to me."

"So what do we do?" asked Marjie. "You could sneak over to our farm and dunk us in the cow tank."

The pastor burst out laughing and nodded. "That's one idea I didn't think of, but it has its pluses." He rubbed his chin thoughtfully. "I don't know. You really feel strongly about this, don't you?"

"Yes," Jerry said.

"And you've considered that there's going to be talk? Some people will be offended, and some of them won't be afraid to let you know it. Are you prepared for that?"

"Without a question," said Marjie.

"Well, then, how does this coming Sunday morning sound?"

"What?" asked Jerry. "Doesn't it need some kind of approval?"

"You won't get it," Pastor Fitchen stated. "I believe it's the right thing to do, so I'm going to do it. If I get in trouble, so be it."

"We don't want you—"

"Let me worry about it," the pastor cut Jerry off. Then he smiled and added, "I've seen more happen in this church over the past six months than I have in the previous twenty years. I'd rather get in trouble with some church members than get in the way of what God is doing. If He's put it on your heart to be baptized as adults, I'm willing to go to bat for you. Just don't go broadcasting it around before the deed is done."

Jerry looked intently into Pastor Fitchen's eyes and said, "I can't tell you how much we appreciate this. We hope we can live up to your faith in us."

"I do have one request," the pastor said. "Marjie, the church has heard Jerry's story, but I think it would be good if they could also hear yours. Would you tell it Sunday morning before the baptism?"

"Oh my!" gasped Marjie, taking Jerry's hand. "That's a tough one. I've never done anything like that in public."

"You were the one who thought I should do it," Jerry reminded her, "and I survived—barely. Time to practice what you preach?"

Marjie pinched his hand, then she nodded. "I'll try. But I've got one request as well. I'd like to be dunked."

Pastor Fitchen's jaw dropped, and he said, "We really aren't set up for—"

"Just kidding!" Marjie broke in with a laugh. "Sprinkling's fine."

————— ✐ —————

The temperature in the Greenleafton church on that last Sunday of July was over ninety degrees, but the congregation sat in rapt silence as Marjie told about how she had come to faith. Despite all of the butterflies she had felt before stepping to the podium, she felt surprisingly comfortable when she actually began talking. When she spotted Ruth and Margaret and Chester, she felt like she was retelling her story to friends, and her nervousness vanished. Even when she spoke about her father's death by cancer, and about those agonizing months when Jerry was at war, and about her terrifying ride with Benjamin to the hospital—fearing he would die—she found a way through the swelling of her emotions.

What made it hardest for Marjie was that there were many in the congregation whose emotions showed plainly. She tried not to look at them, but the tears were rolling down Benjamin's face, and her mother was dabbing her eyes as well. Ruth and Margaret were both in tears, while Chester was beaming a smile. Jerry was somber and focused on her every word.

But the most difficult person for Marjie to look at while she spoke was Betty Hunter, a young woman whose husband had been killed in combat on an island in the South Pacific. Betty began crying so hard that her shoulders shook, and each time Marjie looked her way, she could barely keep going. As Marjie spoke of her own grief and fears, she could feel something of the pain Betty must have experienced.

"I once believed that if there was a God, He must be horribly cruel," Marjie said as she tried to bring her story to a conclusion. "But He came to me, and He loved me when I hated Him. He overcame my doubts and fears, and He opened the eyes of my heart. I want to give my thanks to God today, and I want you to know that I believe in Jesus Christ and in the goodness of God."

Marjie closed her eyes and took another deep breath to help her toward the finish. "And I want to thank two very special people today whose faith and words and life made it very difficult for me to hold on to my unbelief."

She looked at Ruth and choked up. "Ruthie . . . how can I thank you for loving me like a sister and showing me the door of faith? I love you."

Then she turned quickly to Benjamin, but not before her own tears finally overflowed and cascaded down her cheeks. She reached up and pushed the first wave aside, but there was no stopping a second and third wave. "Benjamin . . . I came to your house with a baby on the way, and you welcomed me as a daughter. But even more than that, your quiet confidence in God helped me to stop running away from Him.

"Oh, Benjamin," she told him and God through her tears, "I would never have made it without you."

10

BIG SPRINGS

"How could you wait until the last day of July before bringing me here?" Marjie asked. She had her head in Jerry's lap and was stretched out comfortably on an old checkered blanket under a tall Dutch elm tree. Ruth and Billy were beside them on another blanket, playing with Martha. "I see why you call it the Big Springs. This has to be one of the most beautiful places on the earth, and it's only four miles from our farm."

Towering above them was a high limestone facing, and at the center of the base was a cave out of which an ice-cold spring poured. Crystal-clear water tumbled rapidly over its jutted rock formations, swirled into a deep hole, and then reformed itself into a slender stream that snaked its way through the tangled forest toward the south branch of the Root River. Surrounding the cave and in the shadows of the limestone cliff was the lovely meadow where they had set up their picnic.

"I don't know why we don't get here more often," said Jerry, lightly running his fingers through Marjie's long brown curls. "Guess it's just so far back in the woods, and the farm lane is so rough on the car. If it rains, there's no way you're going to get your car out of here. Plus, having to go through five gates is no treat either, if you recall."

"Marjie, I noticed that you didn't help after that first gate," Billy teased. "Ruthie jumped out and took care of them all."

"You wait till the lady's married. Then see who hops out to get the gates," replied Marjie, throwing a twig over at Billy. "Besides, I hate those rotten old barbed-wire gates that flop around and are so hard to get back into position."

"Like I said, that's why we don't come back in here so often," Jerry said. "But there's never a time when this isn't a beautiful spot. Especially when it's hot. It's so cool tucked back under this wall of rock."

"Jerry," Billy said, rolling over toward them, "we should challenge Marjie to the foot test."

"Sounds like fun," replied Jerry, sitting up a bit straighter against the elm tree. "Want to try, Marjie?"

"Try what?"

"We go to the mouth of the cave, take off our shoes and socks, wade into the water, and see who can stand in the water the longest," Jerry explained.

"That's stupid," said Marjie, shaking her head and sitting up on the blanket. "We'll be there all day."

Jerry and Billy started laughing, and Ruth scooped Martha into her lap.

"Two minutes," said Ruth. "I'll bet you can't last two minutes."

"Come off it!" exclaimed Marjie, then she stood up and laughed as well. "My shoes have been off all summer. Who's brave enough to take me on?"

Billy and Jerry jumped up, and the three of them raced for the cave. Ruth picked up Martha and followed more slowly. By the time she caught up to them, Jerry and Billy had their shoes and socks off.

"Those feet are even whiter than my dad's!" Ruth joked. "How many years since they've seen the sun?"

"This isn't a beauty contest," Billy answered, stepping toward the water. "You coming in, Ruthie?"

"Nope," she replied. "I'll be the timer. Are you all ready to go?"

Three confident nods met her glance.

Holding Martha on one hip and pulling her free arm up to

check her watch, Ruth called out, "Okay. Ready, set, go!"

Marjie, Jerry, and Billy all jumped into the stream at the same moment, and the air was instantly filled with their cries.

"Ahhh!" Marjie screamed as she landed in icy water nearly up to her knees. She grabbed a large boulder that jutted out in front of her and held on with a grimace on her face. "This is horrible!" she cried.

Jerry and Billy had known enough to go for the shallower spots, but they were dancing around on the sharp pebbles and whooping it up. The more they splashed, the more the icy water crept up their pant legs.

Billy hardly lasted any time before he made his move out of the water. "Eeeeh!" he cried, plopping down on the warm rocks and pulling up his pant legs as high as he could. "I forgot about my burns!" he hollered, rubbing his scarred legs. "They can't take the cold."

"Not a smart move," Ruth said. "Thirteen seconds."

"Oh!" Billy continued to groan. "I should have known better. Come on, Jerry. Hang in there."

Jerry had stopped his rain dance as well and was doubled over a large rock in agony. The water swirled around his feet and was quickly turning them from lily white to a pale blue. He looked over at Billy, and his face was a grim contortion of knots and lines. Jerry's mouth was wide open, and his teeth were clenched.

"You can do it, Jerry!" Billy cheered, then both he and Ruth started laughing at the sight.

"How tough are you?" Marjie piped up, looking over at Jerry. Her jaw was set firmly, and she was slowly rocking back and forth against the large round boulder.

"It's her poker face!" Billy yelled out. "She's bluffing, Jerry. Don't let her fool you."

"Come on, Marjie!" Ruth called, cheering Marjie on and waving Martha's left arm in celebration. "He's dying. Give it up, Jerry."

"Time?" hollered Jerry.

"Forty-five seconds," answered Ruth, checking her watch again.

"You're done for, Marjie," Jerry shouted above the din of the water gushing out from the cave's entrance. "I can last long enough to make it inside the cave."

"Lead the way, big boy!" Marjie called back. Then she took her hands off the boulder, stood up straight, and folded her arms. "I'm ready."

"One minute," called out Ruth.

"Are you coming, Jerry?" Marjie asked, stepping toward the mouth of the cave where the water was nearly up to the bottom of her shorts. "It's not polite to keep a girl waiting."

Jerry's face was so convulsed that his eyes were shut. With one of his hands he was squeezing his forehead, and with the other he gripped the rock. Finally he yelled, "I give!" and leaped from the stream, falling to the ground and clutching his frozen feet. "Ahhh!" he cried. "My feet are breaking off!"

While Jerry rocked and rolled on the edge of the stream, Marjie circled the front of the cave and stopped to peer into the dark cavern. "Looks like a great place for snakes," she called to the others. Then she slowly turned and made her way back toward Jerry. "Time?" she asked.

"Over two minutes," said Ruth. "I lost track. But you beat the pants off these boys!"

Ruth and Marjie burst out laughing. Marjie held her hands up over her head in celebration, but stayed in the shallower water.

"And the winner by a technical knockout in the ninth round," Marjie called out, "the new champion of—"

"Marjie!" Billy broke in, pointing to the large rock behind her. "Look what's coming."

"What?" Marjie grumped, turning around. Circling around the rock was a tiny green water snake. "Ahhh!" she screamed, and jumped out of the water, then dashed past Ruth and Martha.

Everyone laughed, including Martha, who seemed to think the splashing water was especially funny.

"I hate snakes!" Marjie cried, then she stopped and turned around when she felt she was safe. The little snake made its way around a few more rocks, then turned toward the current and headed downstream. "Good. Get him out of here."

"That's another reason we don't come down here as much," Jerry said, standing and tapping his thawed-out feet against the grass.

"Water snakes?" asked Marjie, bending to rub her own feet. "Are you afraid of them, too?"

"Nope," Billy replied. He was busy putting his socks and shoes back on. "Rattlesnakes."

"Rattlesnakes!" yelled Marjie, quickly jumping up and scanning the terrain. "Here?"

"We've never seen 'em," Jerry said. "The old-timers claim they're in here, though. I ain't heard of anybody who's seen one in years, but the stories keep you on your toes."

"Goodness," Marjie sputtered. "Is it safe? Maybe we should go somewhere else."

"It's all right," Jerry consoled. "I just keep away from the long grass. Besides, you wouldn't have to worry if you did get bit."

"How's that?" Marjie asked.

"From your performance in the water, it's obvious that you don't have any nerves in your legs," he joked. "How could you take it?"

"You simply need to learn to relax," Marjie stated smugly. "You tell your body that it—"

"Ah, baloney," Jerry broke in. "You're just cold-blooded."

"And you're just a bad sport," Marjie replied. "How about we jump back in and try for two out of three?"

"No thanks," Jerry conceded. "It's time to do some fishing."

"I like that idea better, too," Billy said. "If we can catch some hellgrammites for bait, we'll probably catch some fish. Trout love 'em."

"Not those black ugly things under the rocks?" Ruth asked, putting Martha down on the ground and holding her hands so she could stand. "That's disgusting."

"Maybe so," Jerry said. "But they work. You girls want to join us?"

"Count me out," Ruth replied. "I hate fishing. Martha and I prefer the warm, shallow water back by the blankets. Martha likes splashing around in it—and there aren't any snakes over there."

Marjie shook her head as well. "I'll join you boys at the deep hole there after I get a fire going for the hot dogs. Can you believe I paid thirty-three cents a pound?"

"I paid thirty-eight a week ago," Ruth replied. "Where did you—"

"Excuse us, ladies," Billy interrupted politely and walked past them. "I need to get the fishing gear and get to work. We'll show you how it's done."

"Like you showed me how to stay in the water?" Marjie asked, following Billy toward the cars.

"I hope I'll do better than that," Billy acknowledged with a laugh. When they got to the cars, he stopped and turned around toward Marjie, his green eyes suddenly serious. "I keep forgetting I can't do everything I used to do. Sometimes it's pretty humbling."

Marjie looked at him and nodded.

"I'm sorry your legs are so bad, Billy," Marjie said. "You act so normal, it's easy for us to forget."

"But it's better this way, ain't it?"

"Better what?"

"I'm a better person for it, don't you think, Marjie?" Billy asked. "You remember the way I was."

Marjie laughed and winked at him. "Boy, do I. If you were still the way you were, you can bet I wouldn't let you within a hundred yards of Ruthie."

"It's been worth it all," Billy reflected. "If it only meant that I could get Ruthie, I'd go through it again."

"You got a lot more than just Ruthie," Marjie said. "You got a whole new life. I'm proud of you, Billy. And Jerry and I are delighted that you two are engaged."

"Thanks," Billy said. "You guys mean the world to us."

"And you to us," said Marjie, taking his arm. "Now, you better get back down there before you get me crying again."

"Oops," replied Billy, turning to hold on to his and Jerry's fishing poles and tackle boxes. "Don't want that."

"Are you guys really going to fish with hellgrammites?" Marjie asked as she lifted the picnic basket out of the backseat of their car.

"Sure," he replied. "If we can find some."

Marjie eyeballed Billy hard. "I'll bet you a hot dog that I can catch more fish on corn than you can with your disgusting whatever they are."

"It's a bet. Trout only," Billy challenged.

"You're on," Marjie replied. "As soon as I get the fire started, I'll show you boys. See this?"

Marjie held up one long hot dog.

Billy nodded.

"Kiss it goodbye."

11

MISSING

"Boy, that feels good!" Jerry exclaimed, letting the water pour over his dirty face and hair. "Pump it again."

Marjie gave the long iron handle of the outside water pump another deliberate stroke, and the cool well water washed away another layer of sweat and grit.

"First week of August, and you've got the oats in the bin," Marjie said. "Not bad."

"Not bad at all," agreed Jerry. "Good crop, too. But that combine really kicked up the dirt. I think I swallowed a ton. Get out of the way if I sneeze!"

"Don't you dare," Marjie warned. "Your face is still a mess. Do you want another blast of water?"

"Yeah," Jerry said, bending down and getting his head below the pump's spout. "Man, that feels great," he mumbled as another stroke cascaded the clear water over his brown, summer-tanned face.

"That combine may have kicked up the dirt, but it sure beats the days of steam engines and threshing machines," Marjie remarked. "Do you remember the steam engines belching out all that smoke? I always hoped the wind wasn't blowing toward the farmhouse on those days."

"Whew!" Jerry said, wiping the water off his face and shaking his hair. "I can't say I was sorry to say goodbye to the threshing machine. Talk about a long, hard job in the hottest spells of the summer. I—"

The sound of the phone ringing inside the farmhouse cut Jerry off.

"I'll get it," Marjie said, turning toward the house. "You can bring Martha."

Marjie went on a run for the house, and Jerry bent over to pick up Martha, who had been crawling all over Blue. The little Australian cow dog gave Jerry a look of smiling thanks as he was relieved of his baby-sitting chores.

Slowly carrying Martha up the sidewalk, Jerry was disturbed by the dead silence inside the house. Either Marjie was already off the phone, or she was listening without any comment. And he knew she never listened for long without saying something.

Pulling open the screen door and stepping inside the farmhouse, he found Marjie leaning against the wall with her eyes shut, holding the receiver to her ear with one hand and covering her forehead with the other. She appeared not to be breathing, and her face was sheet white. Finally she moved forward to the mouthpiece and said, "We'll be there as soon as we can."

Marjie's hand trembled as she reached up to put the receiver back on the hook, but she did not open her eyes. Then she leaned back against the wall and took a deep draft of air. Her jaw was clenched tight, and she gave a sudden shudder.

"What's wrong?" whispered Jerry, reaching his free arm around her. "Who called?"

Marjie took another deep breath and sighed. Opening her eyes slowly, she said softly, "That was Benjamin. They got a call today from the war department saying that Paul is—Jerry, he's missing in action. All they know is that three weeks ago he got trapped behind German lines in the fighting in Sicily . . . and he hasn't been heard from since."

"Oh no," Jerry said. "How's your mother doing?"

Closing her eyes again, Marjie shook her head. "I don't know. Your dad said she excused herself from the house and went down by the creek. He thought she wanted to be alone."

"Babe, I'm so sorry," Jerry said, pulling her close. "Maybe it isn't as bad as it sounds, though. According to the war reports, the terrain where they were fighting was pretty rough. Sounds like it would have been easy to get cut off from your unit. Maybe he's just hiding until they push the Germans back."

"When have you heard that someone was missing in action who didn't later turn up dead? Betty Hunter's husband was missing for weeks before somebody stumbled over his body."

"Until we know for sure," Jerry reasoned, "there's no grounds for believing that he's dead."

"Or a prisoner of war."

"Or alive and well."

"Or alive and wounded."

Martha wiggled uncomfortably in Jerry's arm, then reached out to Marjie, who took her into her arms.

"Marjie," Jerry continued, "we have to believe the best. God knows where Paul is today."

Nodding slowly, Marjie looked up and sighed. "My head's killing me. Can you get me the aspirin and some water? We need to get Martha's stuff ready and drive over and see my mother."

"I wish I could go," Jerry said, "but I'm going to have to stay here and do chores."

Marjie looked down at her watch and gave a crooked smile. "Gosh. I even forgot what time it is. I don't even have your dinner ready."

"Don't worry about me," Jerry said. "Are you okay to drive over there?"

"I'm fine. Just take Martha for a minute so I can get her bag."

It was only a few minutes before Marjie and Martha were in the car and rolling down the road toward the farm where she had grown up. But the miles seemed to stretch out endlessly before her. No matter how hard she tried to stop it, a kaleidoscope of images of her brother Paul raced through Marjie's head the whole way. The sight of the Livingstone farmhouse came as a great relief.

Slowing the black Ford to turn into the driveway, Marjie spotted a solitary figure sitting down by the bridge that crossed the marshy creek cutting through the center of their property. "Oh, dear God," she whispered. "What am I going to say to her?"

Benjamin was standing outside the farmhouse in the cool shade of an elm tree and waved as Marjie pulled up. *Boy, am I glad he's here for Ma*, she thought. *At least she's not alone.*

"How's she doing?" Marjie asked as she pushed open the car door, grabbed Martha's bag, and stepped out. Benjamin already had Martha out the other door.

"I'm not sure," he replied. "I figured she needed some time alone. Do you think I should have stayed with her?"

Marjie shrugged her shoulders. "I don't think so. She used to go down there by the creek when she wanted to get away and think. We never bothered her when she wanted to be by herself."

"So you gonna wait for her?" asked Benjamin, lifting Martha up higher on his arm.

Walking around the front of the car and handing Benjamin the bag, she said, "No. I got a feeling that she needs me now . . . and I know I need her. How soon before you start choring?"

"Just listen for the cows to start bawling," he replied. "I can take care of little sweetie till then."

"Thanks," Marjie said, kissing him lightly on the cheek. "You be a good girl," she whispered to her daughter.

Marjie trudged slowly down the driveway, then turned on the road toward the old wooden bridge that spanned the creek. She recalled the many times when she and her older brother Paul and her younger brother Ted had raced down the road to play together in the creek. In younger years, the tiny rivulet had been a lake for sailing their wooden ships, a swimming hole to cool them off, an ice skater's paradise, and the home of a thousand froggy friends. Now it looked like a forlorn marsh that served no purpose except to steal tillable farmland.

She stopped before she got to the bridge and looked down to where her mother sat on the grassy edge of the creek bank. Sarah's sleeping puppy, Tinker, was stretched out on the ground next to her, and Sarah was trailing bare feet in the clear, shallow water. In her lap was the small white flag with a blue star in the center that Sarah had hung in one of the farmhouse windows to symbolize Paul's fighting in the war.

Sarah turned and looked up at Marjie, then she motioned for Marjie to come down and join her. Tinker stirred lazily as Marjie approached but did not get up. A spotted, brownish green leopard frog that had snuck up on the bank leaped into the water and swam beneath it to the safety of the creek's other side.

Marjie took off her shoes and sat down next to her mother, letting her feet drop into the creek. The two sat in silence for several minutes.

"There are a lot of memories down here," Marjie finally said quietly.

"You kids almost lived down here in the summer," Sarah responded. "It was a great place to send you when I needed a nap."

Marjie chuckled. "So that's why you were always shoving us out the door with a little lunch box and telling us to watch out for Teddy. We thought you were sending us on great adventures to conquer the world."

"I was," Sarah said. "And I was getting some rest as well."

"Paul loved it down here . . ." Marjie began, then paused to look at her mother. "He was always coming up with something new to do, another new game. And he was always in charge. He'd get so bossy."

"Which didn't go over big with you," Sarah added. She ran her finger down around the edge of the blue star. "But he was a leader, and he didn't have any problem getting others to follow him. Suppose that's why they made him a sergeant."

Marjie reached out and took her mother's hand, then she leaned against her and put her head against Sarah's head. Both women had their eyes closed, and Marjie welcomed her mother's familiar strength. But neither spoke again for some time.

Finally, Sarah turned and whispered to Marjie, "They said they didn't have much hope, Marjie. But I got a feeling that Paul's still alive."

Until that moment, neither of them had shed a tear, but the

force of Sarah's words broke the restraints. Holding each other, they cried and cried together until the anxieties subsided a bit.

Sarah wiped aside the last of her tears with a handkerchief and exhaled a big puff of air. "Not a day has gone by," she said softly, "that I didn't tell myself over and over that I had to be ready for this . . . or for something worse. Lotta good it did."

"Ma, you can't ever be ready for news like this," Marjie consoled. "And nobody'd ever expect you to be."

"Don't guess it matters," her mother continued. "Suppose it's silly to keep thinking that you've rehearsed it so many times that you're really prepared."

"Didn't work for me worrying over Jerry," Marjie said. "That I know."

"What do I do with this, Marjie?" asked Sarah. "Despite all these confused feelings going on inside me, I really believe he's alive. People are going to think I'm crazy."

"We have to believe he's still alive," Marjie said. "That's not being crazy."

"I know," her mother replied. "But what I mean to say is, in my heart, I really think he's not dead."

"How?"

"I don't know. But I'm sure he's not. When I got the call, it was so strong in my heart."

"Maybe God put it there?"

"I don't know," Sarah repeated and shook her head. "But I believe my son is alive."

Marjie did not know how to respond, but she could feel her mother's faith strengthening her own hope. "I think it's best if we keep this as our secret, Ma," she said. "Other than a few friends, I don't think others would understand."

Sarah looked at Marjie and nodded. "Either way, it probably won't be long before we hear more. The army said that the Germans are being driven from Sicily. Unless Paul's been taken as a prisoner, we should know something by the time Sicily is liberated."

"And in the meantime," Marjie said, "we wait."

"And pray."

12

HEART SOBS

"I'm so sorry to hear about your brother" . . . "I'll be praying for your son" . . . "My sister's boy was missing in Guadalcanal, but it turned out he'd only been injured. . . ."

So spoke a multitude of acquaintances and friends who gathered around the two Macmillan families after church the following Sunday. Pastor Fitchen's announcement that Paul Livingstone was missing in action had generated a large crowd of well-wishers whose sincere words wrapped Marjie and Sarah in a warm blanket of caring.

As Margaret Stanfeld slowly made her way down toward them from the choir loft, Jerry nudged Marjie. Margaret's solo that morning had been "Be Still, My Soul," sung with a delicate strength and a deep awareness of its message. For Marjie, the knowledge that Margaret's own brother was still missing in action in the deserts of North Africa had given the music special power.

"Oh, Margaret, your solo was beautiful." Marjie spoke softly, hugging Margaret and looking into her friend's round blue eyes. "I'm sure it was difficult for you to sing."

Sarah turned to Margaret as well and gave her a gentle hug. "The words are still ringing in my heart."

"You picked it for us, didn't you, Margaret?" said Marjie, before Margaret had a chance to respond to her first comment.

Margaret's slender lips curved into a smile, and she nodded. "Yes, this morning was meant for you. When we first heard that Charles was missing in Libya, I found that hymn brought me cheer. Especially the words, 'Leave to thy God to order and provide; In every change He faithful will remain.'"

Marjie put her arm around Margaret and said, "Thank you. Your words of cheer helped me. I felt so discouraged this morning."

"Waiting can be so dreadful," Margaret replied. "It was especially hard on my good mother."

"Do you ever still hope that one day your brother will suddenly appear?" Sarah asked.

Margaret looked up to the church's high ceiling and nodded slowly. "I hope for it every day," she said. "Until they find his body, I suppose I'll never give up hoping. But my parents were told that after a few days in the desert, there's almost no chance of his ever being found."

Holding Margaret tight, Marjie said, "I don't think I could stand not knowing."

"Me, either," Sarah whispered, hugging Margaret from the other side. "I'm afraid I'd crack in two."

"We'll pray you hear about Paul soon," Margaret said, squeezing both Marjie and Sarah.

At that moment Marjie looked up and saw that Betty Hunter was standing across the church aisle, waiting for them to finish.

"Please excuse me, Margaret," whispered Marjie. Hesitating for a moment, Marjie smiled and stepped across the aisle.

Betty Hunter was tall and slender, with plain features that were softened by a sweep of smooth blond hair. Marjie had never spoken with her beyond a few polite conversations in church. In fact, she had often worried about what to say to Betty. How could a woman whose husband had come home comfort one whose husband had not?

"I'm sorry to hear about your brother, Marjie," Betty was saying. Her clear hazel eyes met Marjie's dark brown ones briefly, then she looked away.

"Thank you, Betty," Marjie responded. "We'd appreciate

your keeping Paul in your prayers."

"I'll do it," said Betty. "I know how horrible all of this is."

Marjie wasn't sure what to do next, and she wished that Ruth was nearby to help, but Ruth had already said goodbye and headed out the door with Billy Wilson. So Marjie took a deep breath, laid a hand on Betty's arm, and said softly, "I'm very sorry for what you've gone through, Betty. I know we don't know each other well, but do you need someone to talk to?"

Betty nodded, took a deep breath, then looked around quickly. "Yes," she said quietly, "but not in here."

"We could go outside and talk in the car," Marjie suggested, wondering what Betty was so nervous about.

"No," replied Betty quickly. "Could I come over to your house this afternoon? Say around two o'clock?"

"Sure," Marjie said. "I'll be home. Would you like it if Ruth came over?"

"No. Just you, please," Betty said. "Is it true you have a horse?"

"Yes. Why?"

"I take my horse out for a ride every Sunday afternoon," Betty explained, looking around again. "We could ride down into the woods to talk."

"Sounds like a . . . good idea to me," Marjie said, but what she thought was, *Sounds strange to me.* "I'll have Charlie ready by two."

"See you then," Betty said, then hurried down the aisle and out the door.

When Marjie tried to explain to Jerry what Betty wanted to do, the first time he simply broke out laughing. The second time he listened in disbelief.

"You can't be serious," he whispered. A few church members were still talking close by with Sarah and Benjamin.

"Why would I joke about a thing like this?" Marjie argued. "I couldn't have thought this one up on my own. I didn't even know she had a horse."

"She has a horse all right," Jerry said. "And she rides a lot.

But you hardly know her. Why would she want to. . . ? This is odd."

"She was acting odd, too," Marjie whispered. "I think we better get going, though. If I'm going to get our lunch together and be ready by two, I need to keep moving."

———— ∽ ————

Just a few minutes before two o'clock, Marjie was outside by the barn, letting Charlie take a long drink from the water tank, when she heard the clip-clop of a horse coming down the driveway. Charlie's ears shot up, then he lifted his head and looked down the lane.

A beautiful chestnut Appaloosa with a white, spotted rump was coming toward them. Betty sat tall in her Western saddle, looking trim and confident in blue jeans, a blue checkered Western shirt, cowboy boots, spurs, and even a whip.

Marjie glanced down self-consciously at her plain pink blouse, blue slacks, and brown work shoes, before looking up and giving Betty a wave. She led Charlie a few feet away from the water tank, keeping him next to the wooden fence. Climbing up to the third board on the fence, she grabbed a handful of Charlie's mane and swung her leg over his broad back. Once mounted, she gathered the reins and turned to Betty again.

"Howdy, Betty," Marjie called out. "That is one gorgeous horse. What's his name?"

"Lucky," Betty replied, then gave a little private laugh. "Mind if I give him a drink?"

"No," Marjie said. "He looks like he needs it. How far is it from your farm?"

"Just a little over three miles," Betty said as she nudged the Appaloosa forward and he bent over to take a drink. His wide-rimmed eyes were fixed on Charlie the whole time he drank. "Makes for a nice Sunday ride. Not too warm today, either."

"It's beautiful for the eighth of August, that's for sure," Marjie replied. "I'm a bit embarrassed, though. I don't even have a saddle, and you look like you're ready for a cattle drive."

Betty laughed, and when she did her face went from plain

to pretty. It struck Marjie that she couldn't recall ever seeing Betty smile before.

"Please don't be embarrassed," Betty said. "People around here have been calling me a cowgirl since I was three. So how do you like ol' Charlie?"

"I love him," Marjie said. "Do you know him?"

Betty smiled again and nodded. "Sure do," she replied as her horse lifted a dripping muzzle from the tank. "I broke him and trained him before Tom Metcalfe bought him. It's a shame it didn't work out with Tom's little girl, but I'm glad you got him. He's a good horse. Smooth and fast."

"Without a saddle, I prefer the smooth," Marjie joked. "Listen, we could ride back on our property. Have you ever been back in our woods?"

"Never," Betty said, pulling Lucky back from the tank and turning him toward the farm lane. "I'd love to see it. You lead the way."

"I think I'd prefer to follow you," Marjie said, "so you don't have to watch me. Just follow the lane, and I'll see if I can keep up."

Marjie felt fortunate that Betty seemed to be content to hold her horse to a gentle canter. She wasn't sure she could hold Charlie back if Betty decided to let Lucky break into a gallop. They followed the farm lane back down through the hills until they reached a knoll that overlooked the farm fields in the valley below.

Betty turned around and pointed to the spot. "I think I'd like to stop here."

The two riders stopped in the shade of two gnarly burr oak trees and dismounted. Betty looped her reins over the wooden fence, then walked to the place where she had pointed and plopped down in the grass. Marjie followed behind and joined her.

Betty pushed her long blond hair back away from her face, then leaned back on her arms and looked around at the lovely green valley. "I appreciate your willingness to come out here with me," she said. "Most people find me hard to be around these days. I know it must have sounded strange, wanting to come out here. But I wanted a place where no one else would be around."

"This is the right place, then," Marjie said, leaning back against a tree trunk and getting comfortable. "It's one of my favorite spots on the farm. You did surprise me in church, though. Was something else wrong? You seemed really nervous."

Betty smiled again and shook her head. "I was afraid my folks were going to suspect something was up. I didn't tell them I was riding over to see you. They just think I'm out for a ride."

"Why should it matter?"

Betty sat forward, cupped her face with her hands, and rocked back and forth slowly. The look of deep sadness that Marjie had seen in Betty's face so many times at church replaced the lovely smile that had made its temporary breakthrough. Tears began to pool in the corner of Betty's almond-shaped eyes.

"They're . . . they're always afraid I'm going to start talking to someone and end up making a fool of myself," she said, taking a deep breath and looking straight ahead. "My father said that once the memorial service for Fred was over, I needed to at least stop crying in public. He got real mad when I cried in church that time you spoke."

Marjie leaned forward, keeping her eyes on Betty's but picking away at the grass by her feet with her fingers. "Like you should push all your feelings down and pretend everything's okay?"

Betty nodded, then turned and met Marjie's stare. A few tears streaked down her cheeks, and she swallowed like her throat was sore. "He says that people get sick of crybabies like me . . . that Fred died proudly for his country, and I should honor his memory by being strong. But I'm not strong."

Sliding over next to Betty, Marjie put an arm around her shoulders as the tears flowed faster. Then Betty let out a loud wail that cut straight through Marjie and echoed in the valley below. Deep heart sobs shook her body, and the tears rained down.

"Go ahead," Marjie urged her. "Cry! Cry! Let it out!"

And Betty did. Months of grief spilled out in a spasm of weeping. Marjie held her tight.

"I can't tell you I know just how you feel," Marjie spoke consolingly. "But I know you've got to let all that pain and anger out or it will poison your soul."

"Oh, God help me . . . oh, God help me," Betty mumbled over and over after she had cried for a long time.

"God *can* help you," Marjie said, rubbing her hand over Betty's shoulders. "I know He can help you, Betty."

Betty had stopped crying but was still rocking back and forth. With both hands she wiped away the tears and rubbed her face. "Marjie, I'm so scared."

"Scared that you'll end up alone?"

"No. I'm scared that I'm going to end up hating God." Betty spoke softly. "When you talked about how much you hated God because He let your father die, that's exactly how I've felt. But I haven't dared to say it to anyone. There was a time when I loved God so much, and now . . . now I don't."

Marjie just hugged Betty a little tighter and gathered her thoughts. Finally she said, "Maybe you've just held your grief down for so long that you've lost sight of God. If you can get the tiniest glimpse of Him, He's very hard to hate."

Through glazed eyes, Betty looked out on the valley and nodded her head. "I just don't understand why. . . ."

"And maybe you never will," Marjie continued. "God doesn't always give us explanations for what He does."

"So what does He give?" whispered Betty, looking at Marjie.

"His only Son," Marjie said slowly.

13

KING KONG

"Why do you have to make such a fuss about this?" Marjie asked.

"Because I don't want a thirty-pound turkey, even if they're giving it away," answered Jerry. "Have you ever butchered a turkey that big? Probably tough as old shoe leather."

"Have you ever done it?"

"No. And I don't want to."

"So, there's a possibility that this turkey has tender, juicy meat?"

"Some, but not likely."

"Tell me, then, what have we got to lose?" Marjie reasoned. "It won't cost us a dime, and we can give away most of the meat if we don't like it. Right?"

"Unload it, you mean."

"Call it what you want, but maybe not everybody's as picky as you."

Jerry shook his head in disgust. "Maybe we're the only suckers the Bransons could think of who would take the thing. Here their kid raises this monster turkey, and then can't stand to see 'em butcher it. It's high time their little Jimmy learns he's living on a farm."

"You never got attached to one of your animals that had to be butchered?"

"Sure, but this is a turkey! For crying out loud, Marjie! Who can love a turkey?"

"Jimmy Branson, I guess," Marjie said. "And I already said we'd come down and get him after dinner. Jimmy will be at the softball game in Greenleafton, and they want to get rid of it while he's gone. Are you going to help me, or would you like me to go there by myself?"

"You figured out how we're going to pluck the feathers?" Jerry returned. "We don't have a tub big enough to dunk it in, let alone keep the water boiling hot."

"We'll cross that stream later," Marjie said. "Right now, all I need is a big gunnysack and some string. If you won't go get that turkey, I'll do it myself."

"You'd try it without me?"

"It's just an oversized chicken. I've handled my share of those."

"I'd like to see you try," Jerry teased. "You and old King Kong Turkey. That would be fun to see."

"If you hold the sack open I can get him in," Marjie challenged. "What are you willing to bet? A week's worth of washing dinner dishes against the fun of watching me?"

"Gentlemen," Jerry mocked, "the table is now open. Place your bets, please. Lady, you are on!"

———————— ✐ ————————

After dinner, Jerry and Marjie and Martha drove into the Branson farmyard and pulled to a stop close to the barn. Mr. and Mrs. Branson had heard their car on the gravel driveway and came out to meet them before they pulled to a stop.

"Harry, how's it going?" Jerry said as he stepped out of the car. "Nora, good to see you."

"We're doing fine, except for that turkey," Harry replied, tugging on his overall straps. "Our Jimmy's having a fit over it."

"You're sure you want us to take him?" Jerry asked. "What's Jimmy going to say when he discovers it's gone?"

"He knows it'll be gone when he gets home tonight," Nora

replied. "He didn't want to know who took it, just so long as we didn't butcher it ourselves."

"Turkey's right inside here," Harry said, opening the side door to the barn. "He outgrew the poultry shed, so I put him in one of the empty calf pens."

Jerry turned around and winked at Marjie, then they followed Harry into the dark shadows of the barn.

"Would you look at the size of that big boy!" exclaimed Jerry, letting out a loud whistle. "What do you say, Marjie?"

Marjie looked in at the thirty-plus pounds of White Holland turkey and started to laugh. The big bird was nervously stalking around the calf pen, and his long wattle was shaking from side to side about his face and neck. At the base of his neck was a large cluster of carbuncles.

"That is the ugliest creature I think I've ever seen," Marjie sputtered. "How could Jimmy ever love such a thing?"

"I have no idea," Harry said. "But he does. That turkey's mean, too. If you turn your back on him, he'll go for your legs."

Jerry burst out laughing, holding up the gunnysack he'd brought into the barn. "Oh, boy," he said. "This is going to be fun. Marjie bet me that she could get the turkey in this sack by herself!"

Harry Branson wrinkled his forehead and shook his head. "I wouldn't mess with him if I was you, Marjie."

Marjie looked over at Nora and smiled. "If Harry would wash the dinner dishes for a week solid, would you try?"

"Not me," Nora answered, shaking her head. "I seen that turkey when he was riled up."

"Well," Marjie said to Nora, "if you'll just hold the baby for me, I'm really sick of doing all the dishes."

Nora took Martha, who was staring at the turkey with fascination. Marjie looked at Jerry with challenge in her eyes. "Ready?"

"You're really going to do this?"

"Harry, would you hold the sack for me?" Marjie asked.

"I'll do it, I'll do it," groused Jerry.

"All right, then," she said. "Time to get to work."

Marjie opened the gate to the calf pen and stepped in. Jerry followed her. He had the gunnysack open and ready.

"I hope this sack is wide enough," Jerry said, sizing up the girth of the turkey.

"He'll fit," Marjie said. She stepped toward the turkey, who had backed into a corner of the pen.

"I hope you don't think you can just grab him and hold his head," Jerry said. "He'll clobber you with those wings."

"Go for the legs, my granny always said," Marjie replied. "You just get the sack ready."

Suddenly Marjie bent down low and stepped straight up to the turkey. Before the turkey could make a dash to the side, Marjie's hands flashed out and grabbed the big tom by both legs. With another lightning move, she jerked the turkey upside down. Surprised, he hung motionless from her extended arms.

"Quick!" she yelled to Jerry. "The bag!"

Jerry swooped the gunnysack under the gobbler's head and pulled it up over his body before the turkey had a chance to respond. Marjie let go of the legs, and the turkey flopped the rest of the way into the sack. Then he suddenly burst to life and started thrashing.

"Tie it!" Marjie cried, grabbing the end of the sack from Jerry and holding it firmly until he could get the string fastened tight.

"Not too shabby, Marjie!" exclaimed Harry, pounding his hand down on the wooden gate. "That old boy never knew what hit him."

Jerry let go of the sack, and the turkey rolled and jerked around until he was standing up inside the sack.

"How did you know how to do that?" Jerry grumped.

"Granny Forrester," Marjie said proudly. "She said that if it works on a chicken, it'll work on a turkey. And she was right."

"Boy, was she," said Jerry, stepping back from the sack. "That was some piece of work. If I help you butcher him, will you help me with the dishes?"

"Today's the day!" Jerry declared as he marched into the

kitchen after the morning chores. "That stupid turkey of yours pecked me in the back of the leg this morning. I've kept him alive in the barn three days longer than I should have."

Jerry pulled up his right pant leg, revealing a large red welt on his calf. "Look at that!"

Marjie burst out laughing. "You knew better than to turn your back on him."

"I forgot," Jerry said, letting his pant leg drop back down. "He hit me like I was carrying a football."

Both Jerry and Marjie laughed again, and Jerry took Marjie into his arms and whispered in her ear, "But now it's judgment day. And *you* will wield the axe."

"I'm not going—"

The loud honking of a car horn and the crunch of gravel in the driveway stopped Marjie's protest, and Blue raced up the driveway barking his announcement of the arrival. Jerry and Marjie went to the dining room picture window and waved as Benjamin and Sarah rolled past. Benjamin continued to honk the horn and Sarah had her head partially out the window, yelling something they couldn't understand.

"What's wrong with them?" Jerry snorted.

"It's Paul!" exclaimed Marjie, dashing for the front door.

Marjie was out the door and down the sidewalk on a dead run. She got to the car just as Sarah was stepping out.

"He's alive!" her mother shouted, jumping up and down. "Paul's alive!"

Marjie joined her mother in a dance of joy, and they were accompanied first by Blue's excited aerial show and then by Benjamin's laughter. By the time Jerry arrived with Martha and joined in the celebration, the big dance was over, but hugs and tears were well in progress.

"Is he hurt?" Marjie cried, holding on to her mother, who couldn't stop laughing and crying.

"No," Sarah gasped, shaking her head.

Benjamin let go of Marjie and Sarah and finally was able to stop laughing. Taking a deep breath, he said, "They said . . . his unit advanced too quickly, and Paul and a few others got caught behind the German lines. He could have probably made it back across sooner, but one of his men was shot up and needed someone to stay with him."

"Paul saved the man's life," Sarah said softly, still shaking a bit in Marjie and Jerry's embrace. "And my boy's alive."

"Just like you felt in your heart," whispered Marjie.

Sarah nodded, looking up through teary eyes. "I did. Like nothing I've ever felt before. But when the call came this morning, it was still so overwhelming. Like I'd never felt anything."

Then the joy came again, and they all erupted into a second round of laughter. Blue even got into the act again with a couple of leaps high up against Jerry's back. Martha was peeking over Jerry's shoulder and nearly got a face washing as the cow dog went flying past.

"So what's next?" Marjie asked when things finally started to die down. "Does he get to come home?"

"I wish," her mother said, letting go of the bodies she'd had her arms wrapped around. "He's back with his unit, and they're driving the Germans out of Sicily. But he's not coming home, that's for sure."

"Why don't you come on in the house? Bet you folks haven't had breakfast yet," Jerry said.

Benjamin wrinkled his forehead and rubbed his ear. "Guess I forgot all about it. Is that an invite, or are you just curious?"

"What do you think?" Marjie said, rubbing her eyes and then running her fingers back through her long brown curls. "I suppose I could fry up some of that liver you like. Liver and eggs!"

"I'd rather have some of that turkey I heard you got," Benjamin joked. "Where's he at?"

"Come with me," Jerry said, stepping toward the barn. "Actually, you're just in time to help butcher him. That gobbler pecked my leg this morning, and I decided it's time for him to meet his Maker."

"You know," Marjie said, "that turkey's way too much meat for us. What if we had a big dinner to celebrate the news about Paul? We can kill two birds with one stone, so to speak."

Sarah groaned. "We'll just ignore that one, Marjie. But I think the idea is wonderful. I feel like a party!"

Everyone broke into laughter again. When they finally dispersed, Jerry and Benjamin and Blue headed to the barn to see the turkey while Sarah and Marjie carried Martha into the house to set two extra places at the table.

After breakfast, Benjamin was the first to emerge from the house. He went out by the barn, set some cement blocks in a circle, and got a fire going in the center. Then he set a large old metal tub on top of the fire and filled the tub with water. It wasn't long before the water began to bubble and steam.

Then Benjamin walked up toward the house and called out, "The water's boiling. Time to pluck King Kong."

Jerry was the next one out the door. He went to the shed to get the axe and a wooden chopping block. Marjie and Sarah came out a few minutes later, and Sarah was holding Martha.

"You want to go in and drag him out?" Jerry called out to Marjie from next to the barn.

"I think I've already shown you how it's done," Marjie replied. "Unless you'd like to wager another week's worth of dinner dishes?"

Jerry shook his head, turned around, and disappeared into the barn. In a couple of minutes, he came hustling back out the side door carrying the oversized turkey by the legs. Blue followed a couple steps back, sniffing the air and cautiously sizing this new turn of events.

"You put gloves on!" Marjie exclaimed and broke into laughter. "Are you scared? Little peck on the leg and—"

"Enough!" Jerry barked. The upside-down turkey was motionless, but at thirty-plus pounds, it was too heavy to hold in this awkward position for long. "When I put his head down on the block, you got to be ready to chop, Marjie."

"I'm not—"

"He's your turkey," Jerry said, wincing from the weight. "Grab the axe!"

"Benjamin, you—"

"He's yours, Marjie," Benjamin said and laughed. "Not scared, are you?"

"Okay, that's it!" said Marjie. She marched forward and grabbed the axe. Pointing to a spot on the block, she said, "Put his head right here. Let's get this done with."

"You may want to back up a step or two, Sarah," Jerry said as he stepped toward Marjie. "This may get a little wild, and I don't want Martha in the way."

Sarah was already giggling at the sight, but she pulled Martha a little tighter against her shoulder and retreated a pace or two. "Better hit him square," she called out to Marjie. "You never were too good with the chickens."

"This is a lot bigger head," Marjie declared, raising her axe and making one smooth practice swing. "Come on, Jerry. Off it goes."

"Okay," Jerry said, lowering the turkey's head down to the block. "Now!"

Marjie took a big swing and brought the glistening axhead down on the block, but her stroke completely missed the turkey's neck and only managed to nick the wattle. In an explosion of white feathers and wings, the turkey lifted off the ground and tried to go airborne. All that held him back from the clouds was Jerry's two powerful arms.

"Help!" Jerry yelled, hanging on for all he was worth. The turkey was straight out in front of him with his wings flapping a hundred miles an hour and blood from his wattle was flying everywhere.

Benjamin rushed in and grabbed one of the turkey's legs to help, but the wind from the turkey's wings blew off Benjamin's old feed cap. "Hit him again, Marjie!" he cried.

Marjie was getting sprayed with blood, but she took a wild swing and only got air. A second swing struck the turkey's head and dazed him, causing him to drop to the ground motionless. She quickly pulled the block underneath the unconscious bird's head, then raised her axe and made a swift stroke that found its target.

"Nice job," Jerry muttered very slowly.

Marjie looked up from the headless turkey and was greeted by the blood-speckled frowns of Benjamin and Jerry, who still had not let go of the turkey's legs. Sarah was laughing so hard that she had to put Martha down on the ground. In a second or two, Marjie burst out laughing as well.

"Nice tender meat, don't you think?" Jerry said, looking up at his father and bursting out laughing.

"Looks like I better sharpen the knives for this meal, thanks to you," Benjamin said, nodding toward Marjie and wiping some of the blood from his face. "Would you care to explain what happened?"

Marjie was still laughing and wiping some blood away herself. "It's pretty simple, really," she said. "Like most other things, this was all your son's fault. He pulled the turkey just as I was swinging."

14

CANNING DAY

"That small plot of a garden really produced the tomatoes," Sarah said to Marjie, wiping the perspiration from her forehead with a plain white cotton towel. She turned back to the double-shelved steam canner and finished loading the last of the glass Mason jars filled with tomato juice.

"Did you get all fourteen quarts in?" Marjie asked, continuing to wash out the next batch of Mason jars. She had her back to the stove, where the metal canner sat tall above the burners. Sarah had just closed the steamer's two doors.

"I always get seven to a shelf," replied Sarah. "That makes forty-two so far. Do you have enough juice to fill the steamer one more time?"

"More than enough," Marjie said. She stopped to try to blow back some long strands of hair that had fallen down over her eyes. "But we better stop at fifty-six. Benjamin's gonna want to be getting home by then."

Sarah had taken the fourteen hot jars that had come out of the steamer and arranged them neatly on a far counter. Then she walked over to where Marjie was standing and looked out the window that was above the sink. "Where'd Ben say he was taking Martha?" Sarah asked. "He's been gone a long time."

"Both he and Jerry are pretty swift on their feet when it comes time to help with the canning," Marjie joked. "Benjamin said he was going to take Martha and Blue for a long walk down through the valley and up around the property line."

"I'm glad he's getting to do that," Sarah replied, taking a couple of Marjie's clean jars and filling them with the tomato juice they had processed into a large washtub. "Those are the two things he misses the most. He's powerful lonesome for his granddaughter, especially in the evenings. Good thing he got me the puppy. Least he's got something to play with."

Sarah paused to grab a couple more empty quart jars. "And he misses the hills. Our farm is so flat and sandy. Just ain't the same."

"That's what he gets for choosing you over us," Marjie teased. "How are things with you newlyweds, anyway?"

Sarah's smile turned to a frown, and she quickly looked down at the glass jar in her hands. "Not so good," she said softly.

Marjie turned around and pulled a towel from the rack to dry her wrinkled hands. "What's wrong? I wasn't being serious. Are you and Benjamin not getting along?"

Her mother took a deep breath and shook her head, still looking away. "It's working fine, Marjie. We really love each other. It's just a little too fine."

"What?" Marjie was incredulous. "How can that be?"

"Pretty easy, Marjie," Sarah said, then turned her attention to Marjie. "I'm pregnant."

Marjie's mouth dropped open, but her eyes refused to blink. She tried to speak, but although her lips moved, her voice did not cooperate.

Then suddenly her mother's cheeks puffed out and she exploded into laughter. Taking Marjie's arm, she buried her head against Marjie's neck and laughed and laughed. "How . . . could you . . . believe such a thing?" she gasped between peals of laughter.

When Sarah's expression changed, Marjie realized she'd been fooled, and she broke into laughter as well. The two of them stood clutching the counter, nearly doubled over with laughter, until the whistle on the steamer began to blow.

"Oops," Sarah said, letting go of Marjie and wiping the tears from her eyes. "Guess I forgot to refill it with water after I loaded this last batch."

"How could you play such a mean trick on me?" Marjie asked as her mother opened the lower door of the steamer and poured water into the bottom. "It could have been true."

"Ain't gonna happen, dearie," Sarah said. "Besides, seemed like you were getting your nose a little too far into our business."

"I just asked how you were doing," Marjie protested, starting to laugh again. "I didn't ask you if you were busy making babies."

"And I sure wouldn't tell you if I was," Sarah replied with a chuckle. "How about you and Jerry? Don't you think that Martha's needing a little brother or sister? She's almost a year old."

"Let's finish loading these last jars," Marjie said, nodding toward the empty Mason jars. "So, you want another grandchild?"

"Sure do," Sarah said. "Me and Ben aren't getting any younger, you know. You and Jerry working on one?"

Marjie laughed. "You're a real stitch, you know. You won't tell me a thing, but I'm supposed to clue you in on what we're up to?"

"I'm your mother, if you recall," Sarah said, mimicking Marjie's smirk and giving her daughter a wink. "I didn't ask for any details."

"Well," Marjie said, "I have nothing to report, but you'll be the first to know if it happens. This time around, though, I'd like to tell Jerry before I tell you. Does that meet with your approval?"

"Sounds good to me," Sarah said. "Boy, my feet are killing me. Let's get this done and go sit down for a while."

Marjie and Sarah stopped talking and went at their task with a new burst of energy. In a matter of minutes they had the rest of the next fourteen quart jars filled with juice. Then they quickly pulled on the rubber rings and screwed down the covers.

"There," Marjie declared, pushing the last filled jar to the edge of the counter. "That didn't take long. Grab the pitcher of tea, and I'll bring the glasses."

Sarah took the pitcher of cold, brown tea to the table and sat down with a big sigh of relief. Then Marjie joined her with the glasses.

"It always gets so hot in the kitchen when the canner is steaming away," Marjie commented. Perspiration shone through her blouse and on the back of her neck. "I remember you used to get us to help you with canning when we were kids. We hated it so bad."

Sarah chuckled and took a sip of her tea. "You kids were really pretty good about it," she said. "You realize there were times when we'd have starved if we hadn't had all those canned goods in the winter. Five mouths to feed, and just about no money."

"I remember," Marjie said, leaning back in her chair. "We were so poor that I thought you would can anything that looked fit to eat."

"Guess I did," Sarah agreed. "And sometimes in huge quantities."

"I still have nightmares about the pile of apples that you and Pa gathered into the cellar that one fall," Marjie joked. "Bushel after bushel after bushel. Paul called it Apple Mountain. Do you remember that?"

"Sure do," Sarah replied. "The three of you kids sat there on the cellar floor peeling and slicing apples for four straight days while I made most of it into applesauce. Then on the fifth day, without saying a word, Paul just put down his knife and walked away."

"And I followed him," Marjie continued, shutting her eyes and smiling. "And Teddy came soon afterward. I always wondered why you didn't come after us."

"I couldn't," Sarah said. "You three little kids had worked like slaves. Seemed like you deserved to go play. And we had over three hundred quarts of applesauce by then, anyway."

"Good night," Marjie said. "No wonder I get tired of applesauce."

"That was the same summer we canned two hundred and fifty quarts of tomato juice," Sarah added. "It made a lot of tomato soup."

"What are you doing with all those jars?" Marjie asked. "I think I'm going to run out of my supply before I get the garden cleaned up."

"Most of them are just sitting on shelves in the cellar," Sarah replied. "I've been canning enough for the two of us. But I've got hundreds of extra jars. You can take whatever you like."

"Thanks," Marjie said. "When the apples get ripe, I'm going to be making a lot of sauce and pie slices. Maybe I can get you to help me again?"

"Be glad to," Sarah said. "For all the times you helped me, I'd say that I still owe you about a million quarts!"

"At least." Marjie laughed.

"Say, I forgot to tell you how much fun it was here the other night," Sarah said, pouring herself another glass of tea. "We don't get to see Billy and Ruthie and Margaret and Chester as much as we'd like. The dinner was good, too."

"That turkey was juicier than I figured he'd be," Marjie said and laughed. "He really gave us a ride, didn't he?"

Sarah burst out laughing again as well. "Reminded me of the first airplane that I saw up close when it was taking off."

"That was really funny, Ma," Marjie said. "I thought Billy and Ruthie were going to die when Jerry tried to tell the story."

"What do you think about Margaret's friends, the ones that are coming over here?" Sarah asked.

"Sounds like they're more friends of Margaret's parents," Marjie said. "Margaret told me they're an American couple who went to Margaret's church while they attended a missionary training school in Scotland."

"And they've been missionaries in Borneo," Sarah said. "Sounds so far away."

"Jerry said he almost got as far as Borneo before the *Wasp* was sunk," Marjie mused. "I guess the Japanese took that island as well. Apparently this couple barely escaped."

"That could be an exciting story to hear," Sarah said.

"Have you ever heard a missionary before?" Marjie asked.

"Never have," replied Sarah. "Never wanted to, either."

"Why's that?"

"Until recently," Sarah said, "I guess I figured that it wasn't any business of ours what religion other people wanted to practice. Now I'm not sure what I think."

Marjie nodded. "Me, too." She took a big sip of her tea. "Jerry told me that when they were in the Solomon Islands he heard some of the tribes out there were headhunters."

"No!" her mother said, shaking her head and rubbing her neck.

"Do you think you would dare go out to talk with somebody like that?" asked Marjie.

"I don't know how you would talk to them at all," Sarah said.

"What?"

"You couldn't talk with them if they don't speak your language," Sarah said. "First, you'd have to learn their language."

"Goodness," Marjie said. "I hadn't thought of that."

Sarah nodded. "But I guess they would have to do it."

"I guess," said Marjie. "Anyway, it'll be interesting to hear what they do. Jerry went to church every Sunday growing up, but he's never heard a missionary. Seems funny for a church to send money to a denominational mission budget and never find out what's being done with it."

"That is funny," Sarah replied. "Stupid, if you ask me."

Marjie and Sarah broke out laughing again. Then the timer that Marjie had set for the canner went off.

"Time to finish the job," Sarah said, rising up out of her chair and following Marjie to the kitchen.

Marjie turned off the timer, then she grabbed two potholders, opened the doors to the canner, and began to pull out the hot jars of tomato juice. Once she got a section of the canner free, Sarah began loading in the uncooked jars.

"That's the last of it," Sarah finally declared, closing the canner's top door. "Maybe we should start cleaning up now."

Marjie surveyed the messy, tomato-spattered kitchen and

groaned. "Ah, don't you hate it?"

"I'll wash, and you dry," her mother replied. "Try not to think about how rotten it is."

"I try, but it doesn't work," Marjie said.

"Then try to think about something that's worse," Sarah offered, starting to load the sink with dirty canning utensils. "Then it's not so bad."

"I've been doing plenty of that lately, but not by choice," Marjie said. "Ever since I talked with Betty Hunter about her husband getting killed, I can't get her out of my thoughts. Seems like there should be a better way to help people like her."

"How?"

Marjie wiped the counter clean of juice and seeds. "I'm not sure," she said. "Seems like the church should have something for families that have loved ones in the service. Like a group that could at least gather together and pray for the ones who are gone. Wouldn't you like that?"

"Sure would," Sarah said, leaning back from the sink and looking at her daughter. "Maybe you should start one."

"I couldn't do that," Marjie retorted. "What do I know about helping people?"

"Apparently enough to make someone like Betty want to talk with you," her mother responded. "Besides, how much do you need to know about starting a prayer group?"

"I have no idea," Marjie said. "I'll bet there's more involved than you'd think."

"Won't know till you try, I guess."

"Wait a minute," replied Marjie, shaking her head. "You're not going to sucker me into this. Besides, I'm not sure that the church would go for it."

"So who said it had to be done at the church? Call the people that you think would benefit most from it and get together here."

"In our house?"

"Why not? It's a free country, isn't it?"

"Sure, but folks around here might not be comfortable with a prayer meeting that's not at the church," Marjie reasoned.

"Then talk with the pastor and see what he can do," Sarah suggested. "My point is that I think you've got a good idea that could help people. So many young men are gone these days, and their wives and parents and grandparents and sisters and brothers and children are worried about them. I think they'd jump at the chance to simply gather together and pray for their boys and for each other." She stared out the kitchen window, her mind obviously on her own two boys in the army. "I know I would."

Marjie joined her mother in looking out the kitchen window at the distant horizon. "I think you're right, Ma. I think it's a really good idea. But there must be someone else who could do it."

15

NO EXCUSES

Marjie leaned forward in her chair and put one hand on the large oak desk in the pastor's study. "Why do you think I should do it?" she asked. "Of all the adult members in your church, I am the least qualified."

"You're our newest member, and you and Jerry hold the record as the oldest adults ever to be baptized here," Pastor Fitchen replied with a broad smile. "But that doesn't mean you're not qualified. I think you should do it because it's your idea."

"And I came here thinking *you* should do it because you're the pastor," Marjie replied.

"Which is another reason you should be the one to do it," he replied, wrinkling his forehead.

"Meaning?"

"First of all, I think that God sometimes puts things on people's hearts," the elderly pastor explained, "but we end up spoiling them by trying to make them fit into our church plans. I know this is going to sound odd to you, but I not only think you're the right person to do it, I also think you should do it in your home."

Marjie squinted and shook her head. "Why?"

"Because if it's in your house, those who come may feel freer to share what's on their hearts," Pastor Fitchen said. "You're probably aware that some of our members put on a religious hat when they step inside the church. In your house, they could be who they really are. Besides," he continued, "what qualifies anyone to do anything? Seems to me that experience is a big factor, and you've experienced a good deal of what others with loved ones in the war are experiencing. Isn't that true?"

"Well, yes, but surely you or your wife or one of the church elders would have much more to offer," Marjie argued.

"That's another reason for you to have it at your home," the pastor replied. "It's no secret people think that because I'm paid to pastor the church, I'm supposed to do everything important in the church. It's time to break that mold. The church should never be so dependent upon one person. And it was never meant to be."

"Oh, great, so everyone's going to get mad at me," sputtered Marjie.

Pastor Fitchen broke out laughing. "No, no," he said, "they won't get mad at you. There'll be some who won't like meetings not being held in the church, but let me assure you that it's me they'll be upset with, not you."

"Have you always been like this?"

"Like what?"

"Well, you were willing to break with tradition when Jerry and I asked to be baptized with Martha," Marjie said, sitting back in her chair. "And you did that knowing that some people were going to be angry with you. Correct?"

Pastor Fitchen nodded.

"And you did the same when Billy Wilson wanted to tell his story. And now you're recommending I begin this prayer group in our house when you know it'll get you in more hot water?"

"I guess I am like you say."

"And you always have been?"

"No."

"Why the change?"

Pastor Fitchen chuckled out loud and rubbed his white, bushy eyebrows. Then he shook his head and rubbed his lower lip several times. "You really want to know?"

"Not if it's something you'd rather not talk about," Marjie

replied, surprised by the pastor's reaction. "I've only known you for a year, but I think I've seen you changing."

"For the better, I hope."

"Yes."

"Good," Pastor Fitchen said, breathing a sigh of relief. "Except for my wife, you're the first person in the church who has dared to say something to me about it. I know I'm changing, but I do get worried if it's for the best."

"You still didn't answer my question," Marjie pressed. "Why are you willing to take the risks when you know you'll pay a price?"

"Would you believe me if I said it's because I'm nearly old enough to retire and I can escape before the fire gets too hot?"

"No."

"That's good," the pastor said, looking out the study window. "I'm doing these things because I believe in my heart that they're the right thing to do. I'm sorry to say that for most of my ministry I've allowed a certain kind of thinking to dictate to me how I did things in the church. It's cheated me, and it's cheated the church out of some things that I think God wanted to do. That day is over."

"Wow!" Marjie blurted out before she could contain her shock. "Your story sounds so much like Benjamin's."

Pastor Fitchen smiled and nodded. "It should," he said. "He's spent many hours where you're sitting, and much of the time he was challenging me to expand my thinking. It worked!"

"So that's where he was going all the time," Marjie reasoned, then she laughed. "He would never tell us, and sometimes he'd just disappear for a while."

"He's become a very dear friend," the pastor said. "And he's convinced me to be brave enough to stop doing the things that the church expects me to do but that I know I don't do well. This is going to rattle some people."

"What things?"

"Like the young people's group," the pastor said. "I've never been good with teenagers, and everyone knows it. But it's assumed that part of my salary includes working with the young people, even though the young people have to suffer along with me. Come Sunday, the congregation's going to find out that someone else from within the church is going to have to take this over."

"You're telling, not asking?"

"That's right," Pastor Fitchen said. "But I think I can convince most of the congregation that this is for the best."

"How?"

"By telling the truth," he replied, closing his eyes and shaking his head, a crooked smile spreading across his face. "Sounds so simple, but it took Benjamin to help me face it. It was painful to see what I had been missing."

Marjie nodded knowingly. "Benjamin's helped us all with that. But my impression is that you're happier now than when I first came here."

"That's an understatement, Marjie," the pastor acknowledged. "I've enjoyed this past year more than all the other years combined. God is reaching into lives and working in ways I marvel at. I wouldn't trade the changes for anything."

"I am so very happy for you, Pastor," Marjie said. "It shows, and it's spreading."

"Good," he replied, looking Marjie in the eye and smiling. "So when are you going to start the prayer group?"

Marjie reached up and covered her mouth with one hand, then she tapped her front teeth with the back of her thumb. "I can't think of any excuse to get me out of this," she finally said. "So I'll do it—on one condition."

"What's that?"

"That if I get in over my head, you'll be available to pull me out. Do we have a deal?"

"Deal."

───────── ⌒ ─────────

"Boy, am I glad you're home!" Jerry exclaimed as the farmhouse screen door slapped shut behind Marjie. He was sitting on the davenport cradling Martha and looking frazzled. "Something's the matter with her. She's been crying since you left, and nothing seems to help."

"What's wrong?" Marjie asked, moving quickly to the davenport and taking Martha into her arms. "I was only gone for an hour."

"You're asking the wrong guy," Jerry replied, shrugging his shoulders. "I think she's got a fever."

"Goodness," Marjie said, shaking her head. "She feels like a little heater. Did you take her temperature?"

"No. I don't even know where you keep the thermometer."

"You're just as blind as your pa," Marjie said, getting up and heading for the bathroom. "Benjamin couldn't find a thing in the medicine cabinet either. It's in the jar on the shelf next to your hairbrush. How could you not see it?"

When Marjie laid Martha down on the bathroom counter to take off her rubber pants, she began to whimper and cry. "Jerry, come get the thermometer and Vaseline. Let's try to do this quickly."

"This is the first time she's really been sick since I've been home," Jerry said as he reached into the medicine cabinet and located the thermometer. Handing it to Marjie, he grabbed the jar of petroleum jelly and unscrewed the top, then set the jar on the counter. "What do you need the Vaseline for?"

Marjie had taken off the baby's diaper and proceeded to dip the tip of the thermometer into the Vaseline. "This," Marjie said, holding it up for Jerry to observe.

"You're not going to put that in her mouth?" Jerry asked.

"Other end, doctor," Marjie replied with a smile. Then she went about her task quickly, holding up Martha's legs and doing her best to occupy the baby's attention.

Jerry's forehead was wrinkled, and he looked a bit disgusted. "How long do you need to keep it there?" he asked.

"Same amount of time on either end," Marjie said, looking up at Jerry and laughing. "Want to try?"

"No thanks," Jerry replied. "You seem to be doing just fine. Is that a rash on her chest?"

"It sure is," Marjie said. "There's a red patch on her back as well."

"Is it serious?"

"I don't know," Marjie responded, kissing Martha on the cheek and trying to keep her occupied. "Could be a lot of things, I suppose."

"What are we going to do?" Jerry asked, rubbing his fingers through his hair. "Should I call the doctor?"

"Just hang on," Marjie said, glancing up at Jerry again. "Let's see what her temperature is before we get too nervous."

"I don't like that rash," Jerry fretted, looking intently at Martha's chest. "I knew a kid who had scarlet fever. Did you ever see what that looks like?"

"No."

"Except for his face, they said he had something like red goose bumps over his entire body," Jerry explained. "His tongue swelled up, and then his skin started peeling, especially his hands and feet. He was really in bad shape."

"This doesn't look like goose bumps to me," Marjie said.

"Didn't Chester say that his rheumatic fever started with scarlet fever?" asked Jerry. "That's what damaged his heart."

"Don't go jumping the gun," Marjie said. She pulled out the thermometer and carefully wiped it with the diaper. Holding it up to the light, she read, "Hmmm . . . just over one hundred and one. This is not good. She's really sick."

"Shoot!" exclaimed Jerry, leaning back against the wall and exhaling loudly. "We'd better get her in to the doctor. Maybe it's smallpox. Doesn't that have a rash? Or—"

"Stop already!" Marjie demanded. She tucked Martha's diaper back together and repinned it. "There's a whole list of diseases that involve fevers and rashes. Maybe it's just the measles. You keep carrying on, and we're both going to be upset."

"Well, we can't just sit and—"

"She's a baby, and babies get sick," Marjie broke in, lifting Martha up off the counter and laying her against her shoulder. "We're just not used to this. I'm sure your mother didn't run you to the doctor every time you had a fever."

"My mother's not here—"

"Take a walk," Marjie said, shaking her head. "Or better yet, you hold Martha and let me make a call. I think I know what it might be."

"What?" Jerry asked. He carefully lifted Martha from Marjie's shoulder and nestled her against his own.

"Just be patient," replied Marjie, stepping out of the bathroom and walking toward the phone. "I can't believe you get so rattled."

"Chester damaged his heart, and you expect me to—"

"Have you heard of one person around here who's had scarlet fever or smallpox in the last year?" asked Marjie. "Don't say another word until I've finished my call."

Martha began to cry again as Marjie rang a number, and Jerry tried rocking her in his arms and humming to her.

Marjie waited for someone to answer, then she spoke into the mouthpiece, "Bonny, this is Marjie Macmillan. Say, Martha's come down with a fever and rash, and I was wondering if you've heard of any of the other babies from the nursery getting sick? ... Ah, sure. That's just what I thought. Thanks a lot. I guess I won't be seeing you on Sunday. 'Bye."

Hanging up the receiver, Marjie smiled and turned toward Jerry. "Well," she said, rubbing her forehead, "I hope you had it when you were little, because you're really going to be miserable if you get it now. And it's not smallpox or scarlet fever or rheumatic fever or polio or—"

"Okay!" Jerry protested. "You made your point. What is it?"

"Buc-buc-buc, buc-buc-buc-bucket," Marjie cackled and laughed.

"Chicken pox!" Jerry exclaimed and groaned. "Jack and I had them when we were little. They're terrible. I itched so bad I just about went crazy. What can we—"

"We can send you out to finish whatever you were doing to the wagon," she said, "or you'll drive me crazy!"

16

PRAYER MEETING

"Why is it that Labor Day never ends up being a holiday?" Marjie asked, shoving a quart jar of applesauce onto the top shelf of the steam canner. Then she shut the canner doors and turned on the timer. "I feel bad that you're slaving away here on your day off."

Margaret and Ruth had finished peeling and coring the last bushel of apples, and now they nearly had the last batch turned into sauce. Marjie's mother was walking around the living room with an exultant Martha holding on to her hands.

"You look real sad about it," Ruth teased. Taking her long wooden spoon, which was covered with applesauce, she reached out and wiped a big glob on Marjie's arm. "Hungry?" she asked.

"Oh, you!" exclaimed Marjie, grabbing the mound of sauce before it rolled off. Then she took steps toward Ruth. "You've been asking for it all morning. Maybe you'd like to try experimenting with this as shampoo."

"Just a second," Sarah called out. "Before you girls make a mess of things, I'm going to take Martha outside for a walk. It's too hot and muggy in here. Feels like another storm."

Marjie looked over at her mother, who was already heading for the door with the baby. "She just got over the chicken pox, you know. Don't get too far away . . . in case it—"

"Trust me," Sarah said and laughed, waving at Marjie with her free hand. "Do you think I'm going to let anything bad happen to my only grandchild?"

"If you find any fresh air outside, send it in here," Ruth said as Sarah and Martha made their exit.

"This really isn't so bad," Margaret said, pushing a few long dark curls back into place. "Sometimes I have to work between the two large ovens in the bakery. I feel like a piece of toast when I come out." Marjie and Ruth laughed, then went back to their tasks rather than plunging into a food battle.

"It must be terrible working down in the sinkhole today," Marjie commented. "I hope the men can get most of that old metal out of there. Can you imagine all the old machinery in this country that's been turned into tanks or guns or ships?"

"The county's scrap metal drive has been pretty successful," Ruth said. "Billy said he heard that we're going to go over our quota on war bonds as well. Fillmore County's already over the million five hundred mark."

"Wow!" exclaimed Marjie. "Not much of that came from this farm. But they can have all the scrap metal our boys can fish out of the junk pile."

"Speaking of giving, I gave blood on Monday," Ruth said. "The Red Cross was at the courthouse. You should have seen all the people."

"How did it go?" Margaret asked.

"Not so good," replied Ruth. "There—"

"Sounds like a story to me," Marjie broke in, looking around at Margaret and Ruth. "Why don't we go sit at the table and drink some cold pink lemonade. We can't do much more until the timer goes off."

Both Margaret and Ruth looked relieved to finally get a break. Nearly the entire counter was covered with cooling Mason jars that represented their morning's labor. Moving to the dining room table, they sat down and poured their drinks.

"Ooh, this tastes good," Marjie said, then she exhaled a big sigh. "So, what happened at the courthouse?"

Ruth started to chuckle and shook her head. "Things got

pretty wild. You know Big John Reymer?"

Marjie nodded. "He's got the gas station out on the edge of town."

"And the large beer belly," Margaret added with a laugh.

"That's him," Ruth said. "Well, somebody talked him into giving blood, even though he'd tried in the past and it didn't go well. He didn't bother to warn the nurses."

Marjie jumped ahead. "And he fainted dead away."

"Not just fainted," Ruth replied, taking a sip of lemonade. "He's lying on one cot, and the banker's wife, Mrs. Stockdale, is lying on the next cot. They're busy chatting away until the nurse comes to take their blood. Everything seemed fine . . ."

A sudden gust of wind pushed back the window curtains, causing the three women to look out the picture window. A few dark thunderclouds had appeared on the horizon, but it came as no surprise on such a sultry day.

"Hope the boys take note of what's coming," Marjie said. "Looks like we're lucky we didn't go on that picnic. So, what happened to Big John?"

Ruth turned her focus back to the dining room and continued. "The nurse came to him first and went through her usual procedure. She got him hooked up but didn't notice that he was starting to get clammy-looking. Then she turned around and went to start on Mrs. Stockdale.

"I was a couple of cots away, and I thought I saw John's eyes starting to close, although he seemed to be struggling to keep them open. Then they kind of rolled back in his head and he was out. I called out to the nurse, and she turned around and immediately saw the problem.

"The nurse stepped back to John and leaned over him and called his name, but there was no response," Ruth said. "Then she patted his face and continued to call his name. In a minute he came to. She got him to take a couple of deep breaths, but then one of the other nurses noticed that Mrs. Stockdale had fainted. Her arms were hanging over the side of the cot, and one arm was twitching."

Margaret and Marjie had broken out laughing at the scene

she painted, and Ruth, too, gave in to laughter.

"So," Ruth finally continued, gripping the table, "Big John is conscious now, but then he looks over at Mrs. Stockdale's twitching arm and bang—he lets out a big moan and passes out again. And by the time he comes to, several other people around the room are fainting. Those poor nurses really had their hands full."

"That sounds terrible," Margaret said. "He must have survived, though. He got a big bag of doughnuts at the bakery yesterday morning."

Ruth nodded. "They eventually got him unhooked and let him lie there for quite a while. He was almost blue."

"Actually, that sounds sort of scary," Marjie said, sobering. "Did you get faint, Ruthie?"

"No," she replied. "But I was a little nervous. I've heard about people having heart attacks when they were giving blood. I thought Big John might buy the farm right there on that cot."

"Why would he buy a farm?" Margaret asked with a perplexed frown.

"Oops," Ruth said, "another one of our Americanisms. Margaret, that's our funny way of saying he might die," Ruth answered. "I'm not sure why we say it that way."

"How did the banker's wife fare?" Marjie broke in.

"She left on her own power and without giving a drop of blood," Ruth said. "But I think she suffered a serious blow to her pride. Too bad, eh?"

All three began to laugh again. Mrs. Stockdale was the small town's reigning socialite, and stories of jerking arms would quickly spread far and wide.

"It's too bad they didn't get a pint of blood out of her," Marjie said, half joking. "With the invasion of Italy and the move to liberate the islands across the Pacific, they're going to need a lot of blood. I hate to think what's coming."

"If the cost of freeing Guadalcanal is any indication, I—"

Ruth was interrupted by the timer, and Marjie jumped up to attend to the quarts of applesauce, which were ready to come out. The tall metal canner was a welcome distraction to their gloomy thoughts about the escalating conflict in the Pacific and European theaters of war.

"One year ago today I was two weeks away from delivering Martha, and guess what I was doing?" Marjie called out as she opened the canner doors. "I was feeding a crew of men who came over to help Benjamin cut corn for silage." Potholder in hand, she reached for a hot Mason jar. "Hard to believe a year could fly by so quickly."

"I was home in Scotland praying for the bonny day when I'd see my handsome Chester again," Margaret added, helping Marjie take out some of the jars.

"And I was twiddling my thumbs on—"

The screen door banged shut, and Sarah called out, "Better close the windows and head for the basement! There's a terrible storm heading our way!"

Marjie glanced out the kitchen window and could see a wall of cloud rushing across the fields straight toward the farmhouse. The huge, menacing cloud was a strange mixture of swirling white and black and green. She could feel the thunder rumbling ahead of it. "Oh no, not again," she groaned.

"Take Martha to the basement!" Marjie called out to her mother. "I'll get the windows upstairs. Margaret—get the windows down here. Ruthie—turn off the stove."

"What about the men?" Ruth cried as Marjie ran for the stairway.

"There's no time!" Marjie echoed back.

Marjie raced up the stairs and dashed from room to room, shutting the wide-open windows. From Martha's bedroom window, Marjie could look down to the sinkhole where the men had been working, but all she could see was the tractor and a hay wagon filled with large chunks of machinery. The wall cloud was already over the sinkhole.

Marjie tore around and headed for the downstairs. By the time she got to the bottom of the staircase, darkness had surrounded the farmhouse and huge drops of rain had begun to splatter on the window. Then she heard the clatter of pea-sized hail outside.

By the time Marjie closed the basement door behind her, wind, thunder, and rain were pounding the house with a deafening roar. Marjie was glad for the light bulb above the bottom of the cellar stairs, but it flickered when she got halfway down and then the electricity went off.

Joining the others who were huddled by the west wall, Marjie took hold of their arms and could hear Margaret and Ruth and her mother all praying at the same time. She joined them, but she also looked out the cellar window.

The large elm tree on the west side of the house was swaying deeply against the rush of the wind and rain. Water was breaking against the window in waves, and an occasional hailstone would crack against the glass and make Marjie jump. Then the light bulb flickered again and came to life.

The thunderstorm only lasted three or four minutes, and the worst was in its initial blast of fury. Soon the sky began to lighten, the winds subsided, and even the rain completely ceased. In the dimly lit cellar, silence replaced the tumult that had briefly reigned over them.

"Whew!" Marjie finally broke the quiet. "That was close."

"Can't get much closer," Sarah added. "We better get upstairs and see what's still standing. I hope the men found shelter."

Heading back up the stairs and into the kitchen, Marjie was relieved that everything in the house looked unscathed. She led the way out the door, and the little group stopped on the front lawn. Countless small branches were scattered all around, but it looked like only one big elm tree had gone down, and that one had fallen straight across the driveway.

"I can't believe there wasn't more damage," Marjie said numbly, scanning the farmyard. "I expected to lose trees and windows, maybe some buildings."

"This is a shock," Ruth said, reaching out to Sarah and running her fingers across Martha's back. "Looks like just one tree. I hope the corn's still standing."

"I hope the men are still standing," Margaret added. "Can we drive out there?"

"Let's go!" Marjie urged.

They all hopped into Jerry's old black Ford, and Marjie drove down the farm lane toward the sinkhole. They rounded a sharp curve and passed a large pine tree, and the sinkhole finally came into view. But only the tractor and wagon were to be seen.

"Where could they be?" Sarah asked.

"There!" Marjie called out, pointing to the wagon. "Somebody's getting out from under the wagon."

First one, then two, then two more bodies crawled from underneath the heavily laden wagon. And one by one they stood up and appeared to be shaking themselves off.

Marjie pulled up by the wagon and stopped. The men were soaked and caked with dirt from head to toe. Car doors popped open, and the women raced to their men.

Someone called out, "Are you okay?" but the laughter of the men was all the answer they required.

"We're fine," Jerry smiled as Marjie grabbed him. He was still trying to wipe the grime from his face. "Chester persuaded us to join him in a prayer meeting under the wagon, and you wouldn't believe how powerful it was!"

17

BLUEY

"Thursday night, in our living room, eh?" Jerry repeated to Marjie, who was busy in the kitchen getting their Sunday lunch together. "What are you going to do if too many people show up? The announcement in the bulletin was so general that most of the congregation may come."

"Half of the members don't think a prayer meeting's supposed to happen in a farmhouse," Marjie replied, pulling open the oven door and putting in the hamburger casserole. "And Thursday is not an official church night, so no one's going to feel like it's his duty to show up."

Jerry looked down at the bulletin and slowly read the select copy, " 'There will be an informal meeting at Jerry and Marjie Macmillan's house on Thursday night at 7:30 P.M. for anyone who wants to join with others in praying for loved ones involved in the armed services.' I think there's going to be a lot more interest in this than you're figuring on."

"That would be wonderful if there is," Marjie replied. She took a freshly washed head of cabbage and began slicing it to make coleslaw. "But I'm guessing only five people will show up for the first night, and the only one I'm counting on for sure is my ma."

"Well," Jerry said, "you got me nervous. I'm betting on no less than twenty."

"Oh, come on, Jerry. That's ridiculous," Marjie muttered, shaking her head and smiling. "Aren't your fingers still wrinkled from the losses you suffered the last time you made a friendly wager?"

Jerry laughed and folded his arms. "You got me on the turkey, but this one's mine. I know there'll be twenty, and the most you can fit in the living room is a dozen. I predict overflow into the dining room."

"I'd really hate to whip you again, but you don't seem to have learned your lesson," Marjie said. "You want to put a second week's worth of washing dinner dishes on the table?"

Jerry puckered his lips and nodded confidently. "And you'll put up digging the potatoes yourself?"

"No, no, no. That's not fair," Marjie protested. "A few hours scrubbing dishes doesn't compare to the back-breaking hours slaving in the garden."

"I thought you were feeling lucky," Jerry needled.

"I am, but digging the spuds was supposed to be your job," Marjie corrected. "The whole summer went by, and you hardly lifted a finger to help in the garden."

"Okay, how about you dig two full rows, and I'll do the other three," Jerry suggested.

"You've got a deal, but you have to promise not to complain about losing this time," Marjie said. "You cried about doing the dishes every night after I did in Mr. Turkey."

"This time it's your turn to cry," Jerry declared. "I'll make sure the pitchfork is sharp so it'll be all ready for those potatoes. You better—"

The high-pitched squeal of breaking tires and slashing gravel on the road beyond the Macmillan driveway cut Jerry off. He turned and stepped quickly to the front door, where he stood gazing out through the screen.

"Wonder what's wrong with him?" Jerry said.

"Who is it?" Marjie asked, dropping her knife and head of cabbage to join him at the door.

"Tom Metcalfe. He stopped almost sideways in the road. Looks like he's getting out."

Jerry stepped out onto the porch with Marjie right behind him. They watched as Metcalfe got out of his car, walked to the far side of the road, and climbed down in the ditch. When he bent over, all they could see was the top of Metcalfe's back.

"Something's really wrong," Marjie said, quickly looking back around the farmyard. "He must've hit . . ."

Jerry was running across the yard and toward the idling car before Marjie could finish her sentence. Wanting to follow him, Marjie first had to listen at the screen door to make sure that Martha was still asleep, then she bounded down the steps in hot pursuit. By the time she got there, Jerry was already down in the ditch with Tom, and the two men were hunched over something.

Marjie could hear Metcalfe talking very fast, his voice cracking. "You gotta believe me, Jerry. It was an accident. He ran right out in front of me. I never had a chance. First the rabbit cut across the road, and then your dog . . ."

"Blue!" Marjie cried out, dropping to her knees beside Jerry. The small Australian cow dog lay motionless on his side in the ditch's high grass and weeds. He was breathing and his eyes were open, but there was blood at the corner of his mouth, on the top of his head, and on his right shoulder.

Jerry hardly seemed to notice that Marjie was on her knees next to him. He had one hand under the dog's face, and with the other hand he was feeling Blue's bones and muscles.

"Honest to God, he popped out of the long grass so fast that I—"

"It's okay, Tom," Jerry assured the shaken farmer, looking up at him. "I'm sure there was nothing you could do. You may as well go on home, seeing as we're here. We'll do what we can for him."

"Oh, man, I feel terrible," Metcalfe said, running his hand across his stubbled face and shifting his weight from foot to foot. "Let me help you carry him back."

"No, that's okay, Tom," Jerry replied, turning his attention back to the dog. "He's not so big. I can carry him easy enough."

"You let me know what happens," Tom said quickly. "I'll pay for him if he don't make it."

"Don't worry about the money," responded Jerry. He was busy feeling for broken bones again. "It wasn't your fault. Let us take care of him."

"You call me," Metcalfe urged, stepping up out of the ditch and toward his car. "I feel awful."

"I'll call you as soon as we know something," Marjie said, nodding to the only farmer in the neighborhood she had never been introduced to.

Slowly Metcalfe got back in his car and pulled away from the scene of the accident, leaving Marjie and Jerry still hunched over the injured dog in the ditch.

"Oh, Bluey . . . you know better than to get out on the road." Marjie spoke softly as she lightly ran her finger down the distinctive blue marking on the dog's forehead. "What do you think, Jerry?"

"I don't know," Jerry muttered. A deep frown shadowed his face as he gently bent the dog's legs, but without any response from the cattle dog. "It don't feel like anything's broken. But he ain't moved a muscle since he landed in the ditch."

"It looks like the car got him above the shoulders," Marjie said. The dog's short, thick black and tan coat was matted with blood where the impact seemed to have done the most damage. "Let's take him to the house."

Jerry gently reached his hands down underneath Blue's shoulders and hindquarters, then whispered in the dog's ear, "You gotta make it, boy. We need you here." Then Jerry slowly lifted the dog to his chest and stood up in the ditch. Blue's thick tail hung limp at Jerry's side.

Marjie raced ahead of Jerry, and by the time he got to the farmhouse she had already turned an old wool blanket into a bed for the dog. Holding the screen door open for him, Marjie pointed to the living room.

Jerry carried Blue to the makeshift bed, bent over, and tenderly laid the dog on the blanket. With his hand upon the dog's head, he said, "There you go, boy. You rest now."

Marjie thought she noticed Blue's eyes follow Jerry as he leaned back away from the dog, but that was the extent of the dog's movement. Then Blue's eyes closed and did not open again. Even the dog's rhythmic breathing stopped.

"Come on, Blue, breathe!" Marjie cried, dropping down beside the dog.

"Bluey!" called Jerry, touching the dog's ribs.

The sudden rising of the dog's chest was met with a burst of relief from both Marjie and Jerry.

"Whew!" exclaimed Jerry, closing his eyes. "I thought he was gone."

"Oh, me too," Marjie said, taking a deep breath of air. "My heart nearly stopped."

The timer on the oven began to buzz, and Marjie jumped up to turn it off. She pulled the casserole out and set it on the top of the stove. Then she opened the cupboards and began to pull out the plates and cups.

"If we can, I'd like to eat in here," Jerry called from the living room.

Marjie pulled out a tin serving tray and arranged Jerry's lunch on it. Adding another dash of salt and pepper to the casserole, she took it in to him. Jerry was sitting beside Blue with his back leaning up against the davenport, solemnly watching his dog and still resting his hand upon Blue's ribs.

"Do you think we should call the vet?" Marjie asked, handing him the tray of food.

Jerry wrinkled his lip and shook his head slowly. "What's he gonna do? He'd probably just tell us we should put Blue out of his misery."

They both fell silent, unwilling to contemplate that possibility.

"Did you get him when he was pup?" Marjie finally asked, sitting down beside Jerry and lightly rubbing the dog's black ears.

"His coat was white, if you can believe that," Jerry said, managing a smile and taking a forkful of casserole. "He was a couple months old before he started to show his colors. Even when he was little, he knew just how to nip at the heels of the cattle to keep 'em coming up from the pasture."

"I love this dog, Jerry," Marjie said, closing her eyes and asking God to heal Blue of whatever damage had been done. "What if he . . ."

Marjie choked up, and Jerry put his hand on her arm.

"If he doesn't make it, I think it's going to be a while before I get another pup," Jerry said. "If he's crippled . . . I don't know. If he doesn't look like he's going to suffer, I want to keep him. But if he's bad, we'll have to call the vet and have him put to sleep. There's no way I can just shoot him."

———— ✑ ————

When Martha woke up from her nap, Jerry carried Blue to the downstairs bedroom and laid him out of her reach on the bed. The dog still had not opened his eyes or moved; he seemed to be in a deep sleep.

Jerry lay on the bed most of the afternoon, hoping that Blue would wake up. When choring time came around, he reluctantly trudged to the barn while Marjie continued his vigil. But the dog did not stir.

"I feel kinda funny about this, but I'm going to sleep with the dog tonight," Jerry said later that night. "Mother would never even let a dog step into the house, let alone have one crawling on a bed."

"You prefer Blue to me?" Marjie teased.

"Only for one night," Jerry answered, putting his arms around Marjie. "I won't be able to sleep unless I'm close by him. If he doesn't wake up soon, I don't figure he ever will."

Jerry did not sleep well, but he found that as long as he kept his hand on the dog's side, he could sleep in short spurts. When morning chore time rolled around, Blue was still sleeping and gave no indication of change. Jerry could see little reason to bother waking up Marjie, so he left the dog on his own.

After chores, Jerry came back into the house for breakfast and called out to Marjie, "Any change?"

"None," Marjie said, shaking her head. "I've checked a dozen times. Go take a look. Martha's in there now, but she can't get up on the bed."

Jerry walked toward the bedroom and Marjie decided to follow. Stopping at the doorway, they found that Martha was on the far side of the bed trying to reach the dog. But her arms were far too short, and there was no way she could pull herself up on the bed.

"I wonder if she could wake him up?" Jerry asked.

"What?"

"I'm gonna try somethin'," Jerry said without explanation. He stepped around to the far side of the bed and picked up Martha. Then he sat down on the bed with her in his arms and stretched her out toward Blue.

Martha let out a giggle and lunged toward her friend who had gotten used to her rough treatment.

"Don't let her—"

Marjie's warning was too late. Martha already had her right arm wrapped around Blue's head, and her face and curly brown hair was in his face. She chattered happily to the little dog, and despite Jerry's initial impulse to pull her away, he decided to let Martha continue.

Marjie could not see Blue's face, but she thought she noticed the dog's tail move. "Jerry!" she cried. "Blue's—"

But Marjie did not need to finish. Jerry could see that, if nothing else, Blue's tail had come to life. First once, then twice, then several more times the tail swished.

Jerry reached out and slowly pulled Martha away from Blue. Although the dog did not try to move anything but his tail, Blue's dark eyes were wide open and watching as Martha moved away from his face.

"Bluey, you're back!" Jerry cried, falling down beside the injured dog and gently taking his face into his hands. Tears began to fall from Jerry's face onto the old blanket underneath the dog. "You're back!"

Blue's tail continued to wag back and forth, and he opened his mouth in a familiar dog smile, but he did not attempt any movement.

"What's up, boy? Where's it hurt?" Jerry asked. "Marjie, get him some water."

Marjie dashed to the kitchen and got a bowl of water, then walked carefully back into the bedroom. Jerry was slowly moving Blue's legs back and forth without any apparent pain showing in the dog's eyes.

"I think his legs are okay," Jerry said, looking up at Marjie with a rare smile after the events of the past day. But when he ran his fingers up over Blue's shoulders, the dog jerked his head and whimpered. "I think he's just bruised badly. There's a big muscle that feels swollen."

"How would you know?" Marjie questioned.

"I know," Jerry replied. "Seven years with this dog, and you wonder how I know?"

"I just mean that you're not the vet," Marjie said. "You think we should try to get Blue up?"

"No," Jerry said. "It's better if we let him try when he's ready. He may need a few more days to mend before he gets up. But let's try to give him some water."

Jerry held up Blue's face, and Marjie held the bowl out to the dog. Blue took three laps of water, but that was all that he seemed interested in.

"Good boy," Jerry said. "Now you rest some more. We're right here, Blue."

"You're going to let him stay in here until he's walking?" Marjie asked.

"Where else?" asked Jerry, squinting up at Marjie.

"The barn is what he's used to," she said. "He's going to get spoiled in here and not want to stay out in the barn when he's well."

"Then we spoil him rotten," Jerry replied. "Maybe he'll be a house dog after all."

The Australian cattle dog gave Jerry a quizzical look and then broke out in another big smile.

18

A Night to Remember

"Jerry, you were supposed to have taken Blue to the barn by now," Marjie said. She'd just come down the stairs after putting Martha to bed for the evening. "The way that dog sheds, I'm going to have to sweep again. If any of the women say a—"

"He's going! Just give me a couple more minutes," Jerry sputtered, buttoning up his shirt and tucking it into his dress pants. "We have twenty minutes."

Blue was resting contentedly on the oval rug by the front door. At the mention of his name, his tail began to wave back and forth, and he turned his head to look at Jerry.

"Okay, boy. Time for you to go to the barn," Jerry said. "Let's go."

But instead of getting up, Blue rolled over on his back and waved all four paws into the air to beg for a reprieve. Then he whimpered and turned his sad dark eyes on his master.

"Oh, goodness, not again," Marjie lamented, watching the drama unfold. "Five days of being inside the house have turned him into a pathetic beggar. He was recovered enough yesterday not to be in the house."

Jerry burst out laughing. "Come on, Blue, get up," he ordered. But all he accomplished was to increase the wagging of the dog's tail.

"We don't have time for this," Marjie said, looking nervously out the dining room picture window toward the road. "Last time he pulled this stunt, you let him stay inside. He's conning you again, Jerry."

"On your feet, boy," Jerry ordered, taking Blue by the collar and gently pulling him up. Pushing open the screen door, he said, "Head for the barn."

Still nursing a sore right shoulder, Blue limped slowly down the sidewalk toward the barn. Jerry followed along to open the barn door.

"He's coming along pretty good, don't you think?" Jerry called back as Marjie stepped out onto the front steps.

"Terrific," Marjie replied. "There's no reason he can't stay in the barn now."

"I kinda like having him inside," Jerry petitioned. "And Martha loves to play with him. Think how bored she's going to be stuck inside the house all winter. She could use a playmate."

"If you want that dog to live a full life, it's going to be somewhere other than under my feet shaking his hair all over creation," Marjie said. "And if Martha needs a playmate, I suggest that a brother or sister might be a better solution."

"I like that idea," replied Jerry with a big grin. "When can we start?"

"Later tonight might work," Marjie said with a nod. "If you're available . . . and the dog is in the barn."

"Blue!" Jerry called out to the dog, who was nearly to the barn door by now. "I'm afraid I've got some bad news for you."

Marjie turned and walked back into the house. She picked up the rug that Blue had been lying on, pushed open the screen door, and shook the dog hairs off it. Stepping back into the house, she went to the stove and put on the big white coffeepot that she normally used only when a crew of men were coming in to work during harvest time.

"Looks like the first car's coming," Jerry spoke out as he returned to the house, the screen door slapping shut behind him.

"They're fifteen minutes early," Marjie said, washing her hands quickly and drying them with a dish towel. She stepped into the dining room and joined Jerry as an old Ford much like theirs rolled past. "Who is it?"

"Harvey and Goldie Turner. Right on time," Jerry replied, glancing down at his watch and chuckling. "Don't worry about them coming in, though. They always like to get to their meetings way early, then they sit in the car until someone else goes in first."

Marjie chuckled as well. "That's an odd thing to do. Guess it beats coming late."

"They're pretty blunt, too. So be prepared for what they might say," Jerry said, wrapping his arm around Marjie. "Are you nervous?"

"Nervous?" replied Marjie. "We have no idea how many people might show up or what's going to happen, and you wonder if I'm nervous."

"Did you really want to put the coffee on already, or is that your nerves?" asked Jerry.

"No, that was planned," Marjie said with a sigh. "The bulletin called this an informal meeting, so I thought I'd fool everybody and start with coffee. Thought it might help break the ice, and then we could get a feel for what to do tonight."

"You keep saying 'we,'" Jerry noted. "This was your idea, and it's your meeting, babe."

"Nope. Wrong again," Marjie said, running her finger down Jerry's forearm. "It was my idea, but we're a team. The men who come are going to need your help."

"Wait a minute. You didn't—"

"Here comes a second early bird," Marjie said, cutting off Jerry's protest. "Looks like my ma . . . and no Benjamin. She was afraid that one of their cows wouldn't have had her calf by tonight and Benjamin would have to stick around and wait. Ruthie can't make it tonight, and neither can Chester and Margaret. Boy, I'm glad you're here."

"What is it that you have in mind that I'm going to do tonight?" Jerry asked. He looked out the window and waved as Sarah Macmillan climbed out of her car. Right on cue, the

Turners opened their car doors as Sarah walked past them and came up the sidewalk.

"I don't have anything specific planned," Marjie answered. "But I've got a feeling I'm going to need you tonight. Just be ready for whatever comes."

"Warn me next time," Jerry growled, letting go of Marjie as her mother pulled open the screen door.

"I did," Marjie whispered, kissing him lightly on the cheek. "You've had fifteen seconds."

"Ready?" Sarah called out as she stepped into the dining room.

"I hope so," Marjie said, greeting her mother with a hug. "Ready or not, here we go."

Jerry had crossed over to the door and pushed it open for the Turners. "Goldie . . . Harvey," he greeted them. "Come on in."

"Are we early, Jerry?" Goldie asked, clutching her big black purse as she came up the steps and through the door. "We hate to be early."

"Just in time for a cup of coffee," Jerry replied, pointing them toward Marjie. "You've met Sarah, haven't you?"

"Surely," Goldie replied, nodding toward Sarah. "We were at the wedding, of course. And we've talked at church once or twice."

"Have a seat at the table, and I'll get you some coffee," Marjie said.

"I'll get the coffee, and you take care of your guests," Sarah piped up before Marjie could make her move.

Marjie and Jerry let the Turners take the chairs they wanted first, and then they all sat down. For a moment an awkward silence surrounded the table, and Marjie glanced quickly over at Jerry.

"What do you hear from Willard?" Jerry asked. "Is he still in England?"

"Yep," Harvey Turner replied. "Their bomb squadron's flying one mission after another. Scary business, boy. He wrote us that they've been torn up pretty bad a couple times. One trip he said they were lucky to limp back across the Channel."

"Wasn't luck, Harvey," Goldie reminded him, and none too gently.

Sarah carried in a tray with five cups of coffee and passed them around, then she sat down next to Marjie.

"My older brother was just a part of the liberation of Sicily," Marjie said, "and my younger brother's still stateside. Sounds like we've got plenty to pray about."

Goldie took a drink of coffee, then pushed her gold wire-rimmed glasses back up on the bridge of her large nose. "You mean we're gonna pray for our boys by name tonight?"

Marjie had expected the evening to have its share of surprises, but she had not anticipated a question like this. She took a drink of coffee to delay her response, then she said, "That was my intention. Is there a reason we shouldn't pray for them by name?"

"Well, we never do in church," Goldie responded. "Someone always just prays for all the boys who have left their homes for the war. That's it."

"That's . . . that's why we're having this meeting tonight," Marjie explained. "So we can pray together specifically about all of our loved ones in the service, and for each other as well. It must be hard on you, your son flying all those bomber raids over Germany."

Harvey squinted his eyes and nodded silently, but Marjie could see that Goldie was still working on the prayer questions.

"There's many nights I've stayed in my rocking chair and never went to bed," Goldie acknowledged. "I dread to get the news that you got, Sarah—that your boy was missing. For fliers like Willard, missing in action usually means dead. But we've never prayed together for Willard."

"Who's we?" Marjie asked.

"The church for one," Goldie replied, setting her jaw and taking a deep breath. "But neither have Harvey and me. We've never prayed together in our whole marriage."

Harvey Turner's face had gone a deep red. Marjie glanced at

Jerry, but his face looked as bewildered as her mind felt. *I should have never let the pastor . . .*

"Then tonight's a good time to start," Sarah responded after a few moments of awkward silence. "Marjie's father and I never prayed together either, although Robert did pray for me out loud a couple of days before he died. We didn't know anything about prayer. But I'm learning now. I still feel awkward about it—maybe I always will—but I *am* learning, and I'm glad."

"I'm sorry, but I can't do it," Harvey mumbled, looking out the window nervously as another car pulled into the farmyard. "It ain't that I don't want to, but I ain't never done it. Guess I'll just go sit in the car."

"No, please stay, Harvey," Marjie pleaded, fixing her dark brown eyes on his gray eyes. "None of us are good at this, and maybe nobody needs to pray out loud. If we simply went around the group and told where our loved ones were, and then we prayed silently for them and for each other, wouldn't God still hear us? Do we have to pray out loud?"

Harvey shook his head, rubbed his chin hard, and then covered his mouth with his hand, looking down at his coffee cup. "I . . ." Then he covered his eyes with his hand and took a deep breath as his wife had.

"This is why we're here," Jerry assured Harvey, putting his hand on the burly farmer's thick shoulder. "Some burdens are just too heavy to carry alone, Harvey."

A knock at the screen door and the sound of tires rolling over gravel in the driveway temporarily relieved the intensity of the moment. But from the Turners' first reaction, Marjie concluded it would be best to let people mingle and talk and pray together rather than gather into one big prayer group.

By seven-thirty, Marjie and Jerry had welcomed more than twenty people into the house, and Sarah was measuring coffee for a second large pot. Meeting the people at the door, Marjie tried to explain briefly what they would do inside. Most of them liked the idea of talking, but some weren't sure about the praying part.

By seven forty-five, thirty-five people had shown up, and

Jerry was worried that there was no more room. When no other cars appeared, Jerry and Marjie stepped into the house and looked around in amazement. People were everywhere, and the house was buzzing. Every chair was filled, and people were even in the kitchen talking in small groups. Some were praying, some couples were holding hands, and a few were weeping.

"Lord, answer the cries of their hearts," Jerry whispered, taking Marjie's hand and stepping awkwardly into the dining room. They were both struck by the sight of Harvey Turner, who was still sitting at the table and seemed to be having no problem praying for his brother's son, who was in the Marines.

The sound of another approaching car broke their wonderment.

"I can't believe this," Marjie said quietly to Jerry. "We better see who's here now."

They went back to the door and out onto the steps. In the dim light, Jerry was the first to make out who it was. "Betty Hunter," he whispered, as if to keep the shock from those who were inside the house.

"She came after all," Marjie said, shaking her head in disbelief.

But rather than find a place to park down past the machine shed where the others had gone, Betty's car slowed to a stop, idled for a minute or two, then backed up, and turned around.

"She's talking herself out of it," Marjie guessed, watching the car lights come forward. Running out to the driveway ahead of Betty, Marjie put her hand up and stepped to the side of the car as it stopped.

"I can't come in!" Betty gasped as Marjie looked in the driver's window. "I'll wreck it for everyone who's come."

"You're not going to wreck anything," Marjie reassured her. "Betty, you've got to give these people a chance to show they care about you. I think you'll be amazed at what's going on in there."

"What if I start crying again like I did the other day?" asked Betty.

"Some people in there are already crying," Marjie said. "The

Bible says there's a time to cry, but it doesn't say you have to cry alone. Please come in. Just pull your car off to the side and leave it there."

Betty looked into Marjie's eyes and slowly nodded. Angling the car to the side of the driveway and turning the engine off, she shoved the heavy car door open and stepped into the cool evening air.

"I'll go in if you stay with me," Betty said. "You leave me, and I leave. Okay?"

"I'm not going anywhere without you," Marjie replied, taking Betty's hand. "But you may find you don't need me."

Marjie and Betty walked silently to the farmhouse porch. Jerry had already gone inside. When they got to the door, Marjie asked Betty, "Do you see what I see?"

Betty was looking through the screen door, her eyes big. "What's going on?"

"Come in and find out for yourself," Marjie said, pulling the door open and stepping in quickly with the hope of not attracting much notice.

But despite several onlookers' best attempts to mask their surprise, the din in the kitchen and dining room and living room slowly died, and every eye was on Betty. Marjie squeezed Betty's hand to reassure her that all was well, but she feared that Betty was about to turn and run.

Then a woman's voice broke the silence. "Welcome, Betty." Sarah Macmillan stepped around the kitchen counter, coming toward her. "You are the bravest of all to come tonight. I'm so glad you did, because I think a lot of us have something we want you to know."

Sarah took the hand that Marjie wasn't holding and looked into Betty's face. "Your loss is so great that we often don't know what to say to you. But you need to know that our silence around you is not because we don't care. Betty, I'm so sorry about what happened to you."

Another hand reached out and touched Betty, and then another. Soon she was surrounded by people. Some were apologizing, others were praying, but all were weeping for the little girl who'd grown up in their midst and had lost the most precious person in her life.

19

BEFORE MY GRANDFATHER'S GRANDFATHER

"Please, just call me Mister," the soft-spoken missionary said in his greeting to the Greenleafton congregation after Pastor Fitchen's formal introduction. "That's what the Dyak people in Borneo call me, and coming from them, it's a name I've come to love."

"He looks so ordinary," Marjie whispered to Jerry as the tall, skinny man addressed the church. She had expected him to be old, odd-looking, and dressed in ancient clothes, but instead he looked like a businessman in his neatly cut black suit. He seemed to be in his early forties.

Marjie and Jerry weren't sure how Margaret and Chester had done it, but somehow they had talked the pastor into letting Anthony Biden speak at both the Sunday morning and evening services. Or maybe it was something about the pioneer missionary story that won Pastor Fitchen over. At any rate, the morning service was dedicated to Biden's story of bringing the gospel to a people who had never heard, and the evening service would feature the American missionary couple's dramatic escape from Borneo past Japanese war boats and guards.

"How beautiful upon the mountains are the feet of him that bringeth good tidings, that publisheth peace" was the text, and to a congregation who had never had a missionary speaker, the message Biden brought was spellbinding. Traveling far up Borneo's great rivers and deep into the exotic tropical rain forests, he and his wife had seen hundreds of animistic Dyak tribal people respond to the good news of Christ's salvation.

"We walked in a land where the sunlight and moonlight never reach the jungle floors," the missionary said. "It's a place where whole villages of people live under one roof—which we called a longhouse—rather than in separate dwellings. It's a land where evil spirits have ruled the people with tormenting fear and the witch doctors have exercised great power for unending centuries. And it's a place where the name of Jesus Christ had never once been spoken . . . until Cynthia and I came."

Biden told how three and a half years of evangelizing had finally yielded one Dyak conversion. But following that one conversion, the entire village had quickly professed their faith in Jesus Christ—and village after village had followed. The minutes flew past as Biden reeled off one incredible story after another.

Marjie glanced down at her watch. *If he rolls on past twelve o'clock*, she thought, *I'll need to go check on Martha. But I don't want to leave!*

"Another village of Dyaks had made a profession of faith," Biden was saying, "and several of them had come to the river that ran past their longhouse to be baptized. For people who have grown up in a totally pagan world, baptism is a powerful declaration that they are breaking from the bondage of idolatry and heathenism. Not surprisingly, the witch doctors often oppose it fiercely.

"On this particular day, I noticed that after being baptized, one of the men was beating his chest and crying out in loud declarations, 'Now it's at peace. Now it's at rest. In here it's at peace.' I looked at him, and I was concerned he might have misunderstood the meaning of baptism. So I asked, 'Why are you saying that? You don't really think that the water washed away your sins, do you?'

"He looked at me as if to say, 'Don't you know any better than that?' Then he said, 'Mister, I have bathed in that river ever since I was a child. My mother took me down there right after I was born. I have bathed myself in that river all the days of my life, and it has never, never washed away any sin. Nothing but the blood of Jesus could wash my sin away. Now it's at peace; now it's at rest.' "

"Goodness!" Marjie whispered, leaning against Jerry. But his gaze remained fixed on the missionary speaker. Against the cruel darkness of the Dyak's paganism, the most basic Christian beliefs seemed so much more powerful and vital than they ordinarily did.

Marjie looked down at her watch again, then spoke softly to Jerry, "I'm going to the nursery to check on Martha. The way he's going, we may be here all afternoon."

Jerry nodded that he understood, then Marjie stepped out of the pew and headed down the side aisle. *Look at these people!* Marjie said to herself as she stepped quietly toward the back of the church. Every eye looked straight ahead as if mesmerized, and no one even seemed to notice that she was passing by them.

When she was almost to the back of the church, Marjie nearly stopped in her tracks. Sandwiched in the center of the last pew were Chester Stanfeld's father and mother. Bill Stanfeld's gaze was transfixed on the missionary, but Clare was smiling at Marjie and gave her a slight nod. "Lord Jesus," Marjie whispered to herself as she returned the smile and nod.

Going up the stairs that led to the balcony and the nursery, Marjie could hear Martha crying even before she got to the nursery door. She slowly pulled the door open and peeked in, then she grimaced and shook her head as the two teenaged girls who were taking care of the children looked up.

"Tough morning, Melissa?" Marjie asked, stepping into the room and taking Martha from the fifteen-year-old who was trying to comfort her.

"I'm sorry," Melissa replied, "but I don't know what's

wrong. She was fine until about fifteen minutes ago. She doesn't seem to want her bottle, but she won't go to sleep either."

"Sometimes nothing works. You don't need to apologize," Marjie replied, holding Martha tight and calming her down. "If you could give me her bottle, I'm going to go out to the balcony door and try to listen to the rest of the service. I'll get her bag later."

Melissa handed Marjie the bottle, then Marjie carried Martha out into the long hallway that ran the entire length of the back of the balcony. Approaching the balcony door, she could feel that Martha was already falling off to sleep.

"My little pumpkin's so exhausted," she whispered in Martha's ear. "I think I'm going to chance it and go in. You be a good girl."

The balcony was actually quite large and as usual was fairly empty. Stepping through the doorway, Marjie decided she'd go down to the front row and hope that Martha wouldn't start crying again. As she made her way to the spot she'd picked out, Marjie looked down. She could see most of the congregation, but the overhang prevented her from seeing where Bill and Clare Stanfeld were sitting.

Marjie took her seat, and her first order of business was to get Martha situated comfortably on her lap. Then to her relief, she got Martha to start on her bottle. *Okay*, she thought as she turned her attention back to the missionary speaker, *back to Borneo*.

"It was very late in the evening," Anthony Biden was saying, "and we were gathered around a fire inside the longhouse. This was a village of well over one hundred Dyaks who had all made a profession of faith in Jesus Christ. My coworkers and I had spent most of the afternoon and the entire evening teaching the villagers the essential principles of Christian discipleship, and we were exhausted.

"Across from me sat the oldest man in the longhouse—an elder whose wisdom and years commanded great respect. His dark skin glistened against the orange flames of the fire, and his wrinkled face was framed by curly, snow white hair. When he spoke, you noticed that he had lost all of his teeth, and it was evident from his eyes and the way he held his head that he was blind.

"The old man had been silent for a long while with his eyes shut, but it was obvious that something profound was bothering him. When he finally opened his glassy eyes, he said to me, 'Mister, how long ago did this Jesus Christ come to die for us? Was it before your father was born?'

" 'Yes,' I told him, 'Jesus came before my father's birth.'

" 'Why then,' he asked, 'did your father not come to tell my father?'

"I wished that I had an answer," Biden continued, "but I had to say, 'I don't know why my father did not come to tell your father.' The old man's head sank down and rested against his chest, then the tears began to stream out of those blind eyes that refused to forget his father's face. For several minutes the long-house elder did not raise his head, but the tears rolled down his brown chest.

"Then he looked up again and said, 'Mister, did Jesus Christ come to die for us before your grandfather was born?'

"Once more," the missionary lamented and shook his head, "I hated to have to answer, 'Yes, He came long before my grandfather's birth. Jesus came long before my grandfather's grandfather.'

"Like he'd been hit with a club, the blind man's head dropped to his chest again, and the tears poured down the wrinkled face. I could see and feel the memories of the man's grandfather spilling through his memory, filling him with grief and loss."

Martha stirred momentarily, and Marjie gently pulled the nearly empty bottle of milk out away from the baby's mouth. Then she lifted Martha to her shoulder and lightly patted her back to sleep.

"When the old man looked up through the glow of the fire," Biden continued, "the tears shimmered in the deep lines of his face, and his blind eyes seemed to struggle to focus upon me. Speaking very slowly, he said, 'Mister, my father died without ever having a chance to hear the story of Jesus. My grandfather died without anyone coming to tell him, either. And you say that Jesus came long before my grandfather's grandfather?'

" 'Yes,' I said.

" 'Why did they not care to come?' the elder asked, and the tears again coursed down the crevices in his cheeks. 'How could they not come?'

" 'I cannot answer that,' I replied. 'I don't know why. But I have come, and I will pray that others will come to help reach the hundreds of other longhouses.' "

Marjie closed her eyes and covered her mouth with her free hand. The story of the old blind man grieving over his beloved family members tore at her heart. *How could nineteen hundred years go by and no one ever go to these people?* she wondered. *How could it be, God?*

When she opened her eyes, Biden was saying, "Tonight, I hope you can come and hear the story of how God miraculously guided our boat through a dense fog and past the Japanese war boats that were searching for us. Word had gone out to the Japanese that American spies were attempting to escape from Borneo, and my wife and I were spared from becoming prisoners of war by the grace of God.

"I've gone long past your normal closing time," he continued, "but I'd like to wrap up this morning by giving you the opportunity to offer yourself to God's service." He paused to survey the congregation. "There are hundreds of tribal peoples across the world who have never once heard the name of our Savior, who have no Bible in their language and no one to translate it, and who remain bound by evil spirits and oppressive idolatry. Not everyone can go to them, but everyone can pray, and many of you can help support someone who does go.

"I also have a feeling that some of you here this morning have never found the peace and the rest of salvation that my Dyak friend declared as he beat on his chest after his baptism. Jesus came to that man along the river in Borneo, and He'll come to you in the same way if you call out to Him today."

Anthony Biden stepped away from the podium and walked

to the center of the front of the church. Then he said, "You need not come forward to meet with God. But if you feel the need for someone to pray with you this morning, I invite you to join me here. I'll stay as long as it requires. Please come now, and the rest of you are excused. Go in peace."

But no one went anywhere, at least for a while. As Marjie looked down upon the congregation from her balcony pew, she couldn't tell if the other church members were as stunned by the stories as she had been or if they were simply curious to see if anyone would venture to the front. Marjie felt like she'd been challenged by so many new things that she didn't know how to respond, but there were others who seemed to know what they wanted to do.

Pastor Fitchen was the first one that Marjie saw make a move. She thought he was simply going to join the missionary at the front and be available for prayer, but instead he knelt down at the steps leading up to the platform where Biden was standing and began to pray silently. He had barely gotten there, though, before Chester and Margaret went forward and joined him.

They were followed by another older couple, then Marjie spotted Billy Wilson stepping out from his pew and moving toward the front. As he passed by Jerry, she could see that was all the spark that Jerry needed. From her elevated post, Marjie felt deeply moved as her husband sank to his knees beside his best friends.

Then Marjie thought she heard some movement directly below her, but she had to wait to see who was coming out of one of the back pews. To her astonishment, it was Bill Stanfeld, holding his wife's hand and moving very slowly and deliberately down the center aisle. He and Clare went right past the others who were kneeling on the steps and up onto the platform, stopping face to face with Anthony Biden.

Marjie held her breath and prayed silently for the volatile man and his scarred wife. At first she thought that Chester's father might be upset with the missionary. But when she saw Bill's hand suddenly reach up and cover his face, Marjie knew that his crusade against God was over.

When the Stanfeld couple dropped to their knees, Marjie began to weep.

And she was not alone.

20

KEEPER OF THE HARVEST

"Where'd you go last night when you got out of bed?" Marjie asked Jerry at breakfast the next morning.

Jerry chuckled and rubbed his forehead. "Let's see. I went to the bathroom about midnight."

"And?"

"And . . . I did what I haven't done in a long time," Jerry continued, looking into Marjie's dark brown eyes. "I went for a long walk around the farm."

"I really wish you wouldn't do that without talking to me first," Marjie said, looking away and giving Martha a spoonful of warm oatmeal. "I couldn't sleep, I got to worrying again, then I got mad. You must have been gone a couple hours."

"Yeah. I was," Jerry replied, pushing his fried egg around on his plate like he'd lost his appetite. "I'm sorry. I hoped you were sleeping. Why didn't you say something when I came in?"

"I almost let you have it," Marjie responded and smiled. "But I was afraid we'd end up not getting any sleep. If Chester and Margaret bring that missionary out here after lunch, I didn't want us to look like we'd been fighting all night."

Jerry took a bite of his toast, then wiped the crumbs from the corner of his mouth. "I'm glad you didn't say anything."

"So, what was the problem?"

Pushing his plate away, Jerry picked up his cup of coffee and took a sip. "Like you don't know."

"You know I know," Marjie replied, giving Martha another spoonful of cereal. "We talked about it most of the afternoon, and it was all I could think about when I was out on Charlie. But I was hoping that you might have more to tell me after your midnight walk."

Jerry shook his head and absentmindedly reached out his hand to Martha, who grabbed onto his index finger. "Not much to add. I'm just so confused that I hardly know which way to turn. I guess I was hoping that if I got my heart still enough or if I prayed long enough, maybe God would show me what He wants me to do."

"You mean us."

"Yeah. I mean us. I'm sorry. I may have slept a few hours, but I'm still zonkered."

"Me too," Marjie said. "I hope you don't think you were the only one who was praying last night. When I got mad in bed last night, it really wasn't about you. It was about me."

"What do you mean?"

"I'm not totally sure," Marjie said softly, reaching out and lifting one of Martha's brown curls. "I guess I was having a hard time being willing to surrender this farm, and our family, and our friends, and the security we have here. But I think I was finally able to honestly say, 'I'm willing, Lord—wherever you want us, and whatever we should do with our lives, and whatever it takes to do that.'"

"Whew!" Jerry exclaimed, looking out the window. "Sounds like I should have stayed in bed. I didn't fare as well."

"I thought you worked through all that after the morning service."

"So did I," Jerry muttered. "But I feel like I keep jerking back and forth on it. I guess I get really afraid that God might take us up on our offer and send us to some horrible place. When I was in the navy, I saw a lot of places I wouldn't want to go, and I heard about places that sounded a lot worse."

Marjie wiped the excess oatmeal from the corners of Martha's mouth, then pulled the tray on the high chair back and lifted her out. "Here's your girl," Marjie said, passing her over to Jerry. "Do you realize that in two days she'll be a year old? And that a year ago you were two days away from the *Wasp* getting torpedoed on the high seas?"

"I haven't forgotten," Jerry replied. "What's that got to do with what I was saying?"

"Well, maybe you just need to start thinking about all that God has done over the past year," Marjie said. "A year ago today you didn't even know Him, and look at everything that's happened since then. God's done a pretty good job so far, don't you think?"

Jerry chuckled and snuggled Martha's plump cheek against his. "Hard to argue with that. But I still don't know what to do with all of this. Maybe Mister Biden will have the answers. What time did you say they were coming?"

"They just said they'd be here after lunch," Marjie replied. "Too bad Billy and Ruthie couldn't get off work today. I think they were as moved by the service yesterday as we were."

"Billy was, that's for sure. He got way too quiet after the service," Jerry said. "You know, I wish Mister Biden could stay around for a few weeks. We really need a guy like him to help us know what to do."

"Maybe you can talk him into it," Marjie said. "I got a feeling he's a man on the move, though. I'm surprised that it worked out for him to stop by here. I sure hope my ma and Benjamin can make it over."

"They'll be here," Jerry replied. "My dad wouldn't miss this for anything."

"They said it's going to be an hour yet," Marjie said, hanging up the telephone receiver. "The cows found a weak spot in the pasture fence and apparently wandered into the neighbor's hayfield. Benjamin's repairing the break now."

"Oh, that's too bad," Chester responded, leaning back in his chair at the dining room table. He and Margaret and Anthony Biden had just arrived and were bursting with stories. "I know you're dying to hear what happened to my father and mother," Chester said, "but I think we'd better save that story until your folks get here."

"So, do I get my tour first?" Mr. Biden asked, glancing over at Chester and Margaret.

"We promised him you'd take him into your bonny fields and let him walk your gentle hills," Margaret explained. "He's an old farm boy."

"I'm only forty-two," Biden complained with a joyful laugh. "That's not old! But I am itching to get a look at the farm. Shall we go now?"

Chester shook his head no. "Margaret and I have to tell them our news first. Then you can walk all day if you like."

"You're expecting a baby!" Marjie piped up before he could say more.

"No, no, no," Chester replied. "I don't think we're ready for babies yet. I'm not sure we're even ready for what we want to tell you."

Marjie and Jerry waited, and Margaret nodded her head. "Since the day that Chester proposed marriage to me, we've been asking the Lord to direct us into whatever He wanted us to do. Chester's desire has been to go into seminary for training as a pastor, and it's what I wanted as well."

Margaret paused and took Chester's hand, then she continued, "But after the Sunday morning service, we believe that God has put it on our hearts to become missionaries. We'd be honored if He'd send us to a people like Mister Biden's dear Dyaks. It grieves me heart to think there are other peoples who have never had a chance to hear of our Savior."

Jerry sat in silence, glancing back and forth from Chester's face to Margaret's. Marjie studied their expressions as well, then rubbed the back of her neck and looked out the picture window.

"We wanted to tell you first," Chester added. "It doesn't look like it was what you were expecting, though."

"You, ah, didn't give us much warning," Jerry mumbled, rubbing his chin and trying to collect his thoughts. He looked over at Marjie who was still staring out the window. "Actually,

I spent most of the night praying about what God wants Marjie and me to do with our lives. If you believe it's the will of God, we're happy for you. Tell me why you feel that way."

Chester puffed out a big breath of air. "I hope this doesn't sound corny," he said. "But when we went forward to pray, we both felt like we knew in our hearts that God was telling us to prepare for the mission field. As long as I've been a Christian, I have never sensed anything so clearly. I can't explain it, but it's like a settled conviction in my heart."

Marjie had turned her attention back to Chester. "For you, too?" Marjie asked Margaret.

"Oh yes," Margaret said. Her round blue eyes shone with confidence. "I couldn't believe that Chester felt the same way."

"Which means you'll be leaving," Marjie said. "Probably for a long time."

Margaret only nodded. Her eyes were fixed on Marjie's.

"I was afraid of something like this," Jerry spoke rapidly, shaking his head and sighing. "I can't imagine you going away."

"Neither can we," Chester said. "Especially with my parents just coming to faith. I'd even thought about going to seminary and then applying to the church here. Pastor Fitchen would be retiring by then. But I don't believe that's going to happen."

"God reminded us both of the burden of the apostle Paul's heart," Margaret added. "He wrote to the church in Rome that his heart's desire was to preach the gospel not where Christ was named but to those who had not heard. We truly feel that is our life's calling."

"Did you and your wife feel the same way when you first started, Mister Biden?" Marjie asked.

The missionary nodded. "As clearly as if it had been written on a sheet of paper. Which has been a tremendous encouragement in the hard times. There have been countless moments when we thought we couldn't go any further."

"If you don't mind me asking," Marjie asked, "where is your wife? We had heard she'd be coming with you."

"That's a long story," Biden replied. "Maybe we should give Chester and Margaret a breather, and we can talk as you show me around the farm. Sound good?"

"Yeah," Jerry said, pushing back his chair and standing up. "I think we can all use a break. And I've got some questions for you."

"You'll listen for Martha?" Marjie asked Chester and Margaret.

"Surely," Margaret replied. "Take your time."

Jerry led the way, and Anthony Biden and Marjie followed him out the front door and down the sidewalk toward the farm lane to the fields. It was a perfect Minnesota fall day. The sun was bright, the sky was a deep blue, the air was clear, and a warm breeze rippled through the overhanging tree branches.

"You were asking about my wife," Biden said to Marjie, who was walking beside him. "Cynthia had planned to come, but her mother has not been well, and the doctors don't seem to know what the problem is. As much as she wanted to come and see Margaret again, she felt she needed to stay with her mother."

"I'm sorry to hear that," Marjie said. "I would have liked to have met your wife. Is she like you?"

"In what way?"

Marjie laughed, then she took Jerry's hand as they walked on down the lane. "I don't know. Courageous, bold, adventuresome, crazy?"

Anthony Biden laughed as well. "It's a shame she couldn't come. She would like you. No, she's not crazy like me. But . . . she's always had more faith than me. She's much more steady than I am. And she's much more intuitive than I've been. A lot of times, she's been the one who's known just the right thing to say to someone. She led the first Dyak to faith in Christ while I was off preaching in the longhouses. I often wonder what would have happened if I had gone as a single missionary."

"Margaret said you grew up on a farm," Jerry said. "Are your parents still farming?"

The missionary had been drinking in the scenery as they walked. "No," he said softly. "I wish they were. I truly loved our farm. But my father passed away four years ago, and my mother moved to a town in Illinois so she'd be close to my brother. He takes pretty good care of her."

"Your father died while you were gone?" Marjie asked.

Biden nodded. "I've only recently been able to visit his grave. Being so far away, it never seemed real. It helped to stand by the tombstone and finally feel like I'd said goodbye. My dad was a very good man. I wish I could've spent more time with him."

The threesome had gotten to the end of the farm lane, and as they stepped out from the trees the full panoramic view of the farm opened up before them.

"My goodness, this is far more beautiful than Margaret described," Biden said, surveying the valleys and hills and fields. "Look at that stand of corn! You should have a great harvest."

"I love this spot, Mister Biden," Jerry responded. "I wish my grandfather would have built our house right here so I could look out over the whole farm whenever I wanted. I stood here for about an hour last night, wondering what God wants Marjie and me to do."

"And what did you conclude?" Biden asked.

"Nothing," Jerry said, shaking his head. "I went home more confused than when I went out. How do you know the will of God, Mister Biden? Everybody seems to know around here except me."

Biden wrinkled his forehead and chuckled. "That is not an easy question to answer," he said. "Much of God's will for our lives is written down in Scripture, but what He wants us to do specifically and where He wants us to go, that He has to show us."

"But how?"

"Look around you," the missionary said. "Who tills these fields, and plants the corn, and cultivates the rows, and guards against destruction, and knows the right time to take out the harvest?"

"I do," Jerry replied.

"You are the keeper of the harvest."

"Yes."

"Well, God is also the Keeper of the harvest, Jerry," Biden

reasoned. "He alone has the authority to call us to His service—where He wants, what He wants, and when He wants. He calls, equips, sends, protects—He's the one that reaps the harvest. The secret is to get to know Him well enough so you can hear Him direct you in the specifics."

"I'm afraid He's going to ask us to do something horrible," Jerry blurted out.

"Like go to Borneo?" Biden asked, then he laughed. "Oh, Jerry, what kind of a Father do you think He is? Do you think that because you've gained this lovely farm that He can hardly wait to tear it away from you?"

"No, but . . . shoot. I wish I knew."

"Take my advice," said Anthony Biden. "The Keeper of the harvest knows all about your life on the farm, and He understands your hearts. If He wants you to go and do the unusual, He will show you. And if He shows you that, He'll give you the grace you need to do what He asks.

"But the mission field is not the only place that needs God's workers," he added gently. "There are all kinds of needy people in this community for you to touch and make a difference in their lives. Perhaps that's what He has for you to do. And to pray for Chester and Margaret and for me and Cynthia, and perhaps to help financially."

He paused and surveyed the lovely panorama once more, his arms lifting from his sides in a kind of unconscious benediction.

"But the Lord of the harvest calls the shots," he finally said. "Our part is to learn to hear Him speak."

21

THREE IN ONE

"One last present," Marjie announced, sliding a little package wrapped in yellow tissue paper to Martha. "From Grandpa Benjamin."

Martha and Marjie were sitting in the middle of the living room floor, surrounded by little mounds of crushed wrapping paper and a variety of stuffed animals, picture books, and other gifts. Benjamin and Sarah, Margaret and Chester, Billy and Ruth, and Jerry sat around the living room, enjoying Martha's first birthday party.

Scooping up the yellow package, Martha immediately popped it in her mouth and began sucking on the paper. Marjie tried to grab Martha's arm, but the birthday girl was too quick.

"Out, out, out!" Marjie cried, tugging on Martha's hand, which was tightfisted around the package. "You can't eat it, sweetie!"

Everyone laughed, including Marjie, and Martha added to the festivity by dropping the present on the floor and clapping with delight. Soon they were all clapping and laughing.

"She really had it right before you pulled it out of her mouth," Benjamin said when the noise died down. "When she opens the present, you're going to be surprised at how intelligent she is. Must be the Macmillan side."

"Okay, let's see what we have here," Marjie said. She held

the small present in a way that Martha could figure out how to pull the wrapping off. Martha made quick work of it.

"Oh, it's a baby spoon with a curved handle so she can hold it easier," Ruth said. "Where did you find something like that?"

"It was in Sarah's silverware drawer," Benjamin said.

"Was it Marjie's?" Chester asked.

"Nope," Sarah replied. "Marjie never had a cute little spoon like that."

Marjie studied the handle and the shape of the spoon more closely. "Benjamin, you made this, didn't you? This belongs to Ma's silverware pattern. You took a regular spoon, ground down the bowl, and shortened and reshaped the handle into this nifty curl. How'd you do that?"

"Just experimented and got lucky, I guess," Benjamin replied. "Do you like it?"

"I love it," Marjie said, passing it to Jerry to look at. "You should go into business and see if you could generate some hard cash. I keep hoping for a big inheritance someday."

Everyone laughed again, especially Benjamin.

"I hope you live a long time, Marjie," Benjamin replied, "because your big inheritance is going to have to come from some other source than us. Say, I think Miss Muffet must be ready for her birthday cake."

Marjie looked back at Martha, who had managed to stuff most of the tissue paper back into her mouth. "Must be the Macmillan side, I guess," she replied for Benjamin's benefit as she wrestled the paper back out of Martha's mouth. "Let's go in the dining room and have some cake, and somebody throw that paper in the trash before she chokes on it."

"Here," Sarah said, bending down to pick up Martha, "let me take her. You go ahead and take care of the food."

"Let me help you," said Ruth in an old granny voice, taking Marjie's hand and pulling her up. "The years just keep ticking past, don't they, Ma?"

Marjie laughed and nodded, then she stretched. "You said it. Sitting on that wooden floor is a killer. But I'll tell you the truth, I feel a lot better today than I did one year ago in the hospital.

You wait, young lady. Your day is coming, and you won't be chirping so loud."

Everyone laughed again, except for Billy, whom Marjie noticed had looked away. *Uh-oh*, she thought. *Not good.*

"Ruthie, you can help me with the cake," Marjie said as the group gathered up the wrappings and then moved toward the dining room. "And Margaret, you can pour the coffee."

When they got into the kitchen, Margaret took the big pot of coffee and went into the dining room to fill the cups. Meanwhile, Marjie leaned against Ruth and whispered, "What's wrong with Billy?"

Ruth shrugged her shoulders and shook her head. "Something happened at church on Sunday," she whispered back. "He won't talk to me about it. It's made him sullen . . . and me nervous."

Marjie nodded that she understood, and she did. Jerry's mood had lightened considerably since their walk with Anthony Biden, but he still seemed to toss and turn a lot in bed. "We need to talk." Marjie mouthed the words, and Ruth nodded back.

"Here, hold these," Marjie said, handing Ruth three candles and a box of wooden matches. Then Marjie opened one of the lower cupboard doors and pulled out three small round cakes. Each was ornately decorated and had "Happy Birthday" neatly written on it.

"Goodness!" Ruth said, nearly gasping. "Did Margaret bring these?"

"Nice, eh?" Marjie replied and smiled proudly. "Margaret and I smuggled them in when you guys were taking turns riding the horse. Chester doesn't even know."

"Why are there three?"

"Three in one!" exclaimed Marjie, laughing and taking the three candles from Ruth, then pressing one into the center of each cake. "Light them."

"Why—"

"Light them. You'll get it soon enough."

Ruth lit each candle, then Marjie picked up two cakes and

Ruth took the other one. "Follow me," Marjie said.

When they came around the kitchen cabinets into the dining room, everyone but Margaret looked up with a measure of surprise. Setting the cakes in the middle of the table, Marjie stood back and smiled with delight. "Aren't they lovely?" she reveled. "Let's give a big hand to Margaret Harris Stanfeld for such a fine talent."

Marjie began to clap, and the others joined in mildly, including Martha, who was fascinated by the burning candles.

"I hate to ask," Jerry said, "and the cakes are beautiful, but why three? And why three candles?"

"Three birthdays."

"What?"

Marjie held up three fingers to Jerry, then she showed them to the others around the table. "We've come to celebrate Martha's first birthday. But there are two more birthdays today that give me joy in my heart. I think you know what they are."

"I got one," Benjamin said. "Jerry coming to faith."

"And Chester being pulled out of a fiery grave," Ruth added. "This is a great day to remember, indeed."

"Yes, it is," Marjie declared. "I want to truly celebrate it. The past few days I've been reminded that we never know how many more times we might be able to get together like this. I'd like to propose a toast. Please take your coffee cups with me and stand."

Everyone around the table stood except for Martha. Sarah had cut off a tiny piece of birthday cake, and Martha was busy getting it all over her face and bib.

Marjie raised her cup and said, "I'm so glad for my baby. She puts a sparkle into every day. And I'm so glad my husband had someone who stepped into his life and showed him the way to faith. And I'm so glad that Chester did not perish, and I promise to pray for you and Margaret as you consider becoming missionaries . . . but it breaks my heart to think . . ."

She could go no further, and instead of an intended celebration of laughter, it seemed like an unlikely moment for them to vent the built-up emotions they had all been experiencing since the missionary's visit. Joy, confusion, sadness, anger, tears, and relief poured out all around the dining room table. Only Martha remained undeterred in her personal celebration.

Jerry brushed away some tears. "What a year it's been. Who can say what the future holds? Here's to each of our desires to make a difference in this world . . . by the way we live and the way we serve. Cheers!"

A chorus of "cheers" followed, then they clinked their coffee cups together. Margaret reached over and hugged Marjie, and Jerry reached out and shook Chester's hand. They both said "Happy Birthday!" to each other.

Then Sarah sat down and tapped her coffee cup with her spoon. Everyone sat down and waited for her to address them. "Aren't you forgetting someone?"

They all looked at Martha, who had managed to embed some of the cake icing deeply into her hair. She was grinning broadly, and in her chunky hand was the spoon that Benjamin had made.

"Looks like she needs some more cake," Jerry offered.

"Oh . . ." Sarah said and groaned. "Now I know why God gives children grandparents." She looked sternly around the table. "We . . . did not . . . sing . . . Happy Birthday to my grand-daughter. I'll spank the first hand that touches a piece of cake until we've done this properly."

Everyone was nearly too tired to laugh, but with Martha's comical grin and a lightening of the mood around the table, Margaret was able to lead them in a rousing "Happy Birthday" song that pleased both Martha and her grandmother.

———— ∽ ————

The birthday party went on much longer than anyone had intended—quite late for a week night. Sarah and Benjamin left shortly after Martha finally settled down and went to sleep, but Margaret and Chester stayed until around ten o'clock. When they left, Billy and Ruth got up, intending to leave as well.

"Just give me a couple of minutes with Marjie," Ruth said as Billy stood at the front door waiting. "I'll keep it short."

"Why don't I believe that?" Jerry asked. "Short for Marjie is measured in hours."

"I'll be in the car," Billy said with a big yawn. "Wake me up before you open the door and scare me. Good-night."

Billy waved and pushed the screen door open, then he slipped into the darkness. Not needing a cue from Marjie, Jerry was right on his friend's heels.

"What a moon, eh?" Jerry said, walking down the sidewalk. "I love—"

"Look, Jerry," Billy turned around and broke in, "I'm sorry if I spoiled your evening. I shouldn't have come. Ruthie talked me into it."

"Talked you into coming to your honorary niece's birthday party?" Jerry asked. "What's wrong?"

"I shouldn't have come. I knew—"

"You didn't spoil anything," Jerry stated. "But you seemed pretty heavyhearted. I was hoping you'd tell me what's wrong."

"I'm not ready to talk to anybody about it," Billy said, turning around and walking on down the sidewalk. "Until I am, I should just lie low."

"What if that makes it worse?" Jerry asked. He followed Billy out to his car, and Billy stopped and leaned against the wide fender of the front wheel.

"I hope it doesn't," replied Billy, "but I'll take my chances."

"Well, I ain't going to force it out of you," Jerry said. "But if you're confused about how to respond to what the missionary preached about, I want you to know I've been struggling with it, too. If I hadn't gotten a chance to talk with him the next day, I think I'd be going crazy. I wish you could've gotten off work."

"Me, too," Billy said, nodding slowly. "With the stories that guy tells, he should stick around for a few weeks to help people sort their lives out. When I was in San Diego, I heard stories from men who'd been on some of the remote islands in the South Pacific, but that was nothing compared to this."

"You should have come out here Sunday night," Jerry said and chuckled. "I needed someone to walk with me. I've never prayed so much in my lifetime."

Billy laughed. "Which probably isn't saying much," he said. "You and I were never much for praying."

"True. But we were good at walking."

"Yeah. Well, I did some walking Sunday night, too," Billy said. "And Monday night. And Tuesday night."

"Why didn't you come out?" Jerry asked. "Not that I can solve anything. But we used to talk stuff over."

Billy threw his hands up in the air and shook his head. "I couldn't, Jerry. It's too big a mess. Anything I say at this point is probably the wrong thing to say, so I ain't saying nothing."

"Man, I don't like this, Billy," Jerry said. "It's not like you to clam up."

"Don't I know," Billy said. "It's eatin' me alive. Listen, if I tell you the heart of it, will you promise not to tell Marjie or Ruthie?"

"Yeah," replied Jerry, stepping toward the car. "As long as you promise not to do anything crazy."

"Don't worry about that," Billy said. "It's other people I'm concerned about with this. I'm afraid of who could get hurt."

"Like Ruthie?"

"Yeah," Billy mumbled, looking up at the moon. "I should have gotten my life together before I asked her to marry me."

"What are you talking about?"

Billy reached up and pulled on the hair at the back of his head. "It's as simple as this. Sunday afternoon was the first time in my life that I truly believed God might want me to go and do something special for Him. But now I'm not sure of anything that I'm doing. Am I supposed to be working at the bank? Am I supposed to stay here or go somewhere? Should I do something like Mister Biden did?"

He looked at Jerry with anguish in his eyes. "If I can't answer those questions, what makes me think that I should marry Ruth and bring her into my confusion? I'm sorry now that I proposed."

22

BUY AND SELL

"Pure misery," Benjamin groused, pulling off his long work coat and shaking some of the raindrops to the floor before hanging it on a hook. "That was about as nasty a day as it gets. Not enough rain to stop you, but enough to keep you damp all day. I'm froze."

Jerry was sitting on an old unpainted chair inside Benjamin and Sarah's farmhouse porch, pulling off his boots. "Froze and beat," he muttered. "Next time you ask me to come over and help the silage cutters, see you if you can order a nice warm day."

"I'll do that," Benjamin said. "Those guys were in a hurry, weren't they? I could hardly keep up."

"Well, maybe a cup of coffee'll help," Jerry said, standing up and slicking his wet hair back with his hands. "Just about time to get home and do the milking."

"Don't remind me," Benjamin replied. He pushed the porch door open and stepped into the living room. "Oh, but that heat does feel good."

Jerry followed Benjamin in and went straight to the oil-burning stove. Pulling one of the side deflectors open wide, he moved as close as he dared and let the heat pour over his body.

"This should help," Marjie called as she stepped out of the kitchen carrying a steaming cup of coffee for Jerry. "You're a mess! Look at the mud."

"I'm fully aware of the mud," Jerry responded, taking a tiny sip of coffee. "Boy, that's hot! You could cut the top layer of skin off your tongue with that stuff."

"You stand any closer to the stove, and you'll be working a patch of skin off your leg as well," Marjie warned, and none too soon.

Jerry suddenly felt an intense spot of heat on his thigh and stepped away. "Ouch!" he cried, rubbing the spot and trying to push the heat around.

Marjie laughed and turned as she heard the tap of Martha's shoes on the linoleum in the kitchen. "Don't let her get too close to that stove. We've been chasing her away from it most of the day."

Martha spotted Jerry as she came to the kitchen doorway, and she started jabbering and coming for him as fast as she could. Jerry quickly set his coffee cup on the stove and reached out to catch her. As usual, she stumbled just before she got to him, and he had to dive to catch her.

"How's Daddy's little girl?" Jerry said as he picked her up and snuggled her into his arms. "Mmmm . . . you sure smell good. Let me guess. Someone wasn't watching, and you got into Grandma's dresser."

"Correct," Marjie replied. "She's been exploring everything."

"Jerry, come on in and have something to eat," Sarah said from the kitchen doorway. "We made some chicken sandwiches. Better get in here before your father puts them all away."

"A sandwich sounds good," Jerry said, moving toward the kitchen. "But we gotta keep moving. Those Holsteins don't like me getting in late."

"Here. Let me take the baby," Sarah said as Jerry came into the kitchen.

Jerry passed Martha to Sarah, then he sat down across from his father at the table. "You look bushed, Dad. You been over-doing it again?"

Benjamin yawned and rubbed the rough stubble on his cheeks. "Between hearing missionary stories that make my hair stand on end and late-night birthday parties and calves being born, I am ready for a nap."

"He hasn't gotten very many since he took over the farm duties when Teddy left," Sarah said. Wiping her finger across the icing on her chocolate cake, Sarah snuck Martha a taste of frosting.

"Say, have you heard from Teddy?" Jerry asked Sarah. "Marjie writes both him and Paul every week, but we never hear from either one."

"I haven't gotten any mail from Paul, but I did get a letter from Teddy a couple of days ago," replied Sarah. "He's still training in Texas, and I hope they keep him there. Least I hope they don't send him out where Paul is."

"I thought you said you hadn't heard from Paul," Jerry said.

"We haven't. But I listen to the radio and read the papers," Sarah responded.

"It oughta help that Italy surrendered," said Jerry.

"Yeah, but those Germans aren't giving it up," Benjamin remarked. "We think that Paul probably landed at Salerno on the ninth of September. They said the fighting there was terrible. They had all they could do to hold the beach."

"That's what we heard, too," Marjie said. "I just wish he'd write once and let you know."

"I know what you mean," Sarah replied. "But then there are times I think it's better not to know what's going on. I walk down to the mailbox every morning and I dread that there won't be a letter, and then I dread that there *will* be a letter."

"With the fighting Paul's been in," Benjamin said, "I doubt that he's had any time to write. And if he's fighting in Italy now, we probably won't hear for a long time."

"We just have to assume that no news is good news," Marjie said. "I just hope we get to see Teddy before he gets sent somewhere."

"I keep hoping he'll be here for Christmas," Sarah said. "But all we can do is keep praying. By the way, that Thursday evening prayer meeting really helped me. I wouldn't have thought so many people could be carrying so many burdens. You'd never know it when you talk with them in church."

"That's for sure," said Jerry. "I saw a side of some folks that I'd never seen before. Chester used to talk about people praying up a storm, and now I know what he means."

"I'm afraid we're going to have to move the meeting to the church," Marjie said.

"After only one time?" Benjamin asked.

"There's just not enough room in our house," Marjie said. "I felt like a sardine in there. I've already heard that a bunch of people who thought about coming but didn't are going to come to the second meeting—packed house or not."

"That's wonderful," said Benjamin, taking the last bite of his sandwich. "I really hated to miss it. But that's going to change."

"You're going to lay down the law to your cows—tell them they can't go into labor during prayer meetings?" Jerry teased. "I'll have to come over and get some lessons on that."

"He's serious," Sarah responded. "We're thinking about selling the herd."

"What?" Marjie gasped.

"Well, we might keep one cow so we have fresh milk here," Benjamin added.

"Whyever would you sell off the dairy?" Jerry asked.

"Partly because of that missionary," Benjamin explained. "Partly because we think we can get along with less income. And partly because I'm old and tired and the doctor told me to stop pushing it. How's that?"

"Back up and try again," Marjie demanded.

"All right," said Benjamin. "I'll start with the simpler reasons. Milking every day really takes it out of me physically, and I can feel it wearing me down again. And now, after four months together, your mother and I are convinced we can get along just fine without the milk check—unless you cut off your monthly farm payments."

"Don't worry about us," Jerry said. "We've got good incentive to pay up. Marjie's afraid you'll want your room back."

Benjamin and Sarah laughed, and Marjie nodded.

"Also, I'm thinking about using the barn to slowly expand

our hog operation," Benjamin said. "We've been thinking that we'd like to try to help support Chester and Margaret if they become missionaries. But it would take some extra income to do that, and I'd rather not have it come from milking cows twice a day. Pigs are a lot easier."

"As long as they're healthy," Jerry replied. "But you say all this is partly because of Mister Biden. What's he got to do with it? Did he say something to you?"

"No," said Sarah. "But we listened real hard to what he had to say. We figured that we're too old to think about being missionaries, but we're not too old to get more involved in other people's lives. We'd like to be less tied down to the farm so we can do more."

"Like what?" Marjie asked.

"Ben would really like to try his hand at teaching a Bible class," Sarah replied. "But he needs more time to study the Bible for himself. And I'd like to be able to invite people over for a meal from time to time or go visit folks when they get sick or have to go in the rest home. Somebody always needs a hand, but who's got the time?"

"After the bull put me out of commission," Benjamin added, "what stuck with me most was how good it was to be able to spend time with neighbors and friends. Having hit sixty now, I figure it's time to do something other than work and sleep."

"Now, this is a switch," Jerry marveled, "but it sounds like a good idea to me. How many milkers you got? Eight?"

"Yeah," Benjamin replied. "But three of 'em are too old to be worth much. I'm thinking about keeping one of the old girls here and selling the other two to the stockyards."

"How'd you like to sell the five good ones to me?" asked Jerry. "Milkers and calves."

"Whoa, there, horsey!" exclaimed Marjie, sitting forward in her chair. "Don't you think the two of us should talk this over before you try jumping over the moon?"

"I didn't make him an offer," Jerry pleaded. "It's just that I been thinking about the same thing, and this gets me excited."

"What haven't you told me?" Marjie asked.

"Well, as far as I can tell, God made a way for us to take over the farm," Jerry replied, his eyes locked on Marjie's. "And unless He shows us something different, I'm planning on staying there and making it a good farm. But I've also been thinking that I'd like to find a way to help support someone like Mister Biden or Chester and Margaret."

"So, you'd add five milkers to increase the milk check," Marjie said, rubbing her cheek. "We've got just enough room in the barn, but are you sure that after we increase the feed and vet costs and make the payments for the cows we'll come out ahead?"

"No," said Jerry. "That's why I didn't make an offer. Plus, I want to see how many pounds of milk the cows have been generating before I 'jump over the moon.'"

"Well, maybe we can jump together," Marjie said. Then she looked at Benjamin and her mother. "If we went home and tried to cost this out, would you be willing to take a monthly payment like you're getting for the property?"

Benjamin looked at Sarah, who nodded back to him. "Sure."

"Give us a day, then," Jerry said, "and we'll let you know. Maybe you can call me tonight and let me know the details on your cows. But right now we need to get home and milk the ones we already got."

———— ✒ ————

"Are you really sure this is what you want to do?" Marjie asked, running her fingers through Jerry's short blond hair. Her other arm was propped up against her pillow in the bed. "It's going to mean a lot more time in the barn."

"I'd be a liar to say I wanted the extra work," Jerry replied, looking up from his pillow to the bedroom ceiling. "But I can handle it. And I'd be thrilled if we could help support something bigger than this farm. What if we could help pay for the Bibles that Mister Biden is trying to get printed for the Dyaks? What if—"

"You're going to keep us up all night with your dreaming," Marjie cut in. "Unless the price of milk goes up, it's going to be

186

a lot of work and not a lot of extra money."

"But it's steady," Jerry replied, "and it's ours to do. Marjie, we can make a difference."

"I like that part," Marjie said. "Maybe I could raise chickens and—"

"Okay," Jerry said. "Enough for one night. If you get going, we won't get to sleep."

"One thing, though," Marjie said. "I'd like to do this without tooting our horn about it. And I don't want us to promise anyone anything until we see if this works. Better that they not know than be disappointed later on. Is that a deal? Mum's the word."

"That's a deal," Jerry replied, rolling over on his side toward her. "Just one more thing. I want you to know that I love you with all my heart and that I'm very excited we can do this together."

Marjie kissed Jerry on the lips and whispered, "You really didn't want to get to sleep right away, did you?"

23

HANDWRITING ON THE WALL

"Mink Slough, Jerry!" Billy Wilson hooted. "What a sight!"

Billy set down the round minnow bucket he was carrying and pushed back the hood on his sweatshirt. A large expanse of the Mississippi backwater on the Minnesota-Wisconsin border near LaCrosse opened before him and Jerry. In the early morning sunshine, a cool autumn breeze rippled across the water and through the yellow and red leaves.

"Look at the ducks!" exclaimed Billy, pointing out over the slough to a large flock of pintails heading south. "When's the last time we were here?"

"I can't remember," Jerry said, watching the ducks disappear behind the tall trees that bordered the broad oval of water. "Must be three years. Man, it's sure beautiful."

"And nobody's here. Can you believe that?" Billy added. "I thought we'd be fighting to get a decent fishing spot."

"There's a war on, in case you've forgotten," Jerry responded. "Most of the guys who used to tramp back in here probably aren't thinking much about catching northern pike today."

"I guess you're right," said Billy, shaking his head. "I feel lucky just to be seeing this place again."

"How are your legs doing?" asked Jerry. "This spot has to be a mile and half back in the woods."

"Feels more like five, but who's counting?" Billy replied. "They're okay as long as I can keep dry and warm. So don't expect me to be jumping in the water after any fish that busts your line."

"Nothing's gonna break my line," Jerry boasted, giving Billy a gentle nudge on the shoulder blade. "And if you don't get moving down the path, I'm going to step right over you. There's some monsters out there who've been waiting for the king to return!"

Billy laughed and picked up the metal bucket, sloshing some of the cold water on his pant leg. "Cotton picker! Look at what you made me do."

"Move it or lose it, buddy," Jerry replied, laughing. "I didn't start milking two hours early to stand and watch you slopping minnow water around. Besides, I'm hungry already."

"You eat better than you fish," Billy teased back. He took off down the heavily overgrown path, pushing aside tree branches and watching for fallen logs in the long weeds that draped over it.

They followed the path around to the southeast edge of the area, where most of the fishermen went. The closer they got to their favorite fishing spot along the Mississippi, the less overgrown the path became and the faster they walked.

"This is it!" Billy finally called back to Jerry, following the path to its end, where a sliver of land jutted out like a pencil point into the water. He dropped his gear down on the grass and sat down on one of the hunks of log that someone else had dragged out from the woods for stools. "It's all ours. We can fish 'em both directions from here. Which way do you want to go?"

"No. You pick."

"Sorry," Billy said. "I want you to pick, because I don't want to hear you crying about how I always catch the biggest fish because I always take the best spot."

"When's the last time that—"

"Just pick."

"Okay," Jerry said, setting down his armload of tackle box, poles, food box, and a big metal thermos of hot coffee. "I'll fish the right side. When the northerns run in here from the channel, they're gonna have to pass by me first. And they'll never even get a look at your minnow."

"Yours will just slow them down for me," Billy countered. "Watch me, now. I'm all set to go, and you don't even have your leader on yet."

While Jerry fumbled to get his tackle box open, Billy took his pole and unhooked his line. Then he let out several feet of line and pulled his large red bobber up about six feet from his hook. Reaching into the round metal bucket, he pulled out a five-inch sucker minnow and carefully pushed the hook through the minnow's back just below the dorsal fin. Billy stepped close to the water's edge, swung the rod back, and then smoothly cast his line twenty yards out from the shore.

"Did you see that cast?" Billy crowed, watching the large minnow dive down and temporarily jerk the bobber under. "I still got the touch, that's for sure. Jerry, how's it going there? Need some help?"

Jerry was sitting on the ground by his tackle box, tying on a twelve-inch steel leader. He looked up and grinned. "You never quit, do you? Maybe you could, ah, get me a sandwich out and pour me a hot cup of coffee. Once my line hits the water, you know I can't afford to be fussing with the food."

Jerry and Billy's bantering went back and forth for quite a while, then they switched over to telling stories of some of the bigger northerns they had caught and carried out from Mink Slough in the past. But after two hours had passed without a single bite, the laughter and the reminiscing slowed down.

"Maybe it's just too perfect a day," Billy said. At the moment he was standing up and stretching. "Or it could be the wind. You remember what your dad used to say? 'When the wind is in the east, the fish bite the least. When the wind is in the west, the fish bite the best.' You might know the breeze is from the east today."

"Ah, just sit down and be patient," Jerry answered, shifting his weight forward on the log he was sitting on. "We both know the big boys are out there patrolling these waters, and they can't resist that big, fat, juicy minnow much longer. It's only a matter of time. But I agree, it's a perfect day. I wish Marjie could have come, but I guess they couldn't get out of that baby shower."

"Yeah," Billy said. "Ruthie's always organizing those things."

"What's going on with you two?" Jerry asked quietly. "Did you iron anything out?"

"No," replied Billy, shaking his head and staring out over the slough toward the Wisconsin side. "I kept my mouth shut, and I haven't told her what's wrong. I don't know which is worse. She's not real happy with my silence, and I can't blame her."

"So what are you going to do?"

"I don't know any more than I did a couple of weeks ago," Billy answered. He sat back down on his log and looked over at Jerry. "It's like I'm lost in the woods and I don't have a clue which way to head. I don't even remember the way back to where I came from. And God's not saying anything. Why can't He show me what to do as clearly as He revealed it to the missionary or to Chester?"

Jerry was squinting from the sun's reflections that danced across the ripples in the water. "Maybe He has already."

"What?"

"Maybe He's already led you down the path, and you're looking back for Him while He's waiting up ahead," Jerry answered. "It's hard to see someone when you're looking the wrong way."

"I agree," Billy said. "But I don't get it."

"Do you love Ruthie, Billy?"

Billy smiled and nodded. "I ran around with a lot of women, especially when I was in the navy, but Ruthie is the only woman I've ever loved. This may sound funny, but if I don't marry Ruthie, I don't think I'll ever marry anyone."

"For the love of money," Jerry muttered. "Don't you see it?"

"See what?"

Jerry stood up and began to pace slowly around where he

had been sitting. "You and Ruthie have both come to love God with all your hearts," he explained. "And although you nearly died, and although Ruthie could have married a raft of other men while you played the field, the two of you have somehow gotten back together. And you love each other. Do you believe that's just a coincidence?"

"No . . . I don't know."

"What do you want God to do?" Jerry asked. "Should He write it on the wall? 'I ordain that Billy Wilson should marry Ruth Buckley.' Maybe you're just scared to face it."

"Ouch!" Billy said. "Now you're stepping on toes. Scared to face what?"

"That maybe God wants *you* to make the decision," Jerry said. "Everything we've talked about here seems to indicate that He's in favor of you and Ruthie getting married. But God isn't going to be Ruthie's husband. You are, or some other lucky guy that beats you to the punch. Maybe God's saying, 'The decision is yours, Billy Wilson. You have to live with her, and she has to live with you. In the tough times that every couple goes through, I want your choice to be the strength that keeps you together.'"

"Did the missionary tell you all this?" Billy asked, sizing up his best friend.

"No. Why would I have talked to him about this?"

"I don't know, but you've never talked like this before," replied Billy. "Do you really believe what you just said?"

Jerry burst out laughing and sat back down on his log. "I'm just a plain and simple farm boy, Billy. I make no claim to understand how God's eternal will works together with all the choices we make. But, you know, I do believe God created us free to make our own choices. And that He's gonna hold us accountable for what we decide."

"So you think God's leaving this choice up to me?"

"Yep," Jerry said. "I do. Have you had any hint that Ruthie is the wrong girl for you?"

"No."

"If God can actually guide us in the right direction, can't He also warn us if we're going in the wrong direction?"

"Yeah, I guess so."

"Well, then," Jerry reasoned. "You tell me one reason why, after all you and Ruthie have gone through, and considering that you love each other and you both love God—why wouldn't God want you to marry her? To torment you? To sucker you into loving someone and then deny that love for no reason? To—"

"All right!" Billy cut in. "I think I got your point. Finally." He stretched his shoulders and rubbed the back of his neck. "I'm afraid that you just might be right. It just seems like it would be safer to have it in writing, like God did to that king in the Bible—where was it? Babylon?"

"The message wasn't all that great, though," Jerry said. "I think that fella lost his kingdom the next day. And you'll lose yours if you keep messing around with this."

"Man, you're tough on me today," Billy responded. "I thought you were my friend. You mean, you think I'll lose Ruthie."

"Well, I'm not an interpreter of dreams and messages, like Daniel was for that king with the funny name," Jerry said. "But if you back out again, I think Ruthie's going to close the door. You burned her once already, and I suggest you realize that this may be it. I'm dead serious."

Billy ran his fingers back through his hair, then one of his hands dropped down to rub the burned area on his right leg. "Sometimes . . ." He spoke quietly and took a deep breath, "Sometimes you really make sense. I think you're right on this one, and I think you may have stopped me from making a very big mistake."

"I have one more thing to say to you," Jerry added, scanning the water where Billy had been fishing.

"Let her fly," Billy said. "You can't do much more damage."

"Your bobber's completely disappeared," Jerry said calmly, still staring out over the slough. "Get up and set the hook!"

Both Jerry and Billy leaped to their feet. Billy grabbed his pole, but the bobber was so deep that neither of them could tell its exact location.

"Slow, now—take the slack out of your line," Jerry coached. "But if he takes off running, let him go. The northern takes a run with the big minnow sideways in his mouth, then he stops and turns it so he can swallow it."

Billy slowly cranked his open-faced reel and followed the direction of the line with his rod tip. "Jerry, reel your line in so I don't get the fish tangled in it."

Jerry picked up his pole and quickly got his line well out of the way. Then he picked up the big net they always brought along.

"Do you feel him?" Jerry asked. "I can see the bobber now, but he's got it down there deep."

"I can feel him," Billy said nervously. "But he's not running with it. He must be sitting on the bottom. Should I set the hook?"

"He's your fish," Jerry replied and laughed. "But I'd take him. He must have swallowed the minnow by now."

"Here goes nothing," whispered Billy. He leaned his rod tip as far out toward the bobber as he dared, reeled in the remaining slack line, and then pulled back hard on the rod. "Got him!" Billy yelled. "He's a good one."

The fish stayed low and swam toward the shore, then veered off and made a hard run away from them. Billy skillfully let out line instead of trying to force it in, then began to reel again as the fish tired. It took two more passes before the fish appeared to be coming in.

"I still haven't seen him!" Jerry cried, gazing intently at the point where Billy's line entered the water. He was bent over with the net already lowered into the water, waiting.

"He's a monster . . . he's a monster!" Billy whooped as he slowly moved the fish in toward Jerry. Then the fish suddenly rose to the surface and splashed before diving again.

"Wow! Twelve pounds at least," exclaimed Jerry. "Bring him head first into the net. Don't let him turn!"

"You just get that net ready," Billy answered. "He's got to be fifteen pounds. All right. This is it!"

Jerry tensed and waited as Billy guided the forty-inch northern pike toward the net. The irregular rows of white spots on the dark green back flashed in the sunlight as the fish tried to turn, and it opened its mouth to reveal razor-sharp teeth.

"Now!" yelled Billy as the lunker's head went into the net.

Jerry jerked up and back, and the fish's long body dropped into the netting. Then he quickly swung the net to shore and flopped it over to make sure there was no way the big fish could work his way free.

Then the two young men started to yell and holler and laugh. Billy was dancing up a storm as Jerry carefully pulled the northern out of the net and took out the hook. Holding up the fish, Jerry whistled. "What a horse! We'll have to stop at the bait store in Hokah and weigh him on the way home. I'd say sixteen, though."

"Great job netting, Jerry," Billy said. "I've never tied into one like this."

Jerry pulled out a rope stringer, tied it through the fish's gills, and then slowly dipped the northern back into the water. Looking up at Billy, he said, "Do you still believe in handwriting on the wall?"

24

BALONEY

"Thanks for letting me go," Marjie called back to the twilight-lit farmhouse and waved to her mother and Martha. "We'll try not to stay late."

"Stay as long as you need," Sarah returned. "Ain't no reason to hurry."

"You can hurry up and get in here," Jerry urged from the driver's seat of the idling black Ford. "We're going to be late as it is."

Marjie hopped in quickly and slammed the door shut, then the car pulled down the driveway. Benjamin, seated in the back of the Ford, was waving out the opened window to his wife and grandchild.

"So what's going to happen tonight?" Marjie asked Benjamin, putting her left arm up over the front seat and looking back at him. "It seems very odd for Pastor Fitchen to call a special church meeting on a week night. Why didn't he wait to bring this up at the annual meeting? It's only a few weeks away."

"I think he figures that he has to start lobbying for it now, or it ain't gonna happen," Benjamin replied. "I already told him I don't think it's going to happen—no matter what. But he's not backing down."

"I just don't understand," Marjie sputtered. "If the church can raise money to help supply Bibles for Mister Biden's Dyak people, how could anyone object? Why would they?"

"You wait and see," Jerry said, rolling up his window as the cloud of gravel dust behind the car rolled into the ditches. "I just hope it doesn't get nasty. I got a bad feeling about this one."

"Come on," Marjie protested. "Not over Bibles."

"My guess is that the discussion is not going to be about Bibles or people like the Dyaks," Benjamin explained. "If that happens, it'll be very unfortunate."

"What do you think it will be about?" asked Marjie.

"The ultimate of sins called 'breaking tradition'," Benjamin responded simply. "Nobody's ever tried to do what Fitch is suggesting, and I admire him for his bravery."

" 'Fitch'?" Marjie and Jerry said in unison.

"He told me that's what his friends called him when he was younger," Benjamin said. "I figured I'm his friend, so that's what I'm calling him. If the shoe fits, wear it, right?"

"I guess," Marjie replied as their car rolled to a stop in the church parking lot. " 'Fitch.' Do you think I can call him that? I kinda like it."

Opening the car door, Benjamin paused and looked back at Marjie. "Are you his friend?"

Marjie stopped for a moment, then shrugged her shoulders and laughed. "I guess I am. Seems strange to think of the pastor as a friend, though. Doesn't seem natural."

"Which is another unfortunate reality that's been around here for too long," Benjamin replied, following Jerry's lead and marching down the sidewalk. "We've treated our pastors as such superiors that no one gets to know them as friends."

"Or their wives," Marjie added, falling behind them.

Jerry held the heavy wooden door open for Benjamin and Marjie. Then the three of them quietly made their way down the basement stairway and opened the door. The meeting had already begun, and most of the wooden folding chairs had been taken. Noticing an open slot toward the middle, the three of them quickly made their way to the available seats.

"What I'm suggesting," Pastor Fitchen was saying, "is that we hold our annual fund-raiser sale as usual, but that anyone who brings an item for sale can mark down whether they want the money to go toward the regular mission budget or toward the Bibles that Mister Biden spoke to us about. That way it's completely up to the individual who's making the donation. What do you think of that?"

One of the church's elders, Orville Manning, was already shaking his bald head decisively. "I don't like it, Pastor," he announced, standing up and surveying the faces gathered in the crowded basement. "We have never allowed individuals to determine where their offerings go. I think that's just the tip of an iceberg of problems that you'd be starting. Besides, the denominational leaders tell us what our budget is supposed to be. We don't have any say over that. And we've struggled every year to meet their goals."

The room went silent as Manning sat down. Everyone in the room knew that he was the biggest financial contributor in the church, and his opinion played a major role in every decision involving the church's money. For a moment Marjie wondered if the discussion had ended.

"Orville, I'm not suggesting that we change our budget relationship with the denomination," the pastor finally replied, "or that we cut back on the mission giving. I just think it would be a great opportunity to allow members to get more involved with what they give. Maybe we have budget problems because people feel too disconnected from the process."

"If we let people decide, you just have the same amount of dollars being split," Orville countered. "There's no way we'll meet the mission budget. Then what do we do? Take it out of your salary?"

"You're assuming that no one might give more, even if they are allowed to direct some of that toward the Bibles?" Fitchen replied quickly.

"That's right," Orville returned. "Pastor, I've known these people all my life. I know who gives and how much. It's not going to happen, and I don't see any point in continuing this meeting."

Marjie had watched as both Benjamin's and Jerry's knuckles

started to get white and their faces began to flush, but she was the first to respond from the Macmillan family. "I think you underestimate your friends and neighbors, Mr. Manning," she spoke firmly, standing up as he had done. "You may know something about the members of this church, but I'm disappointed that you can't believe for something better than that. I think that if individuals can direct money toward the Bibles, you'll see a much larger offering."

"So, we can count on the Macmillans to step up and deliver financially?" Manning shot back.

This time it was Jerry's turn to reply. "Whether or not our church decides to help with the Bibles," he declared, "Marjie and I will find a way to help Mister Biden. But how much we give, and when we give it, and how we give it is our business—not yours or the church's. And if you think you can pressure me into giving, then you've counted your last dollar from this family."

"That makes two of us," Billy Wilson's father piped up.

"Three," Benjamin called out.

There were several others who added their names to the list before things settled back down.

Out of the corner of her eye, Marjie noticed that Edna Miller was standing up. *Oh no. Here it comes*, she thought.

"Pastor, I have a more basic concern." Edna began scanning the room with her schoolmarm eyes. "It troubles me that we'd even take the time to talk about supporting someone whose work is outside our church affiliation. That's never been suggested here before. I don't like the idea of stealing from Peter to pay Paul."

Marjie nearly burst trying to hold back what would have come out either as a scream or a laugh. She closed her eyes so she didn't need to look at Edna, but she couldn't stop her head from shaking.

"I really hope that a church's affiliation with its denomination is not seen that way," Pastor Fitchen replied gently. "Actually, I believe our denominational leaders would be very supportive of our getting involved with the Dyak Bible project. If you recall, Paul warned the Corinthians about ever allowing an 'I am of Paul' or 'I am of Peter" attitude to take over. And I won't allow it here."

"Have you talked with the denominational leaders?" Manning asked. "I have a hard time believing they'd be supportive."

"No, I haven't talked with them yet," the pastor replied. "But I will before the annual meeting. I'm not trying to cover something up."

"Edna," Benjamin asked, "are you trying to say that if some of our own young people wanted to join Mister Biden's work in Borneo or another mission that's doing a good work somewhere else"—here he cut his eyes toward the back of the room—"that we as a church would not support them financially? And that we would withhold our money for the single reason that what they are doing is not part of our denominational mission effort?"

"Well, that's right," Edna stated flatly. "I honestly don't think we should. Why would we ever trust our hard-earned dollars to those we don't know anything about? Besides, our young people should serve through our own missions. That's only right to tell them."

Benjamin had risen to his feet before Edna was half finished. "My father helped build this church," he sputtered, "and it has never seen one of its members go into missionary work—with our denominational mission or any other. We presently have a young couple who are making plans to train for missionary work, but probably not with our mission. Why are we here? To send money to support a denomination that we have almost no personal contact with or to support someone right from our midst who feels called by God to serve with another missionary organization?"

"That's a decision for the church's elders, not for this group," Orville Manning broke in. "It may come down to interpreting the church's constitution. I'm with Edna. Let's not get hung up in sentimentality because we like Chester and Margaret. We need to do what's right as a church. You can do whatever you want personally."

"Oh, for Pete's sake, don't throw that baloney at me,"

Benjamin fired back, stepping into the aisle. "We need to discover what God means a church to be—period. Now, I think this meeting's gone far enough, so I bid you good-night. But if I hear that we have sunk so low that we're not willing to support Chester and Margaret if their plans work out, well, you're not going to see me here again. Call it what you'd like, but that's not a decision a real church would make."

With that, Benjamin turned around and walked out of the basement. Jerry and Marjie were less surprised than the others around them, but it was clear from the tone of the meeting from then on that Benjamin had made his point. Neither Orville Manning nor Edna Miller spoke the rest of the time. But there were several others in the group who were supportive of their positions.

The debate surged back and forth for another forty-five minutes. There were several moments when Marjie wondered why she didn't just walk out of the meeting and join Benjamin in the car. But she stuck it out until the end.

"I'd really like to vote on this tonight," someone finally said. "I got my mind made up, and I've heard enough. Let's vote."

"I'm sorry, but you'll just have to hold on to it for two more weeks," Pastor Fitchen replied. "I made it very clear that tonight was only for discussion, and I'd like that discussion now to come to an end. But I want to say one thing before we close.

"Our church's constitution prohibits me, as the pastor, from having a vote on matters handled by the elders and deacons. But I am allowed to voice my opinion, although I try not to dominate their thinking. So, these are matters for your elders and deacons. But this is my opinion."

Pastor Fitchen paused and rubbed his cheeks, then he puffed out some air and drew in another large breath. "I want you to know that I do feel very strongly on both these issues. My feeling is that if we as a church cannot find it in our hearts to support a Bible project like this one, or if we can't support one of our own fine young couples who happen to go to the mission field with another organization, I cannot find it in my heart to remain in your pulpit.

"I have never considered resigning before," he said soberly. "But I am preparing the papers now in the event that this is the direction you choose to take."

25

HEALING WOUNDS

"Say, whose car is that in the driveway?" Marjie asked as the three Macmillans returned home from the church meeting.

"Looks like Billy's car," Jerry replied. "I kept wondering where he and Ruthie were tonight. Hope they weren't sitting here waiting."

"I'd say they've been here about ten minutes," Benjamin speculated as Jerry's old black Ford came to a stop.

"How would you know that?" Jerry asked.

"I saw that car drive past the church a little while ago," he replied, pushing his car door open and getting out. "But I didn't realize it was Billy's car. Matter of fact, I saw several cars go by while I patiently waited for you to finish with that meeting."

"Somebody had to stay in there so we'd know how the rest of it went," Marjie said. "We couldn't all shake the dust from our shoes and leave the lambs to the wolves."

Benjamin laughed as they headed up the sidewalk. "I was so angry I was shaking when I got in the car. Orville Manning has used his money to call the shots in the church for so long. If that would have been any other place but church, I'm afraid I wouldn't have gone to the door, he popped my cork so bad."

"We noticed," Marjie said, taking Benjamin by the arm. "We wouldn't have to put the car heater on if you were always this hot."

Jerry was already inside the house by the time Benjamin and Marjie came in together. Ruth and Billy were sitting in the living room with Sarah, and all three of them were grinning from ear to ear.

As soon as she saw their expressions, Marjie started laughing and clapped her hands together. Her laughter started Billy and Ruth into laughing as well, and soon even Benjamin had joined in the merriment.

"So what's so funny?" Benjamin finally asked.

"It's congratulations time!" Marjie exclaimed, sitting down and taking Ruth's hand. "We should send the men out to Mink Slough more often. Nothing like good clean air and a big northern pike to clear the smoke out of a banker's eyes."

"I'm going to send this fella out there every weekend," Ruth added. Billy draped his arm around her shoulder, but couldn't seem to stop laughing.

"So . . . when's the big day?" Jerry asked. "Thanksgiving?"

"Nope," Marjie said.

"What do you know about it?" Billy said, wiping tears from the corners of his eyes. "We just decided, so Ruthie couldn't have told you."

"She didn't need to," replied Marjie, looking into Ruth's black eyes. "This lady would never go for a wedding at Thanksgiving. No, sir. She gives the appearance of being strictly practical, but at heart she's a romantic. Try a Christmas wedding with all the trimmings."

"For once you're wrong, Marjie," Billy said with a chuckle. "We can't afford all the trimmings."

Everyone laughed again, and Jerry and Benjamin offered their congratulations as well.

"We're looking for all the help we can get," Ruth said to Marjie and Jerry. "Interested in the job?"

"What's the pay?" Marjie asked. "Interest-free loans, safety deposit—"

"A lovely dinner for two at the Green Parrot Cafe in Rochester!" Billy cut in. "I've heard that anyone who goes in there and whispers the magic words 'Benjamin Macmillan' gets a free steak dinner."

Benjamin laughed and rubbed one of his eyes. "I almost did a repeat performance tonight," he said. "But I'll let Marjie and Jerry tell you that one. My blood pressure will shoot up again if I stick around. Coming, Sarah?"

"Coming," she replied, getting up out of her chair. "Martha's been sleeping for about an hour. She was good as gold."

"Good-night, everyone," Benjamin called out as Sarah joined him at the door. "We'll see you on Sunday."

A chorus of good-nights followed as the two older Macmillans made their exit.

"So, what happened tonight?" Billy asked. "We'd have been there, but we got wrapped up in all these wedding plans."

"Wrapped up is probably about right," Marjie said, scanning Billy's face. "You've got lipstick all over your face."

"No, he doesn't," Ruth protested, but Billy was already rubbing his cheek.

"All right," Marjie said, hands on her hips. "Tell me you were just calmly talking it over."

Ruth looked at Billy, and the two of them burst out laughing. Then Ruth leaned over and kissed Billy right on the lips. "I cannot tell a lie," she said softly. "This boy knows how to kiss."

"You don't look too shabby yourself," Marjie said. "I thought I noticed some fog in the valley, but I guess it was steam coming out of your car."

"Might have been," Billy said. "So, are you going to tell us what happened at the meeting?"

"Oh, man," Jerry groaned. "I'm not sure where to start. It was pretty bad. My dad got so mad that he walked out. Your dad was burning, too, Billy."

"You're kidding," said Billy. "He's never gotten worked up about anything at church."

"Well, they gave everyone plenty to chew on tonight," Marjie explained. "Two big things were debated. There were a number of people opposed to Pastor Fitchen's proposal that we let members designate money to be given to the Dyak Bible project. And most of those same people spoke against the church financially supporting anyone who works with any mission other than our denomination's."

"Mmmm . . . that's bad news," Ruth said. "Who do you think had the most support?"

"Hard to say," Jerry responded. "I'd guess it was about half-and-half. But those who are opposed to it have the stronger voice. The big guns like Orville Manning were smoking tonight."

"But so was Pastor Fitchen," Marjie added. "He drew a line in the sand and said that if the church votes to support the other position, he's going to resign."

"My goodness!" exclaimed Ruth. "A year ago you never could have convinced me that the pastor was capable of standing up to them. They've got the power to hurt him if that's what they decide."

Marjie noticed the reflection of an approaching car's lights on the window, and she stood up to see who was turning into the driveway. Looking out the window, she waited as the car came into the farmyard. "It's Chester and Margaret. No surprise, I guess."

"They were at the center of the fire tonight," Jerry said to Billy and Ruth. "I'm sure glad Chester's dad wasn't there. That meeting would have torn him to shreds."

"Just the report of the meeting will probably send him on a spinner," Marjie said. "I hope Chester and Margaret weathered this thing. I couldn't see them from where I was sitting, and they were gone by the time I got out to the parking lot."

The slamming of car doors was followed by the sound of footsteps on the sidewalk and the muffled sound of voices.

"Come on in," Jerry called, pushing the door open before Chester and Margaret got to the steps. "Glad to see you're still in one piece. That was a brutal meeting."

Margaret stepped through the doorway and went straight into the living room. Seeing Margaret's puffy eyes, Marjie gave her a hug, and Ruthie stood up and followed Marjie's hug with one of her own. Chester walked into the room without his usual good-natured smile and quickly took a chair.

"I'm really sorry you had to go through that tonight," Jerry said. "I can't believe some of the things people said. It must have been horrible to sit and listen to it."

"Yeah, it was," Chester said and nodded. "It was worse for Margaret than it was for me. I got used to it when my father would rip into me, but I didn't expect that kind of attitude from people in my own church. Some of them have been sitting in my Bible class for months. I thought I knew them better than that."

"I'm sorry that Ruthie and I weren't there to support you," Billy said. "I heard my dad got upset, but I'd have been burning up the place."

"We *were* burning up," Chester said, looking over at Margaret. "So rather than come straight over here, we went for a drive and talked our way through some of this. But I'm still sort of shocked. How can people be so narrow and petty?"

"It's pretty easy. Too easy, I'm afraid," Jerry responded. "Chester, I honestly don't believe that most of the people have any idea how trapped they are in their rigid religion. Their faith has gotten so entwined with our particular church that they can't see beyond the walls. It's why Billy and I never had much time for what went on at the church."

"I always figured that if that's what religion was, I could get along just fine without it," Billy added. "The trick is, though, that there's good stuff mixed in with the bad. You can't just lock the doors, sell the property, and start all over again."

"I agree with Jerry," Ruth added. "Most of the people don't realize how much of what they say and do contradicts the values they say they support. How many times have I had to say to myself, 'Father, forgive them, for they know not what they do.' And then I've looked back and had to say that about myself, too."

"Even so," Marjie said, "I'd still like to wring a few necks."

Everyone laughed, including Margaret, although her face was rueful.

" 'Tis a pity," she said, "that Chester and I have become such a problem for them. If we'd known—"

"You're certainly not the problem, and don't let anyone make you feel that way!" Marjie broke in. "The problem is the problem. And the problem won't go away unless people stop pretending it's not there. It's like swimming in a fishbowl and believing it's the ocean."

Jerry was nodding his head in agreement. "I was ashamed of the way you were treated," he said. "I don't know if it's appropriate, but if I could, I'd like to apologize for the church. I can't help but feel that God was unhappy tonight."

"Grieved," Margaret said. "I believe He grieves over us."

"That's how we felt, all right," Chester said. "But that meeting did help us make up our minds. We've decided to apply to the missionary training school in Scotland where the Bidens went."

"How did the meeting do that?" Ruth asked.

"Both the school and the missionary organization connected with it are based completely on faith," Chester explained. "The students, the staff, and the missionaries are committed to not making their financial needs known."

"So how does it work?" Jerry asked. "Like how Margaret received the money for her trip here?"

"That's right," Margaret replied. "They pray. Oh, my, how they pray. I've been to their meetings, and they know how to talk to God about their needs."

"I don't understand," Billy said. "So they go out to the mission field without asking financial support from any denomination?"

"That's what Margaret says," Chester replied. "You'll notice that although Mister Biden talked about the Bibles, he never actually asked for financial support. Yet look at the number of people here who want to help. That's how they do everything."

"I don't know," Billy continued, shaking his head. "I can't imagine it working."

"You'd get a stern argument from Hudson Taylor and George Muller," Margaret reasoned with a warm smile. "They made it work for hundreds of Christian workers. It's just not easy for bankers to balance these books."

"I've never heard of those guys, Margaret," Billy said. "I'm not saying it's impossible, I only said I can't imagine it!"

Margaret laughed. "It *is* amazing, and it can be a powerful testimony of what God can do. We believe that this is how the Father in heaven desires us to trust Him, and we believe that He will put it on people's hearts to support us in what we do. We do not want people or churches ever to feel pressure to support us. And we never want to be a cause for a rift within any church."

"Well, we've got a rift going, that's for sure, but it's really not about you," Jerry said. "I've never been so proud of a pastor as I was tonight. What he said really took some guts. Makes me want to get involved even more."

"Me, too," Billy said. "Everybody that I get a chance to talk to about those Bibles is going to get an earful from me."

"Plus an earful about your wedding date, I'm sure," Marjie added.

"What's this you're sayin'?" Margaret cried. "You didn't say a word about it! When's the date?"

"It's a Christmas wedding," Ruth said, her black eyes flashing with excitement. Then she pointed her finger at Margaret and Chester. "Don't you dare think about packing your bags for Scotland before then. You can talk about faith, but listen to me on this one. I'm telling you in no uncertain terms that you are going to be here."

All six friends laughed once more, and Marjie got up to put together a late snack. But before she got to the kitchen, the phone rang.

"Oh no," she whispered to herself, looking at the late hour on the clock, then stepping to the phone. "Please don't let it be about Paul. Oh, God, please let him be alive. . . ."

Jerry, also alarmed by the lateness of the call, got up to see what was wrong. Marjie was listening somberly at the telephone receiver when he came into the kitchen.

"How bad? . . . Oh, my. . . . Yes, we'll be praying for him. . . . Good-night." Marjie slowly hung up the receiver.

"Is it Paul?" Jerry asked, taking Marjie's arm.

Marjie shook her head no, then she gave a deep sigh and looked into Jerry's eyes. "It's Pastor Fitchen. They think he's had a stroke."

26

TURNING UP THE HEAT

"Blue, stop scratching at the door," Marjie ordered, stepping quickly toward the screen door. "You know better than that. Lie down."

The Australian cattle dog plopped down on the front steps and put his chin down on his paws, looking up at Marjie with sad, round eyes. But his tail was waving back and forth like a windshield wiper.

"Come over here and look at what you did, Jerry. You turned a rugged farm dog into a big baby," Marjie said as he walked toward the door. "The minute it looks like it's going to rain, he's at the door whimpering and scratching. We should call him Bluebird instead of Blue Boy."

Jerry put his arm around Marjie and laughed as Blue's tail went to work even harder. "He's my Blue Boy, even if he is getting soft. After seven years of hard labor, I think he deserves visitation rights to the Big House now and then. Besides, Martha loves to play with him when he's in here. He's a good baby-sitter."

"Right," Marjie replied, putting her arm around Jerry. "Especially whenever I'm gone. You sneak him in here, let her play with him while you drift in and out of a nap, and then you put him out again before I get home. But you're not clever enough to sweep up after he's shed half of his coat on my hardwood floors. Do you think I'm blind?"

"Oops," Jerry said. "Martha really does like it, though."

"You're a sucker for dark curls and beautiful legs, aren't you," Marjie teased. "How about a kiss, big boy. Do you realize that I never got one kiss from you yesterday?"

"Yeah, I don't know what your problem was."

"My problem!" exclaimed Marjie. "The problem was your crazy day. Now, before we lose another whole day, let's see what you got."

Marjie reached up and took Jerry's face into her hands and pulled him down to her waiting lips. "My, that was good," she said, coming up for a breath of air. "Now turn your head a little bit. I hate it when your nose pinches my nose off."

"Picky, picky, picky," Jerry replied, but he was quick to comply with her request. This time he was the one to turn up the heat.

"Whew!" Marjie said, opening her eyes wide and shaking her head, then she gave him a significant look. "Too bad that truck's on its way to deliver Ma's Holsteins this morning. When's that guy supposed to be here?"

Jerry looked at his watch. "Ten minutes or so. Guess we better let this smolder for a while. We can stir the coals later."

"I'll be here," Marjie replied. "But I've got the prayer meeting tonight at the church. You're remembering, right?"

"My turn to watch Martha," Jerry said. "I'll also try to remember to sweep up afterward."

"You keep that dog out of my house," Marjie ordered. "And if you don't, I have ways of reminding you who it is that heats up your fire."

Jerry burst out laughing and let go of Marjie. "There'll be no dog in this house . . . for any reason . . . at any time," he promised, crossing over to take a chair at the dining room table. "Say, did you hear anything more on the pastor?"

"Just bits and pieces," Marjie replied, joining him at the table. "I called around this morning, and the news is better than we thought, but not as good as it could be. The doc believes it was a minor stroke, but he doesn't know how much damage was done. Pastor Fitchen lost only a slight bit of motion, but his speech is slurred. If he talks really carefully, you can understand him. But it's slow gear."

"How long's he gonna be like that?"

"Who knows?" replied Marjie. "As far as I can tell, strokes are a guessing game. One person seems to recover fairly well, and others never come out of it."

"Boy, I hope for his sake and ours that he pulls out of this," Jerry said. "I wonder what's going to happen at the church?"

"Couple of people I talked with thought we'd be calling some of the other churches in the area to see if their pastors could fill in with the preaching temporarily," Marjie answered. "They didn't sound like they cared much for the idea, though."

"You've probably never heard some of the local pastors preach," said Jerry. "Dry as Depression dust. We may end up spending our Sabbath rests at home in bed instead of rushing around to make it to church on time. Especially if I'm milking five more cows."

"You having second thoughts about adding to the herd?" Marjie asked.

"Not at all," Jerry replied. "After telling Orville Manning that I'd find a way to help Mister Biden with those Bibles, you can bet I'll have plenty of energy in the barn. All I have to do is think of his face, and my blood starts pumping faster."

"I guess that's what happened to the pastor," Marjie said. "His wife told somebody that the stroke came about an hour after the meeting adjourned. She said he was still agitated from the meeting, but he was so tired that he crawled into bed anyway. He was lying there, staring up at the ceiling, and he felt it come over him. He couldn't even move at first."

"That's scary," said Jerry. "I tell you, I don't look forward to getting old. Feeling your body give out on you."

"I'm not too fond of the idea, either," Marjie said. "I bet Manning and some of the others are feeling pretty bad today."

"Don't bet on it," replied Jerry. "I've never known that crew to feel guilty about much of anything. But I don't know; this might have dented their armor. You'll probably hear more tonight. Some of them will be at the prayer meeting."

"If they come, they're going to join the rest of us in praying for Pastor Fitchen," Marjie declared. "They probably won't like it, but tonight I'm switching the emphasis from our boys in the service to the pastor. After all the prayers that man has said for these people, I believe it's our turn to say a few for him."

"I think you're right," Jerry said. "And I think it's time for me to get back to work. You hear the truck rumbling up the road? He must have torn the muffler off that thing."

Blue had jumped up from his spot on the steps and was running toward the road barking as the large livestock truck slowly turned the sharp corner into the Macmillan driveway.

Jerry stood up and stretched. "Don't go away, babe," he said, leaning over and kissing Marjie on the forehead. "I'll be back in shortly."

———————— ✐ ————————

Jerry was fast asleep on the davenport when he was aroused by the sound of Benjamin's car rolling down the gravel driveway. For a second, he wasn't sure where he was or what was going on. Jumping up from the davenport, he sighed with relief when he recalled putting Martha to sleep half an hour earlier.

He walked to the door with a slight limp and waited for Marjie and Sarah, but didn't see Benjamin. Rubbing his eyes, Jerry pushed the door open as they came up the sidewalk.

"Where's the dog?" Marjie joked. "I suppose you snuck him out already."

"The only dog inside the house tonight was this old tired one," Jerry replied as Marjie and Sarah stepped into the house. "I was so zonkered out. Hope it's not just from milking five more cows."

"Heard you got kicked," Sarah said with a chuckle.

Jerry nodded. "Big Ethel landed one right on my kneecap. She tried a second time, but I think I got the best of her on that one. Whopped her pretty good."

"I guess Ben didn't warn you about her," Sarah asked with a smirk that reminded him of Marjie.

"Don't tell me she's a kicker," he said, but Sarah was already nodding. "You two birds sold me Big Ethel, the Kicker?"

"She gives a lot of milk, though," Sarah replied quickly. "Your father thought it was a good trade-off."

"And where is my father, by the way?" Jerry asked. "I'd like to chat with him about the price he charged me for a lovely Holstein that may end up as very expensive hamburger."

"Ah, you'll learn how to handle Ethel," Sarah urged. "You treat her right, she'll show you how to fill a bucket with milk. Treat her wrong, she'll make you pay."

"You're a big help, Sarah," Jerry said and laughed. "But where is Dad, anyway? I take it he's not hiding from me in the car."

"No, he's not in the car," Marjie responded. "Ethel's probably the last thing on his mind. He said he was going for a walk. He's pretty agitated again."

"Why?" asked Jerry. "Did something go wrong at the meeting?"

"Nope. It was a wonderful meeting," said Marjie. "We had over sixty people there tonight. And we prayed and prayed for the pastor. I was really pleased."

"So, what got Dad's goat?" asked Jerry.

"I'm not sure. He said he didn't feel like talking about it," Sarah replied. "He was talking to a couple of men after we broke up from our small groups. I think they must have said something to him about the pastor."

"Which way was he heading?"

"Down the lane," Marjie said. "Probably to the same spot you always head for."

"Probably," Jerry agreed, walking over to grab a coat. "If you'll excuse me, I think I'm gonna toddle down there and see what's eatin' my dad."

The outdoor air was cool and dry and still, and it felt good on Jerry's warm face. A brilliant half-moon glazed the landscape with silver, and as Jerry stepped from the sidewalk to the driveway, a great horned owl soared over the barn on its way to the valley below. The farmyard was quiet except for an occasional rattle from inside the hog shed.

Heading down the farm lane, Jerry could easily see his father sitting on a stump, silhouetted in the moonlight. Benjamin's arms were crossed, and he was gazing out over the valley with Blue sitting at his feet. Jerry picked up his pace and quickly reached the end of the lane.

Benjamin did not turn as Jerry approached him, but kept staring straight ahead. Blue got up and gave Jerry's hand a lick. Jerry leaned against a tree and joined in his father's silence.

"You gonna tell me about it?" Jerry finally asked, breaking the quiet, "or should I start yapping about nothing until you give in?"

Benjamin smiled and stretched his head back. "You were never too good at yapping," he said, "but I'll tell you anyway. It's about Fitch. I got a feeling in my gut that some people in the church are gonna suggest we get together a search committee to find another pastor. Soon."

"Why?"

"A couple reasons," Benjamin replied. "First, he's old. He's only got a few years before he retires, and no one knows how quickly he may recover from the stroke. That's if he does fully recover. Plus, he's been stepping on some big toes lately, and they don't like it."

"You actually think that some of the members would use the pastor's illness to get rid of him because they'd like him out of the way?" Jerry asked, looking over at his father.

"I wish I didn't think it but I do," Benjamin said. "And it would be easy as pie, because it all makes sense."

"Did someone say that to you tonight?"

"No," replied Benjamin. "And no one would say it to me. Besides, none of the people I think would do it come to Marjie's prayer meeting. But I heard a comment about Fitch's age and how we really need a younger pastor to attract more young people back into the church. And a couple of people were talking about how hard it is to recover from a stroke."

"That's hardly a conspiracy," Jerry commented. He leaned

over to rub Blue's face and ears and was rewarded with a satisfied dog smile.

"I know," Benjamin said. "But I'm sure it's coming, and they're not going to wait and see how Fitch heals. My guess is that they'll make their move at the next church meeting."

"And my guess is that you're not going to wait to see what they do," Jerry said. "You always used to tell me that if the odds were against me, I should take the first swing and see if I could get an advantage. So, what's your plan?"

"Well, I got something in mind," Benjamin explained, "and you can bet that I'm gonna come out swinging. I ain't gonna let my friend get walked over when he's down."

"Oh, boy. Sounds like you're gonna take the gloves off and go in with your bare hands," Jerry said.

"Not quite," his father responded. "And I can't do this alone. I'm gonna need you and your buddies, Chester and Billy. You think they're game to help?"

"Are you kidding?" Jerry protested. "Pastor Fitchen's become someone special to them. What do you have in mind?"

"I tell you what," Benjamin said. "Give me a couple days to think it over, then I'd like to get us all together to talk. I'm not going to bother if I conclude that there's no way we'd win. But if I figure we can win, then first we have to sit down and count the cost."

He looked up at Jerry with an expression that was hard to read. "I'm not sure that we're ready for this."

27

COUP D'ETAT

Marjie and Jerry stood nervously at the back of the church basement and scanned the large crowd that had gathered. The announcement in Sunday's bulletin that the elders had held a special meeting to discuss how to fill the pastoral duties during Pastor Fitchen's absence was followed by the announcement that Monday evening they would report on their recommendations to any interested church members. From the number of people seated on the wooden folding chairs and the loud buzz of their conversations, it was obvious that interest was running high.

"Benjamin said we should try to not sit too close to each other," Marjie whispered to Jerry. "We don't want to look like we're ganging up on them."

"It looks like we're going to have to take whatever chairs we can find," Jerry replied. "Chester and Margaret are right up front there. Billy and Ruth are pretty close to them. Dad and Sarah are way in the back. I wonder why he picked that spot?"

"I don't know, but let's try to find something in the middle," Marjie said, moving forward.

As they headed about halfway up the aisle and found an opening, Orville Manning stood up and approached the wooden podium. He was wearing his black suit and white shirt, and his bald head shone even in the basement's dim lighting.

Broad-shouldered and over six feet tall with a large frame, he cut an imposing figure despite his sixty years.

"On behalf of the elders," Manning announced, wrapping his large hands around the edges of the podium, "I want to say we're very happy for the large turnout. We have some very difficult matters to discuss tonight. As you're aware, we elders met last Friday night, and now we would like to inform you of our plans."

"Plans or recommendations?" Billy Wilson broke in from near the front of the crowd.

"I'm sorry," Manning retreated. "We have some *recommendations* to make for discussion, and hopefully we'll leave the building tonight with a plan of action."

Marjie looked over at Jerry and winked. "Let's hope it's the right one," she spoke softly.

"Lou, I believe you've spent some time talking with the doc about Pastor Fitchen's condition and can give us an update," Manning continued.

Lou Billingsley stood up from his front-row seat and turned to address the crowd. "Well," he spoke loudly, "the doc gave me a bunch of medical talk, but then he put it to me in plain English. The pastor's stroke was a mild one, but there's no way to predict whether he'll get his speech and motion back fully. At best, it's likely that his speech will always be a little off. And, unfortunately, the reality is that there's a good chance for repeated strokes."

A lot of heads nodded in agreement as Billingsley sat down, and the buzz of conversation rose again as people leaned over to whisper back and forth.

"This is going the wrong way already," Jerry said to Marjie. He craned his neck around to look at his father but found his view was blocked by several heads.

"I think we're all aware of the devastation a stroke can bring," Manning said, shaking his head with an air of understanding. "Even a mild stroke is bad. It leaves the family uncertain of the future, and in this case it leaves our church's future in uncertainty."

"Why is that?" Marjie broke in. She had been leaning forward in her chair, searching for an angle to challenge anything that was being said.

Manning squinted to focus in on who the person was behind the voice. "Because the pastor is the leader of the church," he responded once he had spied Marjie. "He sets the spiritual tone, he brings us the Word of God, he directs us in prayer, he visits the sick and the elderly. He's the key to everything that goes on here."

"But should he be?" Chester asked. "While the pastor is a very important person, I hope you're not saying he's the only one in the church who can do those things. Many people in this room are teaching Sunday school classes, leading others in prayer, visiting the sick, and doing a lot of other things that set a spiritual tone for the church."

"I think we depend on one man for way too much," Jerry added. "We pay someone who's got a seminary education to come in as our pastor, and then he's supposed to take care of everything. But I don't think that's what the church is all about."

"We're really not here to discuss our denomination's policy for the placement of its pastors," Manning stated, standing up tall and leaning hard on the podium. "We have to deal with the problem as it now stands. And the problem is that we must find someone to fill our pulpit while the pastor is out of commission.

"Our first recommendation seems clear-cut," he declared. "We are going to ask some of the other local congregations if we could share their pastors for the Sunday morning and evening preaching. We would have them on a rotating system, and it may mean that our service times will need to fluctuate. This has been done in the past, and we see no reason not to pursue it now. But that only buys us time, of course. We feel that—"

"Excuse me," interjected Ruth, "but I'd like to give my thoughts on your first recommendation. I'm not opposed to other pastors from the area filling our pulpit, but I really don't think it's our best option. I thought that one of the qualifications for elders was that they be 'apt to teach,' and another was that they might be able 'by sound doctrine both to exhort and to convince' others. Isn't that true?"

"Yes, and most of us have taught in our day," Manning responded. "But none of us have ever preached before."

"Doesn't that seem odd to you?" Ruth asked. "Does a person need a seminary degree in order to preach?"

"No, but—"

"What if one of you elders or one of the church members sitting here tonight could preach well?" Ruth continued to press her point. "Would you ask that person to fill in for the pastor, or would you call the other churches in the area and see if their pastors can get on a rotating schedule where they repeat the sermons they've already given to another church?"

"I suppose we would ask our own person," Manning replied. His face was getting red, and Marjie thought she saw beads of perspiration forming on his shiny head. "But, really, this begs the point, Ruth. We don't have anyone here, and we have to—"

"I don't want to be impolite and keep breaking in on you," Ruth interjected again. "But I think your assumption is wrong, Orville. Every Sunday since Chester Stanfeld has taken over the adult Sunday school class, I hustle down these stairs to hear what he has to say. I've never had the privilege of hearing him preach, but he is truly a gifted teacher. I believe, if he's willing to try, that he could fill in admirably until Pastor Fitchen is able to resume his duties, or until it's determined that the pastor must retire."

"I agree!" Sarah's voice called out from the back. Her declaration was followed by a chorus of similar ones, and the room quickly filled with a cacophony of supportive noise.

"Got 'em on the run now," Marjie whispered to a grinning Jerry.

"Just be ready," he whispered back. "Foxes have lots of hiding places."

Orville Manning had gone over to a couple of the other elders and was holding a private session with them. That did not take long, and he soon stepped back to the podium.

"We respect Chester's teaching ability," Manning said, nodding toward Chester and Margaret, "but we do feel that preaching is different. Still, if Chester is willing to try preaching next Sunday morning, we will then decide whether this arrangement might work for the longer term. Keep in mind that this is temporary and without pay. Would you be willing to try, Chester?"

Chester stood up and turned toward the crowd, his square-jawed face red. "I would be very pleased to give it my best," he announced. "I cannot fill the pastor's shoes, but I hope I can honor your pulpit by 'rightly dividing the word of truth.'"

Several members, including Jerry and Marjie, clapped their appreciation, and Chester nodded and sat down. As he was sitting, Benjamin was rising to his feet in the back row.

"I'd really like to say something that's on my heart," Benjamin declared. Everyone turned around to see who was speaking. "I get real excited when I see us moving toward what I think a church should be. Ain't it thrilling to give a young man like Chester, whom God seems to be calling into full-time Christian work, a chance to preach what God puts on his heart?"

Heads all across the basement nodded, but no one turned around to look at Orville Manning.

"I've come to remind us of something," Benjamin continued. "Pastor Fitchen has given us twenty years of his faithful service. He's done everything we've asked him to do and more. He's been at our side when some of us lost our loved ones, and he's been there without fail through some of our prolonged illnesses and difficulties. No one's perfect, and that includes the pastor, but he's been a good man for us.

"Now, I know what's going to be suggested next is that we begin our search for a new pastor," Benjamin continued. "And I can understand the concern. But I'm asking you first to search your hearts about what we owe Pastor Fitchen. This is not a business decision where we simply look at the dollars and cents and realize they don't add up and we have to do something. Marvin Fitchen is our pastor and brother in Christ, and in this hour of his need, I hope the message we send is that we love him and we'll do everything we can to support him. Let's tell him we'll do whatever it takes to help him get back up there into the pulpit. Ain't that the least we can do?"

There was no buzz in the room when Benjamin finished and sat down. No one clapped. A few heads nodded, but most of the people simply looked stunned. The entire group seemed to take a slow, collective breath and then turned around to Manning.

"I . . . ah . . . appreciate what you're saying, Benjamin," Manning started, "but that doesn't solve our problem. We can't limp along indefinitely without a full-time pastor."

"I'd rather limp along and stumble than walk in a way that's less than Christ's love," Marjie piped in.

"So we're just supposed to close our eyes and hope that everything works out?" snapped Manning. "We need a clearer plan than that, or I say we begin our pastoral search."

"I've got a plan, if you'd like to hear it," Benjamin said, rising to his feet again. Every head turned again to listen to him. "Keep in mind that my intent is only to delay any pastoral search until we've confirmed whether or not Pastor Fitchen will be able to return.

"If Chester can take the preaching assignments, it's not fair to ask him to continue the adult Sunday school class. I would like to present myself as a candidate for that job, at least until Chester can return to doing it."

"What about the young people?" Manning asked smugly, looking at Benjamin and then surveying the church members. "Pastor's been trying to get out of that one already. You want to take them on, too, Benjamin?"

"I'd love to give it a try," Billy Wilson announced loudly, standing to his feet. "And Jerry Macmillan and Ruthie have volunteered to help me. We think we can spark things up a bit for our young people, but we won't know until we try."

That offer wiped away any touch of arrogance on Orville Manning's face. "All right," he continued stubbornly, "who's going to handle visitation? We've got sick people and shut-ins to go see."

"Benjamin and I just sold our small dairy herd so we'd have

the time to visit folks," Sarah called out from the back. "We were planning to get involved, anyway. Seems like some of your elders might consider it as well."

Marjie thought that Orville Manning looked like an invisible hand had reached around his throat and was giving him a good squeeze. He fidgeted back and forth, but it was obvious that he had no more ammunition.

"Well, I said we wanted to leave with a plan of action, and I guess we got one," Manning said. "But it's all subject to change, and I personally don't think it's going to work. We elders might need to make some hard decisions in the next few weeks, so don't be surprised."

Margaret Stanfeld had been silent the entire meeting, but she suddenly stood up just when everyone thought the meeting was over.

"Sir, I'm wondering," she began with her gentle Scottish lilt, "if this is a meeting where the church can make a decision."

"Certainly," Manning replied with a puzzled expression. "We had intended to make some major decisions tonight, but we didn't."

"We do want to support Pastor Fitchen, don't we, sir?" she continued sweetly, looking at Manning and then turning to face the congregation.

"Yes, yes," snapped Manning. "So?"

"Well, ye know the good pastor's heart was set on helping Mister Biden with the precious Bibles for the Dyaks," she said, then she smiled. "I think it would honor our pastor if we were to vote tonight for allowing members to make a special designation of their gifts for the annual sale that's coming up."

"I don't think—"

"I second the motion," Betty Hunter spoke out before Manning could block a vote.

Manning rubbed the perspiration from his forehead and took a deep breath. For the first time all evening he spoke quietly. "All in favor, signify by saying aye."

An overwhelming chorus of voices rang out. "Aye!"

"All opposed, signify by saying nay."

Not a soul said a peep, not even the ones who had strongly opposed the idea earlier.

"The ayes have it," Orville Manning declared. "I officially declare this meeting adjourned."

28

A Trade's a Trade

"I'm not going to do it for you. You should have gotten your two rows of potatoes dug before we started seeing snowflakes, but you've been too busy hanging out with that horse," Jerry spoke to Marjie as he lifted the last of the black storm windows high over his head and caught the two metal clips at the top of the window frame. "Okay, get her fingers out of the way."

Marjie pulled Martha's little hands back from the window-sill, then she grabbed the window's metal brackets and slid them over the metal post. Jerry pushed the window into place, and Marjie clipped the hook tight.

"That's it!" Jerry exclaimed, then he stepped back and admired the six windows on the north side of the farmhouse that he had sealed for the winter.

Marjie unhooked the storm window they had just latched and propped it open six inches so she could talk to Jerry. "I hate to tell you this," she said, "but you're mistaking those windows for a work of art."

"Whadd'ya mean?" Jerry retorted with mock indignation. "Those babies look pretty nice with a fresh coat of paint. Real nice!"

"I've got another suggestion for you. Those two rows of spuds would look a lot better in the cellar bin than six inches under in the garden out yonder," Marjie suggested with a smirk.

"If it snows or freezes before you—"

"I did my part!" Jerry retorted. "A bet's a bet, and you lost. Now it's time for you to pay. When I lost, I washed those dishes every lousy night."

"How about we work a trade?"

"I'm listening."

"Come to the window, and I'll whisper it to you. I don't want these young ears to hear."

"Like Martha will understand."

"You never know what a child's picking up. Just come to the window. Like I said, a bet's a bet, and a trade's a trade."

Shaking his head and grousing as he came toward the window, Jerry said, "I'm not gonna dig those rows for you. Now, what?"

He put his face up close to the window, and Marjie said, "You look a little thirsty."

"Yeah. So what?"

"So have a drink of water, grumpy!" Marjie's hand, hidden behind the window ledge, suddenly shot forward and delivered a large cup of water right between Jerry's eyes.

Jerry's face snapped backward, then he reached his dirty hands up and did his best to wipe away the water, not realizing he was streaking his face as well. Marjie was bouncing up and down with laughter on the other side of the window frame.

"That was dirty pool, sweetheart," Jerry said in his best James Cagney voice. "I'll get you for this. You'll be sorry for messing with Big Jerry, see. Don't ever turn your back on me."

Marjie kept right on laughing, and Martha was laughing as well. Marjie pulled the window back into place and hooked it tightly shut. Then she closed the inside window as well.

"Time for you to go in your playpen," Marjie said, chasing after the fleeing toddler. "Gotcha!" she said as she scooped her daughter up and carried her back to the living room.

"No fussing now," Marjie said. She set Martha down in the center of the wooden playpen that was lined with stuffed animals and a couple of inexpensive dolls. "Now, I wonder where your father went to?" she said as Martha picked up one of the dolls and began chewing on its head. "I thought he'd come in and get a drink."

Marjie went back into the bedroom and looked out for Jerry. Spotting him in the garden with a fork, she sputtered, "What's he doing now?"

Checking to make sure that Martha would be okay, Marjie marched out the back door and headed around the northwest corner of the house. "I was just kidding!" she called out. "I'll dig those rows myself. Go on, now. Get to your own work."

Jerry had already turned above several hills of potatoes and was busy digging when she approached, but he didn't look up.

"What's your problem?" Marjie asked, giving him a playful shove from behind.

Jerry caught his balance quickly and turned to face her with a crooked smile. "I was hoping that you'd be a big enough sucker to storm out here and try to get me to stop. When you were a kid, did you ever try swimming in the cow tank?"

"You wouldn't."

"And why not?"

"Because . . . we're going to visit the pastor this afternoon."

"There's plenty of time for you to swim around, enjoy the cool water, and still get cleaned up."

"I don't think so . . ." Marjie said, backing off and then turning to run. But even with her surprise jump, she only made it as far as the back steps before Jerry caught her. Laughing, he wrapped his strong arms around her, lifted her off the ground, and started carrying her toward the barn.

"I suggest you kick off your shoes," he said evenly as he cut toward the cow tank.

"I'm calling your bluff, Jerry," Marjie said. "Just put me down, now. You've had your fun."

Jerry laughed and kept right on walking. "Bluffing, eh? You got one more chance to kick off those shoes. But if you want 'em wet, that's what you'll get."

"You won't do it, Jerry," Marjie told him emphatically, but she did turn her head to look at the tank.

"Well, you've underestimated me, then," Jerry replied, kissing Marjie on the cheek. Then he stretched out his arms, held her over the large metal water tank, and kept her dangling there for a moment.

Marjie looked at Jerry and calmly said, "I knew you wouldn't."

"Don't drink the water," Jerry replied. Then he lifted her even higher and let go.

Marjie screamed as she made her ungraceful descent into the slimy water, but she managed to grab the edges of the tank and keep her hair from getting wet. She stared in disbelief at Jerry, who was doubled over in laughter, wiping tears from his eyes. Then she shook her head and started laughing as well. "You are an idiot!" she cried. "And this water is freezing!"

"And you had it coming!" Jerry said, reaching out a hand to help her out of the tank. "Don't you dare try to pull me in, unless you want to shampoo your hair."

Marjie took his hand and laughed and shivered as she stood up, dripping with water. "This means war, you realize?"

"Or a trade?"

"What's the offer?"

"I dig the potatoes, and you declare we're even."

"You dig, wash, and store the potatoes in the bin," Marjie replied, stepping out onto the grass. "Then a trade's a trade."

"Done."

———— ✐ ————

"Come in, come in," Dorothy Fitchen said, opening the door before Marjie and Jerry had a chance to knock. She looked tired and frail, but her warm brown eyes and friendly smile welcomed them.

"How is he?" Marjie asked, holding Martha's hand and helping her with the big step through the parsonage's front doorway.

"Oh, what a dolly!" exclaimed Dorothy. She scooped Martha up and took her into her grandmotherly arms. "He's . . . better today than yesterday. The words weren't coming out right yesterday, but today he's just slow. And he's itching to see you."

"Here's her bag," Marjie said, handing Dorothy the diaper bag. "Where is he?"

"In the den, of course," Dorothy said and chuckled. "He has to sit at that big desk of his. Can't relax and just sit in the living room. Always the pastor, even when he's not pastoring."

"Should we keep it short?" Jerry asked.

"No, no," Dorothy answered. "He's bored silly. But whatever you do, don't baby him. If he says something you can't understand, make him repeat it."

She led them down the hallway to the den. This time, Pastor Fitchen was not standing at the doorway to greet them. But as Dorothy ushered them into the room he did stand up slowly and extend his hand to Jerry.

"Thanks for coming," he said as Jerry took his right hand and shook it vigorously. The pastor's words were easily understandable, but they came out in slow motion.

Marjie waited for the handshake to stop, then she stepped up and gave the white-haired gentleman a kindred hug. "We've been praying for you," she whispered in his ear. "You are deeply loved, and we're pulling for you."

The elderly pastor gave her a lopsided hug, much tighter with his right arm, and exhaled a big puff of air. When he let go, there were tears in his eyes. "Thank you," he whispered to her.

"Offer them a chair, dear," Dorothy called out. "A lovely young lady gives you a hug, and you forget your manners."

They all laughed as Dorothy closed the door to the study to keep Martha from dashing in. Marjie and Jerry went around the desk and took their seats, and the pastor sat back down in his chair.

"Do you mind if I call you Fitch?" Marjie asked. "Benjamin told me that it was okay as long as you considered me your friend."

Pastor Fitchen raised his white eyebrows and smiled, then he laughed. "Please do." He spoke very slowly. "Both of you. Benjamin . . . told me what you've been up to. I appreciate . . . it."

"When was Dad here?" Jerry asked.

"Yesterday," Fitchen replied. "He stayed most of the afternoon. It's . . . good to have friends."

"You're still our pastor, right?" Marjie asked suddenly.

"Of . . . course," the elderly man replied, a perplexed expression clouding over his face.

"Good," Marjie said, looking over at Jerry. "I want to know what you think of our marriage. This morning—"

"Hold on, here," Jerry broke in, taking Marjie's arm. "You said we were even."

"I said we were even, but I didn't say I wouldn't tell anyone about it," Marjie said with a grin. Then she looked back at Pastor Fitchen. "Now, what do you think of a husband who carries his wife all the way from the house to the barn, torments her by dangling her over a cow tank, and then laughs like a hyena as he drops her into dirty, freezing water? Is that grounds for divorce?"

It took a few seconds for the pastor to figure Marjie out, but when he did, he exploded into laughter. Sitting back in his chair, he laughed and laughed until the tears that had formed earlier came rolling down his face. "Oh my," he said, wiping away the tears. "You've brought some good medicine with you. And what provoked the husband to such a coldhearted act?"

Jerry by now was laughing at the pastor's reaction, but he was able to catch his breath and answer. "The hardworking husband was standing innocently outside his farmhouse, having just hung the last of the storm windows. His beguiling wife whose deceit knows no bounds lured him to the window, and when the innocent young man looked into her beautiful face, expecting to hear words of love and tenderness, she splashed a cup of water between his eyes. His reaction could have been worse, don't you think?"

Pastor Fitchen went into a second long laugh. Marjie and Jerry were roaring as well.

"If I ever write my memoirs," the pastor finally said, "this one goes in it."

"So, what's the verdict?" Marjie asked, then she laughed again. "Will the marriage survive?"

"As long as you're laughing together, you'll be ... fine," Fitchen replied. "Sounds like a healthy home to me."

"That's good," Jerry said. "With Marjie around, there's always something to laugh about."

"Save some of that fun for the young people, Jerry," Pastor Fitchen said. "I'm pleased you've agreed to help Billy and Ruth. If you can win the young people's trust and get them to participate, I'll be the happiest man around."

"We'll give it our best," Jerry assured him. "I'm sort of excited, to tell the truth, but I don't have a clue about how to go about it. I figure Ruthie will give us all the ideas we need."

The pastor nodded and gave a half-smile. "Just your excitement will tell them you care. That's what they need to know."

Marjie had been listening to the men and was troubled to think that the pastor's speech might not improve. Besides the slowness of the words, everything else seemed so normal. *But he can never preach at this rate*, she thought.

She was leaning forward in her chair and noticed that the pastor's left hand looked blue and cold compared to his right hand. In the pause of the exchange, Marjie reached across the table and put her hand on top of Pastor Fitchen's left hand.

"Cold as ice," the pastor said, staring into Marjie's compassionate eyes. "Bad circulation. Your hand feels like a heater."

"I wish I could make it better," Marjie replied, tears forming in her eyes.

The old pastor beamed a smile and winked at her. "You're a character, Marjie. Don't let anyone shut you out of being involved in others' lives. They need your joy. It's infectious."

She nodded, but was too choked up to speak.

"I've had another visitor who spoke well of you," Pastor Fitchen said, still staring into Marjie's dark eyes. "Betty Hunter. I maybe shouldn't say this. But you may have saved her life."

"No," Marjie gasped, shaking her head. "I just let her talk. And we prayed. And then she started coming to the prayer group."

"And you may have kept her from going over the edge," he said. "Sometimes that's all it takes. You opened your heart when every other door seemed closed to her."

"Thanks to you," Marjie replied, squeezing his hand even tighter.

"No," the pastor replied slowly. "Thanks to you. I simply told you that you could do it."

29

RAINY DAY PRAYERS

"This rain better quit soon," Jerry groused, pacing back and forth in front of the dining room window. One light rain shower after another had come through since the early morning hours, leaving puddles in the farmyard and stopping any work in the fields. "Stinkin', rotten, cotton-pickin', miserable—"

"If this was snow, you'd be in trouble," Marjie said as she wiped the crumbs from the table. "It's just rain, and it's Saturday. Relax for a change."

"Just rain," continued Jerry. "Can't get the corn out in this weather."

"You've already got half of it in the crib," countered Marjie. "Most of the men around here haven't even started yet. Besides, this weather's going to blow through, and the sun will be shining tomorrow. You'll be back in the field on Tuesday, Mister Happy."

"If it doesn't start snowing," said Jerry, shaking his head. "With my luck—"

"Okay, okay," Marjie broke in. "I'll give you two choices, farm boy. Either you take off your boots and crawl in the sack for a long nap, or you bundle up and go play outside in the rain. But you're not going to torment me."

Jerry stopped his pacing and looked over at Marjie, then he gave her his crooked smile and a chuckle. "Both sound pretty good to me. You want to come outside with me?"

Marjie laughed and turned to go back to the kitchen. "Not today. The bread doesn't bake itself, you know. I got six loaves going."

"Well, maybe I'll take Martha up to our room and see if the two of us can catch some winks," Jerry said, following Marjie into the kitchen. "I love to snuggle up with her, but she kicks like you do."

"If you get kicked, it's because of your rotten, stinkin', cotton-pickin' bad attitude," Marjie teased. She kissed him lightly on the cheek. "She's in her playpen waiting for you. Sleep tight."

"I will," Jerry said and sighed as he walked away. "Don't let me sleep too long."

Marjie quickly went back to her work, punching the ballooning lump of bread dough that had mushroomed out over the edges of her large mixing pan. She dug her hands deeply into the ball of dough, then she formed out a smaller lump that she plopped down into one of the bread tins.

"One down," she whispered to herself, then she heard the sound of light footsteps behind her. Turning, she saw a very tired-looking Martha coming slowly toward her with her thumb stuck in her mouth. "What's wrong, honey?" she asked, bending down to pick her up.

But then Marjie stopped and looked down the hallway. "Jerry!" she called. "Jerry, come on out."

Jerry's head peeked out around the corner of the living room door. "Help me out with this one," he pleaded as he stepped into the doorway. "I can't handle that stuff."

"How could you even think that you'd get away with this?" Marjie scolded, standing back up with Martha still waiting. "Now come and get your daughter, and you change her, for crying out loud."

"But it's one of those up-the-siders," begged Jerry, wrinkling his face and shaking his head. "I can't do those. She must be cutting another tooth."

"You're going to have to do it," Marjie said, turning back to her bread and punching the big lump of white dough again.

"My hands are full of flour, and I have to finish this bread."

"She can wait for—"

"Look at her!" Marjie interjected. "How can you make her wait? Now, just go do it. You men are all such big babies!"

Jerry laughed and picked Martha up. "If I puke, you're gonna have to clean that up, then. The diaper may turn out to be your best bet."

"The only sure bet at this moment," Marjie replied, "is that I'm not—"

The ringing of the phone cut Marjie off, and she nodded Jerry toward the bathroom with a smile as she headed for the telephone. Picking up the receiver with floury hands, she gave her greeting and then listened. "Sure . . . I suppose we can meet you there. We'll need to bring Martha, but she should be napping. I've got to finish a batch of bread, but that shouldn't take too long. . . . Okay. See you in a hour or so."

Marjie hung up the receiver, then hurried back into the kitchen and set to work getting her bread into the oven with a flurry. By the time Jerry had managed to get Martha cleaned up and ready for her nap, Marjie was already closing the door of the oven and setting the timer.

"No more of these, Marjie. That one was bad enough to make a preacher swear," Jerry muttered, stepping back toward the kitchen with Martha. "Sounded like I'm out of a nap. What's up?"

"That was Margaret," Marjie replied. She grabbed the large, empty mixing pan and set it into the sink. "Mister Biden was on his way to Minneapolis for meetings, and he dropped in to see them. When he heard about Pastor Fitchen's stroke, Biden wanted to stop out and pray for him."

"Sounds like something Mister Biden would do," Jerry replied, rocking Martha in his arms. "Are they stopping by here, too?"

"No. Least I don't think so," Marjie said. "But we're meeting them at the parsonage. Billy's going to ride out with them. I guess Benjamin and my ma are already up there. I don't know if Ruth is going to make it."

"What's the big deal?" asked Jerry. "Is the pastor worse?"

"Not that I know of," Marjie responded. "Margaret says that Mister Biden would like us to join him in praying for the pastor's healing."

"What?" Jerry asked. "Did she explain that?"

"No," Marjie said and smiled at Jerry. "I don't know what it means. But knowing Mister Biden, it should be interesting."

———— ✐ ————

"Looks like we're the last ones to get here," Jerry said as he pulled the black Ford to a stop alongside his father's car in front of the parsonage.

"You come around and carry in the loaves of bread," said Marjie, "and I'll bring in Sleeping Beauty here."

Dorothy Fitchen's eyes immediately widened in understanding when she saw little Martha slumbering heavily against Marjie's shoulder. With a few whispered words of greeting she led Marjie down the hallway to the bedroom. Laying Martha in the center of the double bed, they propped pillows on both sides of her and then made a quiet exit.

Everyone, including Ruth, was gathered in the living room when Marjie and Dorothy returned. Pastor Fitchen was ensconced in a comfortable chair at the end of the room, and Dorothy hurried over to sit on a straight chair next to him. Anthony Biden greeted Marjie as she found a seat and then looked around the room as the conversation subsided.

"I really appreciate your willingness to drop what you were doing today and to come over so quickly," Biden said. "I'm speaking tonight in south Minneapolis, so I'm in a bit of a rush. But I wanted to pray for your pastor with some of the people who love him most, and I think I've got the right group together.

"We've been talking a bit," the missionary continued, "and Dorothy said something when I first came in that I thought you should all hear. But I think she should say it in her own words."

Dorothy Fitchen's brown eyes were glistening as she sat forward in her chair and folded her thin hands on her lap. "I . . . appreciate you coming today and your prayers. This has been a very difficult time for us. Frankly, I felt at first that Marvin's pastoral ministry was over and we should just accept it. As you know, Marvin only has a few years to retirement, and with his health I figured, why wait?

"But the last couple of days," she spoke solemnly, "I've had the strangest impression that Marvin's work here is not finished. I can't explain why I feel that way. I'm not even sure that it's what I desire. In all our years together, I have never sensed anything like this. I . . . I would appreciate it if you would treat this information as confidential."

"I've had the same impression on my heart," Margaret said, nodding her dark head toward Dorothy, then she looked into Pastor Fitchen's face.

The wrinkles around his eyes began to fill with the tears that had begun when his wife spoke, and those tears began to streak down his face. He nodded to Margaret, and his shoulder gave an involuntary shake. Taking a deep breath, he spoke slowly, "My ministry has . . . just got started. It can't be over so soon."

Fitchen's halting words cut through the room. Marjie looked over at Jerry through misty eyes and could see that he was struggling to hold back from crying. Benjamin and Sarah both had tears in their eyes, as did Anthony Biden.

"I . . . ah . . . I'd like to pray for you," Biden said, pushing back the tears. He stood up and stepped toward the big chair where Pastor Fitchen was seated. "And I'd like the rest of you to join me and gather around the pastor."

All of the others, except for Dorothy, stood and awkwardly formed an oval around the pastor.

"I realize," the missionary said, glancing at the pastor's friends, "that you probably have never laid your hands on someone and asked that God heal him. Right?"

"Never," Benjamin spoke for the others. "But I know that Jesus and the apostles did. You also said earlier that you were going to anoint Fitch with oil. Why would you do that?"

"It's fairly simple," Biden replied, taking a small vial from his pocket and unscrewing the top. "Toward the end of the book of James, it says, 'Is any sick among you? let him call for the elders of the church; and let them pray over him, anointing him with oil in the name of the Lord: and the prayer of faith shall save the sick, and the Lord shall raise him up.' Are you familiar with that passage?"

Benjamin nodded. "I am ... but I figured it must be something that wasn't relevant anymore. I've never heard anyone talk about it at church."

"Well, I believe it's very relevant," Biden explained. "The Dyaks in Borneo were afflicted with a tremendous amount of illness, and we practiced this type of prayer all the time along with whatever medicines we had available. We felt that James was very clear with his instructions about how we were to pray for the sick."

"Did it work?" Marjie asked. "Were the people healed?"

Biden smiled and nodded. "Not everyone, but many were. Most of the healings were not instantaneous, but some were. I could tell you stories that make the hair on my arms stand straight up. But I don't have the time today."

"Let's get to praying, then," Sarah said.

"Why the oil, though?" Billy asked, leaning forward. "You don't think . . ."

"No," the missionary said and laughed, "I don't think it's magical. Oil is a constant biblical symbol of consecration to God, and by anointing with oil, I think we're simply saying that this life is totally given to God.

"Oil in the New Testament days was also used for its medicinal value," Biden continued. "I think that means that we're to use all of the sound medicines and scientific techniques at our disposal. But we should always remember that God is our healer. When we pray and anoint with oil, that's what we're saying."

"James said to gather the elders," Marjie said. "We're not elders, and I'm not sure some of our elders would like the oil idea."

Both Biden and Pastor Fitchen laughed together.

"For today, you're going to have to do," Biden replied. "And

God's going to have to figure out the rest. Is everyone here okay with how we're going to pray?"

"Yes," Sarah replied, stepping closer and taking Benjamin's hand. "I've seen God heal my soul from sin. I'd like to see Him touch my friend's body."

"If you can," Biden said, reaching out and touching Pastor Fitchen's shoulder, "move in closer and put your hand on our brother. Then turn the eyes of your heart on Jesus Christ and let your faith reach out to Him. He spoke a word and the raging sea was calmed. He touched the leper and healed him in a moment. And He was moved when the friends of the paralytic lowered the man through the roof so that Jesus could be reached. Look to Jesus, and always to Jesus."

The pastor's friends began to pray quietly. Some shut their eyes, and others kept them open. But all intensely focused their trust in God.

Biden dipped the little vial against his finger, then dabbed a spot of oil on Pastor Fitchen's forehead. Closing his eyes and placing both hands back on the pastor's shoulders, Biden began to pray, "Father, we come to You, as You've told us, in the name of Your Son, Jesus Christ. . . ."

30

SOME THINGS CAN'T BE FIXED

Marjie leaned over next to Margaret and whispered, "He's doing great."

Margaret nodded and smiled, but she'd actually been smiling through most of Chester's sermon. This was his third sermon since stepping in for Pastor Fitchen, and there was little of the nervousness and the stopping and starting to gather his thoughts that had made Chester's previous sermons so choppy.

Looking past Margaret's beaming smile to the rest of the Stanfeld family, Marjie's attention was caught by the proud faces of Chester's parents and his two teenaged brothers. She thought that the hard lines of Bill Stanfeld's face had softened over the past month. But if that wasn't the case, there was no questioning the intense spark of joy in his eyes. Both Bill and Clare Stanfeld were totally focused on their son and his words.

Imagine all that wouldn't have happened if Chester hadn't survived the torpedoing of the Wasp, Marjie thought as she turned her gaze back toward the front of the church. Chester was closing his Bible and evidently bringing his message to a close.

"It's clear in the Bible that different people have different kinds of faith, depending on what kind of knowledge and experience each person has," Chester said. "We've looked at the faith of Abraham and Job with the faith of the Philippian jailer and the one thief on the cross who came to believe in Jesus.

"Sometimes faith isn't much more than just clinging to Christ, being completely dependent on Him," Chester continued, pausing to take a sip from a glass of water that was at the pulpit. "Lots of God's people have enough faith to cling to Jesus with all their heart and soul, and that's all they have. To them, Jesus Christ is a strong and mighty Savior, like a rock that can't move. They hang on to Him for dear life, and this clinging saves them. And God gives His people the ability and the strength to hang on."

Jerry had taken Marjie's hand, and he whispered to her, "I think he's talking about me. I've been hanging on like that ever since I went over the side of the ship."

Chester turned toward Jerry, and Marjie almost wondered if he'd heard Jerry's whisper. Then Chester continued, "This is a very simple kind of faith, but it's complete. In fact, it's the heart of all faith, and it's the kind of faith we're often driven to when we're in deep trouble or when we're sick or sad and our minds are clouded. We can cling when we can't do anything else, and that is the very soul of faith.

"Always cling to what you know," Chester said strongly, then he smiled and relaxed his expression. "If you're just like a little lamb that wades a little into the river of life and not like the great whales who stir the mighty ocean depths, well, take a drink anyway. Because it's drinking and not diving that'll save you. Cling to Jesus, for that's faith. Amen."

"Amen," Marjie murmured and nodded toward Chester. She found that much of what Chester had said spoke directly to her heart and was easy to agree with.

As Chester called out the number in the hymnal for the last song, Jerry whispered to Marjie, "Are you sure you don't want me to come home with you and help get lunch ready?"

"No," Marjie said, shaking her head and then standing as the congregation rose to sing. "You better stay and make sure Benjamin has plenty of support in Sunday school. Last week was pretty rocky."

Jerry nodded. "I'll get a ride with Margaret and Chester. Hope you got plenty of food ready. Chester's brothers look like they can do some damage at the table."

"I think I'm going to throw in a few extra potatoes," Marjie agreed and chuckled. "Maybe you can go light on the meat for a change. Just in case."

Once the hymn was finished and the benediction given, Marjie quickly collected Martha from the nursery and made her exit. When she saw how refreshed Martha was from a cat nap during the service, Marjie wondered if she shouldn't have taken Jerry up on his offer to come home. She had all she could handle trying to drive and keep Martha sitting.

Holding Martha's hand and slowly walking up the sidewalk to the farmhouse, Marjie stopped at the bottom of the steps where Blue was lying lazily in the bright sunshine. He hadn't raised his head as they approached, but his eyes had followed them warily and his tail was wagging cautiously. Marjie could feel Martha's excitement building as they approached.

"Here comes the little tornado, Blue," Marjie warned, letting go of Martha's hand.

Martha let out a whoop of delight and dove on top of the cow dog. She wrapped her arms around Blue's back and her legs around his sides, and then she sat up triumphantly and bounced up and down as if riding him.

"Ride 'em cowboy!" Marjie hooted, then reached down and scratched Blue's head. "What a good, patient dog you . . . say, you just might be able to help me out here. I'll give you a big, round beef bone if you come inside and do some baby-sitting. Wanta come in, boy?"

Blue jumped to his feet, sending Martha on a roll off his back and into the long green grass. Fortunately, she came up laughing. Marjie picked her up and climbed the steps, then looked back down the driveway toward the road.

"What your father doesn't know won't hurt him, I reckon," she whispered to Martha. Opening the front door, Marjie waited while Blue stepped into the house, then she and Martha followed.

Marjie always loved to come home when the aromas of cooking food greeted her. She went straight to the kitchen and checked on the pot roast in the oven while Martha followed Blue into the living room. Then Marjie pulled out three big potatoes and began to peel them to add to the ones she already had soaking in water, ready to boil.

"Let's see," she said to herself, taking inventory of what she had left to do. "Set the table, cut the bread, whip some cream for the pumpkin pies . . ."

By the time Bill Stanfeld's car rolled into the driveway, Marjie had the lunch ready to serve. She'd already ushered Blue out the back door with his prized beef bone and swept away any evidence of dog hairs. Marjie could see Jerry in the backseat with Chester's brothers, but she didn't see Chester's car yet.

I wonder where they are? Marjie thought as she picked Martha up. Balancing the baby on her hip, Marjie stepped out the front door to greet her company.

"Welcome," Marjie called out as the Stanfelds and Jerry emerged from the car. "Where's Chester and Margaret?"

"Delayed," Jerry replied, shrugging his shoulders. "Somebody came up after Sunday school and wanted to talk with both of them. Seemed kind of upset about something. Can lunch be postponed for a half an hour or so?"

"I guess," Marjie said, doing her best to mask her disappointment. "It's ready, but we can keep it warm."

"Wendell and Bob would love to take Charlie for a ride," Jerry said. "What do you think?"

"Fine with me," Marjie responded, "if you watch them close to make sure they know how to handle him right. And don't get too far away. Once the others get here, we should eat."

"Let me take Martha in the house," Clare Stanfeld offered, coming up the sidewalk to meet Marjie. She took Martha from Marjie's arms. "Kind of cool out here for her. Thanks for letting my boys take the horse. They love to ride."

Jerry and the Stanfeld teenagers had headed for the barn, and Bill Stanfeld was walking over to the garage.

"When did you get the garage door on?" Bill spoke out to Marjie. "Looks pretty nice."

"We got it back in . . . early September," Marjie replied, walking toward the garage. "Figured we better get it done before the snow started flying. Had just enough paint left over to cover it."

Bill had gone to the door and was surveying the inside. "Looks mighty good," he offered. "This should last a long time."

"Thanks to you," Marjie said, coming up alongside of Chester's father.

"Ah!" Bill sputtered, shaking his head and looking into Marjie's face. "It's the least I could do. I owed your husband more than I could ever pay, but my bill keeps going up. I owe you, too."

Marjie fixed her brown eyes on his. "What are you talking about? You don't owe me a thing, Mr. Stanfeld. If you did, I'd make you pay, though."

Stanfeld chuckled and leaned against the back of the Macmillans' black Ford. "Oh, I owe you, all right, but I don't have any idea what kind of payments I could make. Do you remember when I came up to you before the Fourth of July parade?"

"Sure," Marjie responded. "You were offering to help with the garage supplies."

"What else?"

A large grin spread across Marjie's face. "You asked me if I believed that the rain on the night of the garage fire was a miracle."

"And you said, 'Without a doubt.' I'll never forget that as long as I live," Bill Stanfeld said, squinting his eyes and nodding. He reached his large hands into the pockets of his dress pants and rattled his keys. "I figured you'd get flustered and back down on what the paper said. When you didn't, I'm not sure why, but it caused me to want to try to believe again."

Marjie looked at Bill Stanfeld but was too overwhelmed to speak.

"Maybe it was just a combination of things," Bill continued. "I saw the change in Chester's life, and I wasn't about to let my son know something I didn't know. But it was hard to listen to

Jerry's story and just toss it aside as a coincidence. Then you come along spoutin' about miracles. Sounds crazy, I know, but for a second or two, I almost thought I could see God in your face."

Marjie laughed a little nervously. "You hadn't been celebrating early, had you? A few cool beers before the big parade?"

"Not me," Stanfeld replied. "I've had a terrible temper and swore with the worst of 'em, but I ain't a drinker. I think I saw what I saw."

"Maybe you saw and heard Mister Biden," Marjie offered. "If anyone walks close to God, that man does. I've never met anyone more humble in my life."

Bill Stanfeld closed his eyes and took a deep breath. With one of his hands, he reached up and rubbed his forehead, then he puffed out some air and shook his head. "Don't I know" was all he was able to whisper.

Marjie swallowed the lump in her throat and waited for Chester's father to recover. Eventually he opened his eyes and stared down at the ground.

"Did you know that King David wrote a psalm about my life?" Bill asked. "He even put my name in it."

Marjie shook her head no.

He closed his eyes and quoted, " 'The fool hath said in his heart, There is no God. They . . . are . . . corrupt, they have done abominable works, there is none that doeth good.' "

Stanfeld opened his eyes and looked up at Marjie. "I am the fool, and the damage I've done as a result is just awful. What Mister Biden said went direct to my heart."

"And you've . . . you've come to faith?" Marjie ventured.

Bill pursed his lips and nodded.

"It just takes some of us longer, right?" asked Marjie.

"You said that, too," Bill replied with a smile, "the morning we first met. Made me really mad at the time. But I never hit a woman, so you were safe."

Marjie paused and wondered at the change that had swept over Bill Stanfeld in the year she had known him. "So," she asked, "what's it been like since that Sunday morning when

Mister Biden was here? I mean, it's not my business to pry, but it sounds like there were a lot of things in your past that made you mad."

"What's it been like?" Bill repeated, looking out the garage and staring toward the hills on the horizon. "It's kinda hard to describe, Marjie. When I went forward in church that day, I realized how much I've hurt the people I love the most and how much damage I've done to myself. I knew I'd wrecked just about everything beyond repair. I knelt down and knew I couldn't fix it. It was too busted up."

"We had a pine tree down in the woods that got struck by lightning," Marjie said softly. "It shattered right at the base, and all we have left now is a stump."

"Sounds familiar," Stanfeld said, still gazing out as far as he could see.

"Anyway, I stopped by the stump the other day," Marjie continued. "Guess what? There's a new shoot growing out of it. It's alive."

Bill looked over at Marjie and nodded. "Thank God for a new life. I been trying to start all over again. I done a lot of apologizing. My boys and Clare . . . I put them through hell. Especially Clare. I really took my problems out on her the worst."

"And she forgave you," said Marjie.

"Yeah," Bill said, choking up again. He clenched his jaw and took a shaky breath. "I don't deserve the woman. She had a lot of good reasons to leave me years ago. By the way, she told me she had a talk with you and your mother about our little Mary."

Marjie looked at Chester's father and spoke carefully. "We didn't mean to—"

"No, I'm glad you talked," he broke in. "I was so mad at God when Mary died that I couldn't deal with it. I left Clare on her own, and I never visited that little grave again. Every year I watched Clare make her trips to the cemetery, but I wasn't about to go.

"We went together—Clare and me—a week ago."

Marjie's eyes filled with tears as she heard the pain in his words.

"Nobody was there but us and the pine trees and the wind. We just stood there and we grieved. And we laid our little Mary to rest."

31

THRILLS AND CHILLS

"Look at all the cars!" exclaimed Marjie to Jerry and Martha as their Ford rolled down the little hill into Greenleafton. "Half the county must be here today!"

"Wait till you see all the corn and oats and soybeans people brought," Jerry said. "When I unloaded my wagon of corn this morning, it was like a beehive around here. People just kept hauling the stuff in, wagon after wagon. This is gonna be some sale."

A large crowd of people was already milling around the outside of the church building when they arrived, and many more were coming and going out of the church basement where all the baked goods and crafts were to be sold. Marjie had baked two cakes for the sale, but from the looks of the armloads of goods being carried into the church, she thought her cakes would hardly be noticed.

"Now that's a pile of corn," Jerry declared with a big grin as he turned the corner by the grocery store.

Marjie looked to her left and shook her head in disbelief. There were actually three small mountains of bright yellow ear corn in the north parking lot of the church. A half-dozen boys were doing their best to become king of the hill on the tallest pile, but none of them seemed to have the upper hand. Beyond the corn was a smaller pile of soybeans and another of oats.

"Everything's going to be sold to raise money for the church's budget?" Marjie asked as Jerry pulled the car into a parking slot near the parsonage.

"Everything except what's designated for the Dyak Bibles," Jerry replied, shaking his head. "That biggest pile of corn is all going to the Bible project. Should bring in a pretty penny."

"I guess," Marjie agreed. She retied Martha's bonnet, then opened the car door and got out with Martha on her hip. "Looks like allowing everyone to designate their gifts has paid off. There's a lot more stuff than last year."

"Yeah. I love it," Jerry said, coming around the car and taking Martha from Marjie. "Can you carry both of those cakes in by yourself?"

"Sure. But I'm embarrassed already," Marjie said, reaching into the backseat and carefully pulling out the two boxes. "Looks to me like everybody else is bringing in a baker's dozen."

"Ah!" Jerry spat. "This is plenty. With all the corn I hauled up, we've done our share."

"I hope you're right," Marjie said. "You coming in?"

"Nope," Jerry replied. "I see Billy over there with some of the boys from the youth group. It's a good chance to spend some time with them."

Marjie nodded and headed for the church, but she looked back and watched as Jerry walked up to Billy and the group of teenagers and laughed at the comical way the young men responded to little Martha. Some of them made faces, some took her hand or touched her cheek, and a few hung back bashfully.

Just like boys, she thought, feeling a flash of loneliness for her two brothers. *Paul's never even seen Martha*, she caught herself thinking wistfully, *and Teddy wouldn't believe how she's grown. Oh, well. . . .* With a sigh she turned and carried her two cakes over to the main doorway.

When Marjie got to the basement, she looked around in amazement at the array of platters, boxes, and jars that crowded the long wooden tables, waiting to be auctioned to the highest bidder. Behind the tables was more food that would be loaded up as the food was sold off.

"I don't believe it!" Marjie whispered, but her words were lost in the buzz of the room. Then she felt a tap on her shoulder and turned to see Ruth.

"This is staggering, eh?" Ruth said, taking one of Marjie's cakes and heading toward the tables. "Here, we'll put these with the other baked goods. Do you want them to go to the general fund or the Bible project?"

"You're kidding, right?" Marjie asked, following Ruth. "Give me the Bibles any day, honey."

Ruth was chuckling as she led Marjie to the table that had the most food on it and behind it. "This is it, and the next table," she said to Marjie, setting the chocolate cake down on the floor behind the table. "There has to be at least twice as much food as we've ever had at one of these sales. I'll bet that Orville Manning and a couple of other folks are surprised."

"Embarrassed, I hope," Marjie added, bending over to put her coconut cake on the floor beside the chocolate one. "If the dollars match up to what we're seeing, Orville and his cronies will be crawling under the tables."

"Maybe, but don't count on it. Where's the rest of your gang?" Ruth asked.

"I don't know where Benjamin and my mother are," Marjie said. "But Jerry and Martha are outside with Billy and some of the church kids. Talk about two guys being an instant hit."

Ruth burst out laughing, and her black eyes sparkled. "What a pair of characters. But they are so good with the kids. The only reason I'm needed with that bunch is to try to restore order every once in a while."

"You guys must be doing more than fun and games with the kids," Marjie said. "For somebody who didn't care much for school, Jerry sure is doing a lot of studying these days—it's almost funny. Says he wants to make sure he's able to explain whatever they're going over together."

"Billy's doing the same thing," said Ruth. "I didn't think he could get so serious about anything—except me."

"*Smitten* is the word, I believe," Marjie added. "Six weeks and counting. When are we going to get together to plan your wedding?"

"Now you're kidding, right?" Ruth asked and laughed again. "I've had this wedding planned for five years—right down to the dill pickles."

Marjie laughed and nodded, then she stopped smiling and got serious. "Who's going to be in your wedding party?"

"Well, you and . . ." Ruth answered, then paused and put her hand on Marjie's arm. "I cannot believe it. We didn't ask you, did we? I'm so sorry. I—"

"Don't blubber on, now," Marjie broke in and laughed. "You've had a lot on your mind lately. Besides, we knew you'd want us to be there."

"What's that got to do with it?" asked Ruth.

"Everything," Marjie teased. "I wouldn't come unless you let me be up front with you. It just wouldn't be proper."

Ruth laughed and put her arm around Marjie. "I love your friendship, Marjie," she whispered. "My life was dull-dull until you came along."

"The feeling is mutual," Marjie responded. "But I think Billy Wilson also had something to do with taking off the dull edges. Just don't go forgetting about me all alone on the farm once you get hitched to that rich young banker."

Ruth shook her head at Marjie and then she noticed something toward the back of the basement. "Say, there's Pastor Fitchen and Dorothy sitting all by themselves. Let's go see how he's doing."

Marjie followed Ruth toward the solitary white-haired couple who waved at them as they approached. This was the first time that Marjie had seen the pastor in public since the stroke.

"What are you sitting out here in left field for?" Marjie joked as they sat down near the Fitchens. "Don't tell me you're back here necking?"

Dorothy and the pastor laughed and shook their heads.

"You never stop, do you?" Dorothy said. "We just couldn't stand sitting at home when we saw so many people bringing in so many things to sell, but I was hoping to conserve a little bit of Fitch's energy by keeping him away from the main action. We can't believe what's going on here."

"Neither can we," Ruth said. "I'm so excited about the response to the Bibles for the Dyaks. I wish Mister Biden could be here."

"I'm sure we all do," Dorothy agreed. "This day is certainly an answer to a lot of prayers."

"Speaking of prayers," Marjie said, looking pointedly at Pastor Fitchen, "how's our favorite pastor doing?"

Pastor Fitchen smiled at Marjie, but then he gave his wife a quizzical expression and shrugged his shoulders.

"Go ahead," Dorothy said. "We can't keep it a secret from everyone."

"What are you hiding?" Marjie asked.

"I'm really doing fine, except I still tire out so quickly," the pastor said, but this time his speech was without pause or hesitation. "I've had no problem with my words since the day you all prayed for me. Feel my left hand."

Marjie reached out and put her hand on his. "It's warm," she marveled out loud. "It was so cold the last time. Why haven't you said anything?"

"Oh, boy, you don't know how hard it's been to keep the lid on it," Fitchen replied with a warm smile. "We wanted to make sure it lasted, so we thought we should give it time. We didn't want people to make a big fuss about it and then discover things hadn't really improved. If I could just get my strength back, I'd be in business again."

"This is so thrilling it gives me the chills," Ruth spoke softly, with a shiver of her shoulders. "I'd really like to go up and bring Billy and Jerry down to hear what's happened. Do you mind?"

"Not . . . if . . . you'd . . . like it," Pastor Fitchen stuttered along slowly.

"I thought—"

"Gotcha!" exclaimed the pastor and laughed. "Why do you doubt, oh ye of little faith?"

"I forgot to warn you," Dorothy apologized, laughing along

with her husband. "He's also regained a sense of humor that I haven't seen for a decade or two. He's threatening to do stand-up comedy when he retires."

All four of them laughed, and Ruth stood up to go outside. But as she did, she spotted Sarah coming through the basement door with Martha in her arms. Ruth waved at Sarah, who headed their way.

"Why's everybody hiding out back here?" Sarah asked, sitting down in the chair next to Ruth. "Something tells me that some folks at this table are telling each other secrets."

"Yeah, a doozie," Marjie replied. "Didn't I tell you, Ruthie, that you can't hide anything from this woman?"

"So what's the secret?" Sarah asked as she loosened Martha's bonnet.

Looking over at Dorothy and Pastor Fitchen to see if they were going to tell it, Marjie and Ruth were surprised to see that Dorothy was shaking her head no. "We'd rather not," she whispered.

Marjie and Ruth glanced at each other with an instantaneous, awkward bewilderment, but neither spoke. Marjie's attempt to clear her throat only compounded the awkwardness of the moment. Then Pastor Fitchen suddenly burst out laughing, followed by both his wife and Sarah.

Ruth looked at Marjie again and said, "I think this is twice I've been had in five minutes. So, how long have you known about this, Sarah?"

When Sarah finally stopped laughing, she said, "Ben and I knew the next day."

"And you didn't tell us?" Marjie sputtered. "What's wrong with you?"

Sarah shrugged her shoulders and smiled. "We were asked to keep it a secret, and we did. You two would have blabbed it all over the county. I could see that on Ruthie's face from the basement doorway."

They all broke out laughing again, and Ruth nodded ruefully that Sarah's words were true.

While they had been talking, the buzz and laughter in the

basement crowd had increased significantly, and whole groups of people were heading for the door.

"By the way," Sarah said, looking over at those who were exiting, "I came down here to tell you that you're missing all the action in the parking lot."

"I thought they were going to start selling down here and do the big stuff at the end," Marjie said.

"They are, I guess," said Sarah. "I'm talking about your father-in-law. You know, the crazy fella I married."

"What's he doing now?" Marjie asked, standing up.

"You have to see it to believe it," Sarah said. "I'm sworn to secrecy."

"How about you leave Martha with us?" Dorothy Fitchen asked. "I think we'll just sit here and save our energy."

Sarah gladly surrendered Martha over to a delighted Dorothy, and the three women headed for the stairs.

"Look for Teddy's pickup," Sarah called out, lagging behind Ruth's brisk pace up the stairway and out the door. "It took Ben two days to get it running, but he was bound and determined to do it."

They had no problem discovering where Teddy's old truck was. A huge crowd had encircled the pickup, and Marjie could see Billy, Jerry, and Benjamin standing in the back. Jerry was just lifting off one of the high wooden side gates and setting it down.

Something like a roar went up from the crowd as Benjamin held up a large white sign that neither Marjie nor Ruth could read from their angle. Marjie heard her mother breaking out in loud laughter behind her.

"What is going on?" Marjie demanded as she and Ruth got to the edge of the crowd nearest the back of the truck.

"There's a huge boar in there!" Ruth cried, pointing with her finger and starting to laugh. "Look! Billy's sitting on its back."

Billy spotted them and waved, but kept right on with his theatrics. Jerry leaned over and said something to Benjamin, who was showing the sign to the people on the other side of the truck.

Then Benjamin turned toward Marjie and Ruth with a beaming smile and swung the sign with its huge letters in their direction.

"BACON FOR BIBLES!" Ruth and Marjie screamed together as the whole crowd erupted in applause.

32

THANKSGIVING PRODIGAL

"So we're not going to get to see you and Billy today, Ruthie?" Marjie asked, speaking into the telephone mouthpiece. "Sounds like we're in for a quiet Thanksgiving Day. Margaret and Chester are going to Chester's folks', and Ben and my ma won't be coming over until around three. They're invited to the Fitchens' for lunch. Could you have imagined that a year ago?"

Marjie paused to listen to Ruth and turned her head to watch Jerry rock Martha on the lovely wooden rocking horse that Benjamin had made for Marjie's baby shower. The sounds of Martha's giggles and Jerry's laughter combined with the sweet and savory smells of turkey baking in the oven and the apple pies she'd finished early in the morning to fill the old farmhouse with rich pleasure. *If we're all alone today, this is just fine with me*, she thought.

The sound of Blue's muffled bark from outside the house cut short Marjie's daydreaming, and she looked out the window to see the cow dog slowly walking across the lawn toward the driveway. Whatever had roused him from his nap didn't appear to be troubling him now.

"Sure, we'll be here this weekend. Where else would we be?" Marjie joked with Ruth. "Maybe you and Billy would like to take care of the farm for us some weekend, and we'll go to Minneapolis and take a second honeymoon. . . . No, I was just joking,

261

but you're right; it *is* a good idea. . . . Well, stop in anytime. Have a Happy Thanksgiving, and don't forget that you have to fit into your wedding dress in three weeks. . . . See you later. 'Bye."

Marjie hung up the phone and crossed over to the dining room picture window. "I wonder where Blue went?" she said to Jerry. "He was walking down the driveway, and I don't see him at all now. He doesn't go down to the road much since he got hit by the car."

"I thought I heard a car go around the corner a little while ago," Jerry said, gently helping Martha dismount her steed. "Who knows? Maybe Blue got a whiff of something and went to investigate. So . . . what are Billy and Ruthie up to?"

"This afternoon they're down at Billy's folks', and tonight they're with Ruthie's pa," Marjie responded, still gazing down toward the end of the driveway. "Looks like we'll have to suffer through part of this day by ourselves."

"Now, that's my kind of suffering," Jerry responded. He leaned back in his chair and yawned. "If you could get me a piece of that fine-looking apple pie, I think I'll force that down and then see if I have the strength to drag my body to the davenport for a nap."

"I wish you'd drag that body outside and see where Blue went," Marjie said. "He doesn't—hey, there's somebody down there sneaking through the pine trees! Looks like . . . a soldier."

Jerry stood up and stepped toward the window, but Marjie was already heading out the front door. "It's Teddy!" she cried. "It's Teddy!"

The screen door slapped shut behind her, and Marjie raced across the lawn and down the driveway. Ted Livingstone and Blue stepped out from behind a large pine tree, and Ted dropped his green army bag.

"Teddy!" Marjie cried, jumping into her brother's arms and burying her head into his shoulder. "I can't believe it!"

Ted was laughing, and he squeezed her tightly. Blue started barking wildly, and Jerry and Martha made their approach across the lawn.

"This was supposed to be a surprise!" Ted protested as he

put Marjie back on the ground. "I can't believe you caught me. That stupid dog of yours never could keep a secret."

Marjie was laughing and nearly crying as she stepped back to look at her brother. "You are one handsome-looking rat!" exclaimed Marjie. "Why didn't you let us know you were coming?"

" 'Cause I thought it would be more fun to just show up on Thanksgiving Day," Ted answered, straightening his hat and standing tall. "What do you think of the beer belly?"

"It's gone!" Marjie wondered aloud, prodding her brother's midsection. "They must be working you hard."

"Day and night," Ted said, looking up at Jerry and Martha. "Oh, look at my little lady—she's all growed up. Let me have her."

Jerry handed Martha to Ted and then shook Ted's one free hand. "Boy, this is a shock," he said. "Welcome back. You must have gotten a good pass."

"Ten days," Ted answered, hugging Martha up tight against his neck. "Trains, buses, and I got a ride out from Preston from some guy who's going to visit his folks in Cherry Grove. He dropped me off down at the corner. I thought if I cut through the trees I could walk right in the front door without knocking. But Marjie caught me, just like she always used to do."

"So Ma doesn't know anything about this?" Marjie asked.

"Nope," said Ted. "Not unless she spotted me when we drove through Greenleafton."

"How could you know she was there?" asked Marjie.

Ted laughed. "You know the army's given me special intelligence training. I've got a source that told me they were going to be at the preacher's place for lunch and here this afternoon. Two sources, actually, and they're very reliable."

"Come on!" Marjie muttered. "Tell me the truth. How did you know that?"

"I'm telling you the whole truth and nothing but the truth," Ted answered with a smile, then he winked and nodded to Jerry. "I got a letter from Ma a few days ago telling me their plans.

And if you recall, my dear Mrs. Watson, I got a letter from you as well."

"Fair enough," she conceded. "But come on up to the house." Jerry picked up Ted's bag and put it over his shoulder as they started up the driveway and across the lawn.

"I hope you got that kitchen of yours full of goodies," said Ted as they walked. "I'm starving. Haven't eaten since last night, and that was a bogus meal. I swear it was a greasy pigeon masquerading as a baked chicken."

"We got plenty of everything," Marjie replied. "But the turkey's not ready. Jerry was just about to sample the apple pie. How's that sound?"

"Like heaven," Ted said. "I haven't had a home-cooked meal since I left. That army food tasted good for about a minute."

Jerry opened the front door of the farmhouse and said, "If I never see another baked bean, I'll be a happy man. Blue, you stay out here."

The Australian cow dog had followed closely behind Ted and Martha and was nearly successful in his bid to make it inside the house. He looked up, forlorn, but Jerry shook his head and said, "Not today, buddy. We'll call you if we need you."

"You let that dog in here?" Ted asked, looking at Marjie.

"Only when we need a baby-sitter," Marjie replied with a smile. "Martha loves him. Ma's got a dog now, you know. Name's Tinker."

"Yeah, so I hear," Ted said, sitting down with Jerry at the dining room table. "That ain't all she's got since I left."

Marjie was heading for the kitchen to dish up the pie, but she stopped and turned around to study Ted's expression. He was looking straight at her, but his face gave no hint of what he was thinking. Jerry squirmed in his chair and looked at her as well.

"So, is it okay with you, Teddy?" Marjie asked carefully. "Ma was worried about what you and Paul were going to think of her getting married and all."

"And if I'm not okay with it?"

Marjie shrugged. "Then ... you're not okay with it, and

she'll be sorry about that. But she's very happy now—whatever you think about it."

Ted's poker face gave way to a crooked smile. "Not to worry about me," he said. "I'm just sorry they didn't get together sooner. Maybe my leaving wouldn't have been under such rotten circumstances."

"Or maybe they wouldn't have gotten together at all," Marjie said, turning to step into the kitchen.

"Oh, they'd have gotten together," Ted called after her. "I just sped things up. I think Ma was holding back with me in the way."

"Well, they didn't hold back once they made up their minds," Marjie said as she put the pieces of pie on small plates. "Wish you could have been here for the wedding. It was a perfect day—out in the fields, the birds singing. Hundreds of people showed up, and then we had a barn dance."

She came around the corner from the kitchen and placed Ted's pie and a cup of coffee on the table.

"Thanks," Ted said, picking up his fork as Marjie went back to the kitchen. "Yeah, I would have loved to have been there, but no way was the army going to let me go during basics. Besides, I was in the doghouse right about then."

"Why?" Marjie asked.

"With my record. Guess."

"Let me guess," Jerry responded. "The fastest road to the doghouse that I know is to hit an officer. You didn't!"

Ted nodded his head as he buried a large forkful of apple pie, then he grinned. Marjie brought two more cups of coffee and Jerry's plate of pie, then she sat down to listen.

"We went out to the bars one night," Ted said. "As usual, I got plastered and didn't know where I was. Some big-shot lieutenant came in, and I ended up taking a couple of swings at him. They locked me away for a while, and then they put me on a short leash. I was lucky they let me come home for the holiday."

"You were lucky you didn't get court-martialed," Jerry added. "It looks like it helped, though. The last couple of times

I saw you, your eyes were glazed over and I thought your face looked puffy."

Ted took a sip of coffee and nodded toward Jerry. "You're right. I was hitting the bottle almost every night, and if that wasn't killing me, it was certainly wearing me out." He set the cup down in the saucer. "But I haven't had a drink in two months."

"What?" gasped Marjie.

"Two months, going on three," Ted said. "While I was sitting in the brig, I finally decided that enough was enough. Then after I got out, one of the guys in our barracks was found dead in his cot. He just drank so much it killed him. I got to see him before they took his body out . . . it was bad news, I tell you."

Ted shook his head and puffed out a deep breath of air.

"I watched them carry out a guy who'd picked up a case of VD on one of his leaves in Norfolk," Jerry said. "I can still hear him yelling about how much it hurt. Penicillin usually knocked it out, but not for him. He never came back, and I never heard what happened to him. It made you think twice before going to the red-light district."

"You never told me about him," Marjie said. "What else don't I know?"

Jerry laughed and took a sip of coffee. "I'm sure there's plenty more that you'd just as soon forget about. It was pretty bad."

Ted nodded his head. "I seen some of that, too. It's like playing Russian roulette with a pistol. You just never know when your turn's coming. You have to stay away from it."

"I . . . ah . . . I'm amazed to hear you say that, Teddy," Marjie said, looking into dark brown eyes that were so like her own. "There's no way I would have thought you could quit."

"Why not?" asked Ted, wrinkling his lips into another crooked smile. "Ma's letters and your letters all ended with, 'Our prayers are with you.' What are you expecting?"

Marjie eyeballed Ted hard, but she wasn't sure how to respond. Ted bailed her out by answering her unspoken question.

"No, I didn't get religion, if that's what you're wondering," he said. "But I did get my head back on my shoulders. That seems like enough for now."

"What are you doing with your spare time, then?" Marjie asked. "No bars, no booze, no wild women, no religion. You're not one to sit around and twiddle your thumbs."

Ted laughed, then he sat forward in his chair with a glint in his eye. "You're gonna think I'm off my rocker," he said softly, "but I've had a chance to get involved with electronics—and I'm good at it. I bought a bunch of books, and every chance I get I read and read. One of the guys in our division is an electrical engineer. He's helping me."

Marjie kept staring at Teddy after he finished, and she blinked a couple of times before she said anything. "You sold me on this whole story until you got to the electrical engineer business," she said, then smiled. "You're going to have to re-vamp that if you're going to try it on Ma. She'll see right through it."

"Marjie, I think he's serious," Jerry said, watching Ted's face. "Why would he kid you about that?"

"Because he thinks I'm a sucker, and he loves to set me up," Marjie said.

"True," Teddy admitted. "But I'm not conning you, this time, Marjie. Don't you remember I said I had to get away from the farm because I didn't want to be a farmer?"

Marjie nodded.

"Well, I think I've found out what I *do* want to do," he said. "At least I'm going to learn everything I can."

"Electronics?" Marjie whispered. "You didn't just stick your finger in a socket and take too big a jolt?"

"No. This is for real."

For the next three hours, off and on, they traded news. Jerry and Teddy swapped service stories while Marjie put Martha down for her nap. Then Teddy followed Marjie into the kitchen so she could put the finishing touches on the turkey and tell him more details of what he had missed at home. Then they all shared another cup of coffee while Ted gave them an update on what he knew about the war effort, particularly their brother Paul.

"So you and Ma haven't gotten any letters since he was in Sicily?" Ted asked.

"No. Have you?"

"Me? Of course not," Ted replied. "But I've got a friend who's listening for me. Paul didn't land at Salerno like you thought. His group landed farther south in Italy. It wasn't nearly as bad where he was as what the other group faced at Salerno. A lot of guys got killed there."

"So, where are they now?" Marjie asked. "Do you know?"

"Yeah, but it's not good," said Ted, shaking his head. "They're about seventy-five miles south of Rome at Cassino— they haven't been able to break through the German defenses yet. My friend says the fighting's brutal there. So don't waste your prayers on me. Paul's the one that needs 'em."

"And you don't pray for Paul?" Marjie asked.

"I didn't say that," Ted answered. "I said I haven't got religion yet. That doesn't mean I don't believe in prayer."

"You're just as stubborn as Pa, aren't you?" said Marjie.

"I hope not, but—"

Blue's barking cut Ted off, and the sound of Benjamin's car on the gravel driveway was like an alarm going off.

"Where'm I gonna hide?" Ted called out, ducking down so he couldn't be seen through the window as the car went past.

"I don't think you should hide," Marjie said, jumping up and going to the window. "Ma just might have a heart attack if you jump out and scare her. Just go outside and sit on the front steps. That's good enough. Quick!"

Ted jumped up and ran out the door. He sat down on the steps and put on his army hat and started to laugh as he waited for his mother to spot him. Blue quickly sidled over to sit behind him.

Marjie and Jerry watched from the window as Sarah finished her discussion with Benjamin and slowly turned to push the car door open. She was halfway out of the car when her eyes focused in upon her son. The sight of him froze her in place.

"She's going to faint!" exclaimed Marjie, but the scream of delight that followed proved her wrong.

Teddy raced past the window and his hat went flying off as he grabbed his mother and twirled her in the air. The two danced around, but there was no way that Sarah would let go of her boy.

"Looks like the prodigal's come home," Marjie whispered.

33

ONE WILD RIDE HOME

"So what do you think of the Christmas tree now, banker boy?" Marjie called out. She and Ruth had finished hanging all of the large red and blue glass balls on the lower half of the eighteen-foot blue spruce that was positioned at the front of the church to the right of the pulpit. "Good enough for your finer tastes?"

"I think it'll do," Billy answered, pulling back the long step-ladder he had been using to decorate the upper half of the tree. "I just wish you could have picked a better-looking tree," he said, cocking his head critically.

"Oh, you!" Ruth scolded him. "You know very well that it's a perfect tree." She draped an arm around Marjie's shoulder and stared at the light gleaming off the ornaments. "It's absolutely beautiful," she said, "so strong and majestic."

"It was all Jerry's idea," Marjie replied. "Benjamin's been supplying the church with a Christmas tree for years, but Jerry would never let his pa take this one. He said it was the prettiest tree on the farm and there were plenty of other ones that would do for Christmas."

"But then you had to go and put together a Christmas wedding," Jerry said. He lifted his wooden extension ladder from against the back wall of the church and carefully swung it away from the tree and down to the floor. "I was thinking about cutting down that scrawny one on the corner of the driveway, but I was afraid the snow might drift through without it. So I guess this one'll have to do."

"I believe I saw some anguish in the man's eyes when he started sawing," Marjie said. "This is his wedding present to you. No one but someone dear to his heart could have coaxed him into giving away this tree."

"Thank you so much," Ruth said, letting go of Marjie. She stepped over to Jerry and gave him a big hug, then she planted a kiss on his cheek.

"Wow!" Jerry sputtered, breaking into a laugh and blushing crimson. "That's a sure way to cure any anguish I may have felt."

"Your face looks like one of these big red glass balls on the tree," Billy said with a laugh, stepping over to shake Jerry's hand. "Thanks for the tree, Jerry, but keep your mitts off my lady. If I recall correctly, you and Ruthie used to smooch fairly regular in the old days."

"What?" Marjie gasped. "So there were other women."

Jerry got even redder and shook his head no, but Ruth nodded her head that it was true.

"He may have been shy," Ruth said, her black eyes flashing, "but he had a thing for me when we were in first grade. Whenever he thought no one else was watching, he'd kiss me on the cheek like that. I liked it, too. Did you—"

"Stop it!" Jerry said, holding up his hands. "Billy dared me to do it and called me a chicken. I was chicken, but I did like it!"

They all burst into laughter, and Billy put his arm around Ruth.

"Billy still does," Ruth said softly, looking into Billy's face. "A lot."

"Always did, always will," Billy replied. He leaned over and kissed his girl on the lips, wrapping both arms around her.

"Whoa!" Jerry blurted out, stepping back and putting his arm around Marjie. "That's a hot frying pan, babe."

Marjie and Jerry started laughing again, but that didn't seem to faze their best friends.

"Mmmm, mmmm," Marjie commented as Billy and Ruth finally finished their kiss. "Should have put the timer on that one. What time is it, anyway?"

"Goodness," Jerry said, looking down at his watch. "It's after ten. We better get moving. Your mother's probably itching to get home, Billy."

"She's fine," he said. "She loves to baby-sit. Dad's probably up there by now."

"You're sure we got that tree tied down good?" Jerry said, stooping down one last time to survey the wooden platform they had built and the wire straps that held the tree in position. "If she tips over, we're in big trouble."

"That thing will still be there on our twenty-fifth wedding anniversary unless somebody tears it down," Billy replied, shaking his head. "Don't worry about it. Let's get home."

"I wonder if it's still snowing," Marjie said as they found their coats and headed toward the back of the church. "Good thing you hauled the tree in early this afternoon. Think of how much snow we'd have dragged in here."

"The janitor would shoot me," Billy replied, "and Ruthie would remain a single country schoolteacher. Unless you became a Mormon, Jerry. Remember what Chester's dad was telling he'd read about? I still don't believe him."

"You're suggesting I could be Jerry's second wife?" Ruth asked. "You're full of great ideas, aren't you? What do you think of that, Marjie?"

Marjie laughed as they headed down the steps to the big wooden doors. "That is the stupidest thing I have ever heard. I don't believe they do that. You wouldn't have to worry about the janitor shooting somebody. I'd shoot the guy who pulled that on me."

"I take it you disapprove," Billy said, pushing open the door and stepping into eight inches of fresh snow. "Yikes, look at this!"

Billy lifted his one foot back into the church doorway, and they all stared out in wonder. There was not a trace of wind to disturb the steady deluge of huge, wet snowflakes. The pine trees outside the church were bowed with the weight of armloads of snow, and the lights from the houses twinkled against the falling flakes.

"I can't believe it's done all this while we were inside," Ruth said. "Are we going to make it through the hills?"

"The question is, are we going to make it to the car?" Marjie corrected. "None of us brought boots. Bunch of dingdongs."

"Hop on board," Jerry said, kneeling down for Marjie to jump on his back. "No sense in us both getting wet feet."

"No, it's okay," Marjie protested as Billy bent over for Ruth to hop on his back. "I'll wreck your back."

"Billy, your legs," Ruth said. "You can't carry me."

"Oh no?" Billy countered. "Just try. I'll stop if it hurts."

"You're crazy," Ruth said with a grin. "Here goes."

Ruth hopped on, and Billy launched out into the deep snow without any apparent problem. They both were laughing as Billy chugged a path toward his partially buried car.

"Hop on!" Jerry said. "Let's catch 'em."

"I think I should walk," Marjie said. "I'm not feeling so hot."

"What?" asked Jerry. "You getting the flu or something?"

"No, no," replied Marjie. "Probably just something I ate. Tell you what, if you'll be careful, I'll take the ride."

"Sure," Jerry said, giving her a perplexed look. "Slow and steady."

Marjie hopped on Jerry's back, and he took off in pursuit of Billy as fast as Marjie's shouts allowed. But Billy had already made his deposit safely into the car by the time they got there. He opened the back door, and Jerry gently set Marjie in.

"Her Majesty, the Queen," Jerry said, bowing to Marjie as the snowflakes dropped on his head. "That's what they said when we were in Scotland."

"Help me clean the car off," Billy said. "My legs are starting to tingle already."

"Just hop in," Jerry said. "I can get it. I don't want you limpin' around on your wedding day."

Billy didn't protest. He disappeared around to the driver's side and started the engine. Jerry had wiped as much snow off the car as he could, then climbed into the backseat and snuggled up to Marjie.

"She's spinning," Billy said as he let out the clutch to back up. "We ain't gonna make it this way."

"Rock her," said Jerry.

Billy shifted into first gear and gently let out the clutch. The car moved a few inches forward against the wet snow, then he popped it into reverse and gave it more gas. They swung backward several more inches, then he popped it back into first and rocked forward. Shifting back into reverse, he gunned the engine. The green Plymouth made it up over the packed wad of snow and into the clear.

"Whew!" Billy called out as he pulled the car to a stop and shifted back into first.

"Don't get your tires spinning now," Marjie said from the backseat.

"Excuse me," Billy said, holding the clutch in and turning to look at a laughing Marjie and Jerry. "Would you like to try?"

"Touchy, touchy, touchy," Marjie chided. "Go ahead. Just thought you'd appreciate my advice."

"Thank you," replied Billy, laughing and turning back around. "I didn't."

Billy slowly let out the clutch, and the car inched forward. Marjie felt the muscles in her face straining to help the wheels keep turning. Slowly the car picked up speed, and Billy was able to shift into second gear.

"Boy, it's really coming down," Billy said. "I can hardly see the road."

"Just try to keep her in the center," Jerry urged, peering through the frosty front windshield from the backseat. "There's no tracks to follow."

"Nobody else is crazy enough to be out tonight," Ruth said. "The hills are going to be murder."

They made it up the slight incline out of Greenleafton and left the lights of the small burg behind them. There was a long flat stretch before the hills, and Billy used it to build up his speed.

"I'm going to have to roll down the hills pretty fast or we'll never make it up the next ones," Billy explained. He had hit third gear and was doing around forty miles per hour. "This is gonna be a wild ride. Better hang on."

As they whooshed down the first hill, Billy gave it all the gas he dared, but the car slowed rapidly as it climbed the next hill and they barely made it up. Billy let out a yell of relief as they cleared the top of the hill and headed down the other side with the same abandonment. Up and down they went, slipping and sliding, hanging on for dear life, gasping and congratulating, but Billy pulled them through.

"I won't be giving you any more driving tips," Marjie said to Billy as they slid down the driveway into the Macmillan farm-yard. "Look at the snow in the yard. You're going to have to stay here tonight."

The car passed the Wilsons' tractor on the way to the garage. "Well, looks like Dad came to get Mom," Billy said. "I'll bet he's at the door ready to go home when we get there."

Feeling lighthearted from the release of tension, all four friends whooped as they took off running for the house. Sure enough, Bud and Ella Wilson both had on their coats and were standing by the door as the four tree-decorators burst into the farmhouse.

"Here, step on the rugs," Ella said, pointing to the extra ones she'd moved around to handle the snow. "Glad you made it."

"Thought I might have to come and fetch ya younguns," Bud said. "Got my chains on the tractor. We gotta go, though. It's late."

"Thank you for watching Martha," Marjie said, taking off her coat and trying to shake down some of the wet snow. "Did it go okay?"

"Wonderful," Ella said. "Want me to take her along for the night?"

Marjie chuckled. "If the road wasn't so bad, maybe."

"Well, good-night," Ella said, but Bud was already out the door with a wave. "You want to stay with us tonight, Billy? We got an extra fender you can ride home on."

"That's okay, Mom," Billy replied, giving her a sheepish grin. "They've got two extra bedrooms here."

"Two?" she teased. "You're sure."

"We'll watch 'em like hawks," Marjie promised, laughing as Billy started to squirm. "Ruthie's going upstairs close to me."

"Good," Ella said. "I'll sleep a lot better."

She waved and ducked out the doorway. By the time the four friends had their wet shoes off and appeared at the dining room picture window, the Wilsons were on the tractor and headed down the driveway on their way home. Ella was waving from the right fender.

"I can't remember your mother ever being so happy," Jerry said. "Or your father."

"They can't believe I finally got smart enough to see who really loved me," Billy said. "Ruthie wasn't the only one I hurt in the past. Mom hated the way I treated the girls I dated—I think she felt responsible. She chewed my leg off sometimes, but I really didn't care." He reached out and put his arms around Ruth, pulling her close to him. "So, how 'bout it? You sure you want to marry someone who's as damaged as me?"

"I can't wait," Ruth said softly, watching the snowflakes falling outside the window, then she turned and looked into his deep green eyes.

Marjie looked on and shook her head. "Let me remind you love birds of one thing: You can wait—and you *will* wait."

34

A LITTLE SURPRISE

Marjie and her mother stood silently at the back of the candlelit sanctuary and watched as the ushers began to escort people to the pews. Besides the church's traditional Christmas decorations and the lovely Christmas tree, there were red candles on all the windowsills and in glass holders mounted on the inside entrance to each of the wooden pews. Red velvet bows adorned each glass holder. At the front of the sanctuary stood two large metal candelabra with their long-stemmed red candles still unlit.

"Now I see why Ruthie wanted an evening wedding," Sarah whispered. "The candlelight makes the sanctuary feel sort of eerie ... holy. Look at how quiet people are when they sit down."

Marjie nodded. "Like God is here," she spoke softly.

"Isn't He usually?" Sarah teased.

"Not quite like this," Marjie said. "You know what I mean."

"Is Ruthie here yet?" asked Sarah, turning to look at the church's back office, which doubled as a bridal room for weddings.

"She and Margaret just arrived," Marjie said. "I need to get back there, too. I can't believe Ruthie's so calm. I thought she'd be over here directing everything with her checklist."

"Maybe here comes the reason why she's calm," Sarah whispered as Betty Hunter came up the stairway and stepped toward them.

"Marjie, you look beautiful," Betty said, pushing her long blond hair back. "Where did you get the outfit?"

Looking down at her tailored tweed suit and her rayon crepe blouse, Marjie started to laugh. "It's two years old. This was my wedding dress, and it's remained 'the wedding dress.' I wore it to Margaret's wedding, Ma's, and now to Ruthie's. Pretty good, eh?"

"You're squeezing your money back out of it, that's for sure," Betty said. "Will you tell Ruthie that everything's ready downstairs for the lunch? I need to get back down there to finish getting the cake together."

"I'll tell her. You've made the wedding preparations so easy for Ruthie," Marjie said. "It means a lot to her."

"I'm glad," Betty said, putting her hand on Marjie's arm. "It's getting easier for me. Gotta go."

Betty winked and away she went.

"She made the wedding cake?" Sarah whispered.

"Margaret made the layers, but Betty is putting it all together," Marjie replied. "Plus, she volunteered to organize the whole lunch for Ruthie. You should see the tables. She really has an artistic touch."

"It's amazing she's even at a wedding," Sarah said. "It took me a long time after your father died to be able to sit through a wedding. Just a part of grieving, I guess."

"Yeah," Marjie spoke softly. "Hard to believe it's only been a few months since she finally let herself grieve. Now she's baking wedding cakes."

"And your husband's alive, and I'm married, and we sold a pig to raise money for Bibles," Sarah joked and laughed. "It's . . . all . . . so . . . amazing!"

"I guess God *is* here," Marjie whispered, bending close to her mother and giving her a kiss on the cheek. "By the way, after the wedding, I've got a little secret to tell you. I'll see you in a bit."

Sarah tried to protest, but Marjie slipped away before she

could get her hand on her daughter. Sarah went down the stairs to join Benjamin, who was letting Martha run around the basement.

Marjie went to the back office and knocked on the door. The lock clicked, and the door was slowly pushed open from the inside. The round, blue eyes of Margaret Stanfeld were peeking through the crack.

"Got room for one more in there?" Marjie asked.

Margaret's slender, curving lips bent upward in a smile. "Surely," she said as she quickly pushed the door open. "We're waiting for you."

"Oh, my goodness!" Marjie gasped. Ruth was standing in front of a long, upright mirror. She wore a full-length wedding gown, and her reflection was shimmering in creamy satin. Delicate ruffles softened the sloping neckline, and a narrow waistline highlighted Ruth's slender figure. Red baby rosebuds shaped into a garland adorned her black hair, and in her hands was a bouquet of the same baby rosebuds.

"Is that the best you can do?" Ruth joked, turning her flashing black eyes toward Marjie.

Marjie walked over to Ruth and gave her a careful hug. "I'm speechless," she whispered. "Whatever happened to my friend, the old-maid country schoolteacher? And where did you manage to find the fabric?"

"Your friend is right here," Ruth replied, hugging Marjie in return, "and the fabric's been in my aunt's cedar chest since way before the war." She straightened her shoulders. "Tomorrow I'll look like I looked yesterday. But today we give 'em our best shot."

"I hope Billy can handle this," Marjie said, then she looked over at Margaret. "Do you remember the look on Chester's face when he saw you? I thought we'd have to get the doc to put his jaw back in place."

The soft curls of Margaret's dark hair began to bounce as she and her friends broke into giggles. Margaret covered her mouth with her hand, but it didn't help. "I was afraid his face was going to crack in two," she sputtered, which got them laughing even more.

"Wherever Marjie is, someone's laughing, or crying, or both," Ruth said, touching the corner of her right eye to make sure that no tears had snuck out while she was laughing. Then she reached over, set down her bouquet, and picked an old wooden jewelry box off the desk. "I'm so glad to have such wonderful friends as you with me today. My mother was the most special woman in my life, and having special friends like you here helps make up for the loss I feel not having her with me."

Ruth stopped talking and looked seriously at the jewelry box, but she said nothing.

"Is this from your mother?" Marjie asked.

Ruth looked up and nodded. "My father brought it out this morning and said I'm to wear what's inside on my wedding day—my mother's family heirloom that she kept hidden from me. I've never seen it, and I thought I'd wait to open it until we were all together."

"Are ye sure ye want us here?" Margaret asked. "It's a very private moment."

"No, please," Ruth said. "I want you here very badly. And I wish my dad would come in. But he said he couldn't take it."

"Just a second," Marjie said, stepping back toward the office door. "He's right outside the door."

Marjie pushed the door open and walked quietly over to Harold Buckley, who sat on a folding chair waiting patiently for the time to give the bride away. He looked up at her, somewhat surprised.

"Is everything okay?" Harold asked.

"Everything's great except for one thing," Marjie smiled and said, "You have to be there when Ruth opens the jewelry box. I think your wife would have wanted you there."

The rawboned, balding farmer grimaced and looked away, and for a moment Marjie regretted being so forward. "I know she would," he whispered hoarsely. "I just don't think I can hold up."

"This is not a day where you have to hold up, Mr. Buckley,"

Marjie said. "Don't miss the joy of it."

Harold Buckley finally nodded. "You're right. I can't miss this . . . even if it kills me."

"Well, it probably will—all of us," Marjie warned as Harold stood to tower over her. "But it's a great way to go."

They stepped back into the office, and Margaret quickly pulled the door shut. Ruth looked up at her father and instantly choked up. "Oh, Daddy," she whispered.

Harold Buckley went to his daughter and wrapped his long arms around her. "Dear God, you're as beautiful as your mother was the day I married her," he mumbled. "I wish she could be here," he said brokenly.

Ruth nodded mutely, then composed herself and looked up. "I want you to open the box for me, Dad. Will you?"

Her father nodded and stepped back, taking the jewelry box in his big hands. "This is your mother's wedding gift," he said formally. His long, thick fingers trembled slightly as he grasped the lid and gently lifted it.

Ruth's mouth dropped open, and the tears instantly began to streak down her face. Marjie and Margaret stepped closer to see. In the box was an ornate gold pendant of overlapping gold and silver ovals set in a delicately wrought circular frame. It glimmered in the light.

"Put it on," Ruth's father said. "I polished it myself."

"Oh . . . my," Ruth breathed as she carefully lifted the pendant by its fine gold chain. Margaret stepped around Ruth and reached up to help her with the clasp. Then Ruth looked in the mirror. "Thank you, Momma," she whispered.

All four of them fought against the tears, but it was a losing battle. Marjie and Margaret gathered around Ruth, their faces wet from weeping.

"It's so beautiful," Marjie said, trying her best to catch the tears with her handkerchief.

"I gotta get outside," Harold said, stumbling toward the door. "I love you, Ruthie girl."

Left to fend for themselves, the three young women took several moments to regain their composure.

"Your mother saved for you a wonderful memory," Margaret said gently.

Ruth nodded, still blotting her tears and taking a deep, ragged breath. "She was a wonderful mother. If I become half the woman she was, I'll be very pleased."

"You ladies without rouge have an unfair advantage," Marjie complained, stepping close to the mirror and studying her streaked face. "Let's hope the candles give off a little less light than usual. My face looks a mess."

"Paint it, baby," Ruth joked, finally breaking into her bright smile. "It's almost time already."

Marjie went to the desk and found her purse, then she pulled out her small container of rouge. "Say, I forgot to tell you that Betty's got everything ready for the lunch," she said.

"Good," said Ruth, looking in the mirror and adjusting the position of the gold pendant. "She's been wonderful. I just hope Pastor Fitchen does all right. I don't know if it was such a good idea to have my wedding be his first service since the stroke."

"He is so excited about doing it, you couldn't have kept him away," Marjie said. "Besides, Chester's gonna be close at hand if something goes wrong."

"Nothing will go wrong," Margaret said calmly. "But I want to tell you some exciting news before we go out there. It looks like Chester and I will be going back to Scotland in February. My father has asked Chester to help him run the church's outreach to the servicemen until our missionary training starts in the fall."

Marjie's hand stopped midstroke while applying the rouge. She glanced up in the mirror at Margaret and tried to smile. "Margaret, that is wonderful news for you, and I'm going to do my best to be happy about it. But if you don't want me wrecking my face again, and Ruth's wedding, don't you dare say one more word about leaving us. It overwhelms me, so please. No more."

"I didn't mean—"

"No, no, no," Marjie broke in, holding up her hand. "I'm really glad I know now. The service will be that much more special for me. But I have to tell you that it tears me up inside, too. If we can leave it here for now, I'll be fine. I'm sorry."

"I understand," Margaret said. "Thanks."

There was a light knock on the door, and Harold Buckley poked his head in. "It's time."

Marjie, Ruth, and Margaret took one last look in the mirror and nodded to each other.

"Just one more thing," Marjie said, her patented smirk back in place. "After the service, I've got a little secret for you."

With that Marjie turned quickly toward the door and escaped her two friends' complaints. She smiled at Ruth's father as she passed him and kept going right on through the foyer until she reached her position at the back of the long sanctuary aisle. The candles were flickering brightly, and the church was packed right to the front row.

Margaret came up behind her, followed by Ruth and her father. They only had a moment's wait until the organist moved into the processional piece. As she had done at Margaret's wedding, Marjie smiled and stepped softly down the aisle to the rhythm of Wagner's Bridal March.

Benjamin and Sarah were seated on the end of one of the pews near the back, and as she went by, Marjie reached out and touched little Martha's outstretched hand. When she let go, she was relieved that a squeal didn't follow. But Benjamin did take a couple of vigorous kicks to the midsection before Marjie was too far down the aisle.

Jerry was waiting for her at the front of the sanctuary, and behind him stood Chester and Billy. Pastor Fitchen had gone up the stairs to the platform and was standing in the center. The candelabra had been lit, and the softly glowing red candles surrounded him with a halo of light.

As she reached for Jerry's arm, Marjie carefully stuck a piece of paper in his hand, then slipped her own hand into his elbow. The two of them stepped up the stairs in the front, then stayed together and went to the right side of where Billy and Ruth would stand. Turning toward the crowd, they waited for the others.

Jerry rustled the piece of paper in his hand and looked at Marjie suspiciously. With every eye on Margaret, who was only halfway up the aisle, Marjie whispered to him. "Open it. Quick!"

Being as discreet as possible, Jerry turned the paper toward the light from one candelabrum and squinted at the message. He stood blinking hard, then his eyelids froze open. His hand let go of the piece of paper, and it slowly dropped to the wooden platform. Marjie's foot was on it like a flash, but not before Chester and Margaret gave them funny looks.

Jerry raised his eyes as Chester and Margaret ascended the steps and walked to their places on the left side of the platform. But until the congregation stood and turned to watch Ruth and her father come down the aisle, Jerry's eyes did not turn to Marjie.

Marjie took Jerry's hand, and he slowly broke out in a ridiculous grin and began to silently chuckle. Marjie had all she could do not to laugh. He finally gave in, looked deep into her dark eyes, and whispered, "A baby!"